Martha Rogers has written a cl generosity, and young love. Fr Texas town we receive a beauti love others as we love ourselve for the Christmas holidays or any day!

—SANDRA ARDOIN
AUTHOR OF *THE YULETIDE ANGEL* AND *A RELUCTANT MELODY*

Martha Rogers is an extraordinary writer and storyteller. She brings characters to life and draws readers into the story with an invitation to make themselves at home. In this charming story Joe Fitzgerald first appears as a bedraggled old man on a train. Tom Whiteman, however, suspects much more behind that rough hobo exterior. As Tom and his close friend, Faith Delmont, begin to explore the man's deeper side, they are drawn to one another in a way they hadn't expected. This many-faceted story finds its fruition at Christmas, as secrets are revealed in the joyous Light of Truth.

—KATHI MACIAS
WWW.KATHIMACIAS.COM
AUTHOR OF MORE THAN FIFTY BOOKS, INCLUDING
THE 2011 GOLDEN SCROLLS NOVEL OF THE YEAR, *RED INK*

Martha Rogers has done it again! From the first scene until the last page *Christmas at Stoney Creek* captured my attention and wouldn't let go. Tom and Faith's love story is as sweet as the cinnamon rolls that Faith's family bakery serves and as interesting as any story Tom reports on for his local newspaper. If you love Christmas tales, this book is a must-read!

—KATHLEEN Y'BARBO
BEST-SELLING AUTHOR OF *FIREFLY SUMMER* FROM THE PIES,
BOOKS & JESUS BOOK CLUB SERIES AND THE RITA
AWARD–WINNING *THE SECRET LIVES OF WILL TUCKER* SERIES

I thoroughly enjoyed *Christmas at Stoney Creek*, which follows some of the characters in Martha Roger's The Homeward Journey series. When a bedraggled yet benevolent stranger comes to town, the townsfolk, though curious about the mysterious stranger, embrace the man with friendship and the practicalities of food and a place to live. The people of Stoney Creek live out their faith in genuine, daily practice and are a shining example of what it means to be a believer. Visiting the delightful townsfolk in this series reminds me of a gentler time in which putting the needs of others before one's own was a way of life. Without giving away anything, the romance is lovely and sweeter than all the sweets in the town bakery. This wonderful story touched my heart but also leaves me longing for one of Mrs. Delmont's cinnamon rolls.

—LINDA P. KOZAR
AUTHOR OF THE WHEN THE FAT LADIES SING MYSTERY SERIES
AND *BABES WITH A BEATITUDE: DEVOTIONS FOR SMART,
SAVVY WOMEN OF FAITH*

Christmas

AT

STONEY CREEK

Christmas

AT

STONEY CREEK

MARTHA ROGERS

REALMS

Most CHARISMA HOUSE BOOK GROUP products are available at special quantity discounts for bulk purchase for sales promotions, premiums, fund-raising, and educational needs. For details, write Charisma House Book Group, 600 Rinehart Road, Lake Mary, Florida 32746, or telephone (407) 333-0600.

CHRISTMAS AT STONEY CREEK by Martha Rogers
Published by Realms
Charisma Media/Charisma House Book Group
600 Rinehart Road
Lake Mary, Florida 32746
www.charismahouse.com

All Scripture quotations are from the King James Version of the Bible.

This is a work of fiction. The characters portrayed in this book are fictitious unless they are historical figures explicitly named. Otherwise, any resemblance to actual people, whether living or dead, is coincidental.

Cover design by Studio Gearbox
Design Director: Justin Evans

Visit the author's website at www.marthawrogers.com.

Library of Congress Cataloging-in-Publication Data:
An application to register this book for cataloging has been
submitted to the Library of Congress.
International Standard Book Number: 978-1-62998-758-3
E-book ISBN: 978-1-62998-759-0

First edition

16 17 18 19 20 — 9 8 7 6 5 4 3 2 1
Printed in the United States of America

CHAPTER 1

Stoney Creek, Texas, October 1892

HE SCRUFFY AND somewhat dirty old man shrank into the corner of his seat on the train. Instead of the foul air surrounding him, Tom Whiteman's journalistic nose smelled a story.

Tom contemplated the bedraggled figure a moment longer then folded the notes on the article he had been writing and stowed them in his coat pocket. He'd go over them later, but for the moment this stranger aroused his curiosity. He didn't appear to have much money, so how had he bought a ticket?

Instincts borne from reporting unusual events kicked in, and Tom sensed a story behind the tattered clothes and dirty exterior. Other passengers moved away to give the man more room and to escape the odor surrounding him. Snow-white hair needing a haircut as well as a good combing covered the man's head, and a droopy, discolored mustache graced the man's upper lip. Although his hunkered-up state gave no clue as to height, his form didn't carry extra weight.

While observation gave some clues, Tom would have to sit with the man to learn more about him. He'd make a good personal feature story for the Stoney Creek paper.

Tom crossed the aisle and settled into the seat next to the stranger. He extended his hand in greeting. "Hello, I'm Tom Whiteman. I'm on my way back home to Stoney Creek, Texas. Where are you headed?"

The man's blue-eyed gaze searched Tom's face before answering. "Name's Joe."

"Hmm, I see." Rather evasive. This man strangely dressed in shabby, well-worn clothes hit a chord deep inside that prodded him to dig behind the man's countenance and learn more. The man's outward appearance may be ugly and worn, but the serenity in the man's eyes grabbed Tom's heart and wouldn't let go.

A scripture from First Samuel pressed into Tom. "Man looketh on the outward appearance, but the Lord looketh on the heart." That's where he'd start. Find out more about Joe's life and how he came to be on this train.

Tom tried his question again. "Are you headed for Stoney Creek? I've lived there most of my life and know near about everybody in town."

"I'm not headed anywheres in particular. Just wanted to take a train ride. What's Stoney Creek like?" Joe's eyes darkened to a deeper blue as he waited for an answer.

"It's a nice town, really. We've grown quite a lot over the years. My pa's been the town doctor since I was a baby, and my sister teaches school. We have a newspaper, a library, a number of stores, and an especially good bakery." Tom's mouth salivated at the last addition. He'd sure like one of Delmont's cinnamon rolls or a slice of carrot cake about now. Breakfast had long since disappeared.

"Maybe I'll make a stop and see it for myself. Must be named after a nearby creek." A tentative smile played about Joe's lips.

Tom laughed and slapped his knee. "Well, you got that right, even if it is a little obvious. That creek running outside town has more rocks and stones in it than you could ever begin to count. It's good water too. Always tastes fresh, sweet, and cool even in the heat of summer."

Joe nodded and glanced out the window. He flexed his hands then curled his fingers into a fist. Brown spots and veins stood out among the wrinkles. Those hands had seen hard work.

"What line of work are you in, Joe?"

"Oh, I dabble in this and that. Did some carpentry work back in the days when my hands weren't so old." He held them up then dropped them to his lap. "Ain't of much use anymore."

"I wouldn't say that. I'm sure there's plenty you can still do." Names of people in Stoney Creek who would be willing to help Joe raced through Tom's mind. In years past their town had taken in more than one stranger and made them welcome, and this time should be no different.

Joe simply shook his head and stared out the window. Tom glanced around the train car to find passengers staring at him and covering their noses. The old man did reek, but curiosity and a nose for the unusual spurred Tom to stay.

The conductor came through announcing arrival in Stoney Creek within ten minutes. On impulse Tom reached over and grasped the man's hand. "Joe, get off at Stoney Creek with me. We'll find something you can do in our town."

Joe nodded but said nothing. He reached under the seat and pulled out an old knapsack and settled it on his lap. This time moisture filled his eyes as he peered at Tom. "That's a kind invitation, Tom."

The train whistle blasted the air and signaled their approach to the station. Now that he'd invited Joe, Tom had to figure out what to do with him. Ma would know. She could and would take care of anyone or anything her children brought into her home. She'd proven that starting with all the stray animals his younger brother, Daniel, had dragged home.

The train pulled to a stop, wheels screeching in protest against iron rails. Tom peered out the window, his heart filling with pride. The trees all around seemed to have put on their finest fall foliage of orange, yellow, and red to welcome him home after a week of travel.

He spied a pretty girl in a blue dress searching the windows. His heart swelled, and a grin split his face. Could Angela Booker have come to meet him? Then his brow furrowed as another young woman stepped into view. Faith Delmont. He hadn't expected one, much less two young women to meet the train.

He hopped down to the platform then turned to help Joe maneuver the steps. Now that he stood, Tom noted that Joe wasn't as short and fragile as he'd appeared slumped in his seat, but he still didn't come near to reaching Tom's height of a little over six feet.

With Joe by his side, Tom doffed his hat and smiled at Faith and Angela. "And to what do I owe the pleasure of seeing you two young ladies today?"

Faith sent a sideways glance toward Angela and pursed her lips as though she'd bitten into a sour lemon. Tom swallowed a chuckle. Could that be jealousy in his friend?

Angela's smile lit her face, and her blue eyes danced. "We did miss you, Mr. Whiteman, but I'm here to greet my aunt coming from Austin for a visit. Excuse me, there she is." With that she stepped around Tom and hugged an elderly woman.

So much for Angela coming to meet him. Tom turned to speak to Faith, who tried to hide her smirk but didn't quite get her mouth reset before being caught.

"I'm glad to see you amused to have me home, Faith." He pulled Joe forward. "Welcome to our town, Joe. This is Faith Delmont. Her family owns the bakery."

Without hesitation, Faith reached out and grasped Joe's hand. "Pleased to meet you." She tilted her head to the side. "You must be worn out after your travels."

Admiration for Faith jumped a few notches. Not a flicker of distaste or revulsion at the sight and smell of Joe. "Yes, he is, and I'm taking him down to our house so he can rest and clean up from his trip."

"That's nice." She smiled at Joe again then turned back to Tom. "How did your trip go, Mr. Ace Reporter?"

"Fine. You'll see my full report in the next edition." Out of the corner of his eye he saw Joe stiffen at the mention of his job. Could the old man have something to hide?

Time would tell.

⇶⇷

Faith swallowed hard to mask her reaction to the odor emanating from Joe's body and clothing. Never had she met someone so in need of a bath. Even the tramps who sometimes camped by the railroad seemed cleaner than this old man. Tom had given no last name, so she would have to call the man by his given name, although Mama might not approve. Nor would Mama approve of judging the man before finding out more about him.

Tom headed toward town with Joe on his right, so Faith situated herself on Tom's left in an attempt to distance herself from the smell. It didn't help much, but she kept walking.

At least she had Tom somewhat to herself. Angela had not been on the list of people Faith wanted to see today. Relief had flooded her when Angela stepped away to meet her aunt.

For so many years Tom had paid attention to Faith and escorted her to social events in town. She'd hoped that he would have declared his intentions by now, but that had not happened. Then Miss Angela Booker and her family moved to town a few months ago, and since then Tom seemed distracted by the pretty new arrival.

The new church Reverend Booker started was already drawing a nice crowd that had no effect on the attendance at the older church in town, which pleased the leaders of both churches. If Angela weren't so sweet and nice to everyone, ignoring her or disliking her would be easy. But Faith found herself befriending Angela, welcoming her to the community despite the little tentacles of jealousy that threatened her heart whenever Tom paid attention to the newcomer.

Tom touched her arm. "Do you think it might be possible to stop at your place and pick up a cinnamon roll? I've had a hankering for one all day."

"Really? Your mother makes them as well as Mama does, but if that's what you'd like, then by all means we'll stop in." Tom's mother was one of the best cooks in town and rarely used the bakery except for special occasions. Still, she'd seen Tom put away a cinnamon roll or two at the bakery more than a few times.

"How about you, Joe? Would you like to have one of my mama's fresh-baked rolls?" At his grin, Faith gulped. That smile exposed white, very straight teeth. They didn't match the other bits of his appearance at all. Who was this man?

Before she had a chance to inquire further, Mrs. Whiteman stepped out from Hempstead's Mercantile carrying a string bag of groceries. She stopped and grinned at the trio before her.

"Hello, Faith." She reached out with her free arm and hugged Tom. "I heard the train and figured you'd be coming this way soon. It's good to have you home, Son."

She turned her gaze to Joe. Her nose wrinkled slightly, but a smile graced her lips and eyes to erase the reaction. "And who do we have here?"

"Ma, this is Joe. I met him on the train and invited him to visit Stoney Creek. He's a carpenter." Tom visibly held his breath waiting for his mother's response.

Faith's shoulders tensed then relaxed as Mrs. Whiteman grasped the man's hand. "Welcome, Joe. I'm Tom's mother. We can always use a good carpenter around Stoney Creek. We'll be having supper shortly, and I imagine you're tired from the journey." She turned to Tom. "Bring him with you, and he can freshen up and have dinner with us."

Joe pulled off his battered old hat. "I don't want to be any trouble, ma'am. Perhaps I can find a room at the boardinghouse."

"Pshaw, no trouble at all. I'll go on ahead and tell the others you're coming. I might even stop by and see if Emma Hutchins has an empty room if you'd like, although we could find a place for you at our house. Oh, and Faith, you're more than welcome to come to supper too."

"That would be wonderful, Mrs. Whiteman, and I thank you, but with Mrs. Gladstone's big party tomorrow, Mama and I have a lot of baking to finish up tonight." How she'd love to spend the evening with the family and perhaps have some time alone with Tom, but duty came first.

Mrs. Whiteman's hand flew to her mouth. "Of course. How could I have forgotten that? It's practically all Clara's talked about the past few weeks." She clutched her package to her chest. "I'll be off then. Don't be too long, Tom. Your sisters will be delighted you're home."

As soon as she left, Tom herded Joe toward the bakery, and Faith followed along. If only Tom would invite her for a walk Sunday after church, she'd be happy, but lately his attentions seemed to be everywhere but on her. Of course his job as a reporter for the weekly newspaper kept him busy and sometimes out of town, like the past week.

When they walked into the bakery, two patrons grabbed their purchases, wrinkled their noses, and hurried from the shop. Faith cringed but couldn't blame the women. Joe didn't just smell; he reeked as bad as a riled-up skunk.

Mama frowned and glanced over at Faith, who shrugged slightly by way of an answer. At Faith's request Mama reached under the counter to grab two cinnamon rolls. "These are from this morning, but they're still fresh." She wrapped them in paper and handed one each to Joe and Tom.

"Thanks, Mrs. Delmont. I sure have missed these." Tom stuffed his hand into his pocket and came out with two coins. He placed the coins on the counter then grabbed Joe's arm. "C'mon. We can eat these on our way home."

Faith stared after them as they sauntered down the street, each one munching on a cinnamon roll. When she turned, her mother peered at her with narrowed eyes and one raised eyebrow.

"Who was that, and what was he doing with Tom Whiteman?" She waved a hand in front of her nose. "Phew, I can still smell him."

"His name is Joe. Tom met him on the train and invited him to visit Stoney Creek. I don't know anything else, but Mrs. Whiteman invited him to her house to clean up."

"Well now, isn't that just like that sweet lady to take in a stranger like that." She dusted her hands together. "Now, let's look at what we need to do tonight."

Faith reached for an apron. This would be a long night and one she'd much rather be spending with Tom than up to her elbows in flour and sugar. She strode to the window for one last look up Main Street in the direction of the Whiteman house. For late afternoon the town certainly had its share of people milling around, which made it impossible to tell if Tom and his new friend were still about.

With a sigh she tied the apron strings about her waist and hastened to join her mother in the kitchen. With Aunt Ruby not feeling well, this evening Ma and Faith would tackle the baking alone. Papa stayed out of the kitchen except to sample a bit here and again. He took care of ordering supplies and kept the books.

Curiosity nibbled at Faith as she measured and poured. Who was Joe? Something didn't add up, but she couldn't put her finger on it. Although he tried to speak like a vagrant, he sometimes slipped into more formal speech, and his teeth and manners all spoke of someone with more refinement than a hobo wandering around on the railroad.

Stoney Creek was a fine town with friendly people. It'd be interesting in the next few days to see how others in town accepted Joe. Most people probably would be nice, but certainly some would complain and ask all kinds of questions. She punched down a large mound of dough and sighed. Best get her mind off the old man and onto the sweets for the party hosted by the mayor's wife.

≫ CHAPTER 2 ≪

OM SHOWED JOE where he could clean up before supper. When asked, he said he did have one pair of good pants and a shirt in his knapsack, so Tom left Joe to himself and sauntered back downstairs. In the parlor he found his youngest sisters, Alice and Juliet, engrossed in a jigsaw puzzle.

Juliet glanced up from the table and wrinkled her nose. "Is that man staying for supper?"

Tom placed his hand on her shoulder. "Yes, he is, and I expect you to be nice to him. I don't know how long he traveled on that train, but I think he was there when I boarded it in Austin. So he's probably tired from the journey."

Alice shivered and shook her head. "I hope he cleans up good. He stinks."

Tom frowned, but Alice had always been one to speak her mind. At age fourteen, with chestnut hair and brown eyes, she stood on the threshold of becoming a most attractive young woman. Papa would have his hands full when the boys started calling on her.

His sister Clara pushed through the swinging door from the kitchen and addressed the girls. "Supper's ready to put on the table. We need your help setting the places."

Juliet hopped up and headed to help, but Alice looked toward the ceiling and sighed. "I suppose I have to, but I'd rather work on the puzzle."

Tom chuckled as she trudged her way across the room as though headed for the worst thing in her life. With four girls in the family, there was usually plenty of help in the kitchen. Clara, two years behind him, had taken over most of the chores since Molly's marriage.

Tom raised an eyebrow at Clara. "Alice has never liked helping around the house. It makes me wonder what she plans to do with her life."

"No telling with the way things are changing for women. By the time she's our age, there'll be even more opportunities." Clara glanced toward the hallway. "Joe hasn't come down yet?"

"No, and I didn't want to bother him." Tom furrowed his brow and started to mention the strange feeling he had about the man but clamped his mouth shut. Telling Clara would be like telling the whole town. Keeping secrets was not one of her virtues.

Behind him footsteps pounded the staircase accompanied by two male voices.

"I think that's him coming down now. Daniel must be with him."

"You greet him. I'm heading back to finish helping Mama." She turned on her heel and strode across the parlor and through the dining room to the kitchen.

Daniel's laughter preceded his appearance with Joe. Tom sucked in a breath at the change in his new friend. His clothes were still worn and threadbare, but the odor had disappeared, his hair was neatly combed, and his mustache had been trimmed.

"Well, I must say you look a sight different from when I met you on the train."

Joe beamed and shook Tom's hand. "I do thank you for the bath and fine hospitality. Does make a man feel better."

Ma clapped her hands. "Time for supper." She beckoned the family to gather around the table. Alice and Juliet had a difficult time keeping their eyes off Joe, disbelief in their eyes at the transformation rendering them speechless.

Pa joined the group. "All our patients gone for the day, and I'm ready for a good meal." He grinned at Joe. "I'm sorry I couldn't say hello earlier; I saw you come in but was busy with patients." He held out his hand. "I'm Doctor Whiteman, and you're welcome to our table. I say, you're a different man than I saw come through our door a bit ago."

"That I am. Your family has been very nice to this stranger." His gaze traveled around the group assembled at the dining table.

Pa nodded and took his seat with the others following suit. "Now we thank the Lord for this bounty and our guest." He bowed his head and extended his hands to those on either side of him.

When Joe clutched Tom's hand, Tom noted how Joe's hand bore the strength of one who knew hard work but a certain softness of a man who had known easier times. Everything he'd seen in Joe since the train ride contradicted what he'd seen in an hour or so on the train. That only served to intensify Tom's natural curiosity.

After the blessing the girls began chattering and Daniel reached for the bowl of potatoes. At Mama's frown, he turned and offered it to Joe. "Here, help yourself."

As Joe did so, Pa leaned forward. "Joe, do you have a last name to go with your first?"

Joe hesitated and glanced around the table where all conversation had stopped. "It's Joe Fitzgerald. My last stop was Chicago, and I was a carpenter and builder by trade."

Tom smothered his chuckle. Smart man. He'd answered three questions to the one asked. That should satisfy Papa.

Ma beamed and passed him the ham. "Like I said earlier today, we can always use someone with those skills around here. Oh, and I stopped by the boardinghouse, and Mrs. Hutchins said she had a room available if you'd care to have it."

Red crept up Joe's face. "That's mighty nice of you, ma'am, but I'm not sure how I'm going to pay for it."

"I told her that, but she said if you'd do some odd jobs for her, she'd provide the room for free. She's another of Stoney Creek's fine cooks, so you'll do well with both food and a good room."

Joe swallowed hard. "I do appreciate that, Mrs. Whiteman." He held up his hands. "I'm not sure how much these old hands can still do, but I'd be pleased if I can be of service to Mrs. Hutchins."

Once again, everything about this man belied the first impression of Joe being a homeless, penniless drifter. Something else lurked beneath the surface, and Tom would search until he found it.

⫸⫷

Joe savored the creamy potatoes and smoked ham and listened to the conversation around him. It'd been awhile since he'd had a meal like this or met such friendly people. Maybe he'd said too much with his name and what he did, but he didn't want to lie to them. At least his middle name sounded like a surname, so he could get by with that for now.

By the prayer Joe deduced Dr. Whiteman and his family to be Christians. That would account for their initial hospitality. So far the people of Stoney Creek had been friendly and welcomed him despite his appearance. He'd found the same in a few other towns, but it hadn't lasted long. It'd be interesting to see how long these nice folks accepted him for who he was now without trying to change him to fit their ways.

He'd have to be careful around Tom though. If he had realized before getting off the train that Tom worked for the newspaper, Joe would have avoided Tom completely. The young man had a reporter's natural instinct and curiosity, and it wouldn't do for him to find out who Joe really was. He'd have to be extra careful around Tom, for sure.

The family sitting around the table reminded him of happier days many years ago when he'd been a young lad. The three girls were all pretty but very different in their personalities, and their parents were warm, gracious people. He hoped he'd get a chance to know them much better in the days ahead.

Mrs. Whiteman spoke his name, and Joe blinked. "Excuse me, my mind was elsewhere for a moment."

Her laughter rang in the room. "That happens all the time around here, but I did ask if you'd like to attend church with us Sunday morning. We have two churches now, and if you'd prefer to attend the other one instead of ours, that's fine with us."

Church hadn't been on his agenda in recent months, but maybe it should. "I'd be delighted to attend church with your family."

"Wonderful, and then you can come and have dinner with us and meet more of our family. My sister and her husband have a ranch not far from town, and my daughter Molly and her husband live in their own home on another part of the ranch."

More family to meet meant he'd have to be careful about answering questions, but then the more people he met, the better he'd get to know the town. "Thank you, Mrs. Whiteman. You are indeed a generous woman."

He cut a sidewise glance in Tom's direction, and the expression on his face caused Joe to catch his breath. Those eyes missed nothing. What had he done to warrant such scrutiny from the young reporter? If anyone could ferret out the truth, it would be Tom. More thought needed to be given as to what Joe would do in the days ahead. If Joe didn't take extra precautions, Tom might indeed uncover the secrets Joe wanted to hide.

Faith helped her mother clear the table after supper. Family meals hadn't been the same since her brother Andrew had married Clarissa Elliot and moved away from home to set up practice in New Orleans. At times like this she missed her brother more than she had ever imagined.

They still had two cakes and two batches of cookies to bake. She'd take care of the cookies while her mother mixed up the cakes. She dried the last of the dishes and stacked them in the cupboard in the dining area. Pa patted her shoulder before draping his arm around Ma's shoulders.

"Do you need my help down in the bakery this evening?"

Mama grinned and leaned into Pa's embrace. "No, Faith and I can handle it. Ruby is down with her back again, but we don't have much left to do. Besides, you'd want to sample everything, and you don't need the extra sweets." She patted his chest and stepped back. "Don't forget you'll need to go down to the ice house and pick up a block of ice for the punch bowl tomorrow."

"I won't, and I'll have it all chopped up for you too." He kissed her cheek. "Since you don't need me tonight, I'll work on the books and bring them up to date. This looks like it will be a good month for the bakery."

"Wonderful, because after tonight Faith and I will need to stock up on supplies for our regular baking next week." Mama dried her hands and hung the towel on a hook by the sink. She nodded toward Faith. "Are you all ready for a few hours of mixing and stirring?"

"Ready as I'll ever be." Saturday would be a long day with the last-minute preparations and then the setting up at the town hall. Mrs. Gladstone's servants would take care of the rest, much to the relief of both Faith and her mother. Mrs. Gladstone had even invited Faith to attend as a guest.

She followed her mother downstairs to the bakery and checked the stove to make sure it would be hot enough for the cakes and cookies to bake. The old stove had become less reliable in the past few weeks. Faith tied an apron around her waist then reached up for the biggest crockery bowl to make her cookie dough. "Mama, what did you think of the old man Tom brought into the store?"

Her mother measured flour and sugar into a large bowl. "I'm not really sure what to think. I've seen some dirty men in my time, but not quite like him. Sallie Whiteman has such a big heart. I'm sure she treated him to a nice meal."

Probably so. Everyone in town turned to the doctor and his wife for help when they needed it, whether it was for their health or some other reason.

Faith cracked eggs into the lard and sugar mixed in her bowl. How she longed to be a part of that family. They had so much fun together, and there never seemed to be a dull moment around their house. With Andrew her only sibling, her family seemed rather dull in comparison.

She and Clara Whiteman had been friends since they were little, but Faith's childhood crush on Tom had turned into much more as they had grown older. What she had hoped would develop into a lasting relationship with Tom now stood at a standstill. Especially since Angela had come to town.

⁂⁂ Chapter 3 ⁂⁂

OE TURNED OVER on the soft feather mattress and sighed. It'd been awhile since he'd had such comfortable sleeping conditions. Opening his eyes, he found sunlight streaming through the window to his second-floor room. It was later than he'd thought! His feet hit the floor, and he grabbed for his pants, hoping he hadn't missed breakfast.

Mrs. Hutchins had been gracious and hospitable last evening when Tom had escorted Joe to the boardinghouse and introduced him to the landlady. She couldn't have fussed over him more if he'd been a lost child. However, she had warned him that breakfast on Saturday was served promptly at eight, and if he missed it, he wouldn't eat until noon.

The aroma of frying bacon wafted up the stairwell, arousing a grumble in Joe's stomach. He didn't want to miss out on the breakfast feast one of the other boarders had assured him was the best of the week. After washing his face and deciding he didn't need another shave this morning, he tucked in his shirt and headed downstairs.

As soon as he stepped through the door of the dining room, conversation stopped. The eyes of all four lodgers centered on Joe. Heat crept up his neck, but he sat and nodded to the others. No doubt they'd been discussing their newest resident.

Joe had met the women last evening when he'd arrived. "Good morning, ladies." Joe smiled and reached for his napkin.

Mrs. Rivers, the tall, slender woman with a pinched look on her face, said nothing, but the attractive younger woman beside her smiled and bobbed her head, sending her golden curls to shaking.

"Good morning, Joe. We're glad you made it in time for breakfast."

Joe remembered her as Ethel Simmons, one of the teachers at Stoney Creek school. The other one was Josie Rivers, a widow and the town librarian. Joe hoped her sour expression didn't reflect the way she dealt with patrons of the library.

The younger of the two men extended his hand across the table to Joe. "And I'm Herbert Spooner, a teller at the bank in town, and I believe you met this gent beside me, Zachariah Morton. He owns the tailor shop in town and makes fine-looking clothes for gentlemen. Sorry I wasn't here when you came in last night."

Joe shook the man's hand, surprised at his firm grip. "Glad to make your acquaintance." A tailor, a teller, a teacher, and a librarian: now that was as diverse a group as he'd ever seen. It made the side trip into this town all the more interesting. Already he had concluded that Stoney Creek had a leg up on the other towns he'd visited in the past few months.

Mrs. Hutchins swished into the dining room with one platter heaped with bacon and the other with eggs. She set them on the table and turned back to the kitchen. "Ah, glad to see you made it in time, Joe. Biscuits will be right out. Go ahead with the blessing, and then I'll bring in the coffee too."

Mr. Spooner took the lead with the blessing. "Shall we thank the good Lord for our bountiful breakfast?" Without waiting for answer, he bowed his head and offered thanks for the meal.

Joe sat next to Miss Simmons, and his nose wrinkled in pleasure at the scent of lavender surrounding her. She had a kind look about her, which he'd found in the people he'd met thus far in Stoney Creek. Couldn't quite say the same for Mrs. Rivers. No smile had crossed the woman's features yet.

At the conclusion of the prayer Herbert and Ethel picked up platters and began passing them around. Herbert handed Joe the bacon. "How long you planning to stay in town, Mr. Fitzgerald?"

While serving himself from the platter, Joe had a moment to consider what answer he should give. Might as well tell the truth since it wouldn't reveal anything about his plans. "I don't know. It depends on the amount of work I'm able to find." As well as how the townspeople accepted him.

Mr. Morton eyed Joe with a raised eyebrow, his partially bald pate shining in the light. "When Mrs. Hutchins told us about you this morning, she mentioned you once did carpentry work. There's a need for a man with carpentry skills around here. In fact, if you'll build me some more racks and shelves for my store, I could tailor you up a fine suit of clothes."

Joe swallowed the chuckle that bubbled in his throat. Trust the tailor to notice the condition of his clothes and suggest new ones. "That sounds like a fine idea." A new suit wouldn't be a bad thing to have, especially if Joe planned to stay around any length of time and attend church with the Whiteman family.

Back from the kitchen, Mrs. Hutchins passed the platter of biscuits to Joe. "I hope you like buttermilk biscuits. They're my specialty." Before Joe could reply, she continued. "Didn't Tom say you came in on the train with him yesterday? Where's your home?"

The flaky biscuit split apart into two perfect halves which he slathered with butter. "Yes, I met Tom on the train. I came from Austin." Which, while true for the train trip, Austin was not his home. He wouldn't reveal that bit of information just yet, but then he remembered he'd told the Whiteman family he came from Chicago even though that wasn't his home. It had simply been his last stop. Best to make notes and keep his stories straight if he didn't want Tom breathing down his neck.

He turned his attention to the food while the others chatted about the big party the mayor's wife was putting on that afternoon. He'd heard mention of the affair several times, and his curiosity was aroused as to who would be attending. He remembered benches in front of a few businesses on Main Street. One of those would be the perfect place to sit and observe the good citizens of Stoney Creek as they arrived at the party. More often than not, body language told more about folks than they might suspect.

»»»«««

Clara slid into her chair. "Sorry I'm late."

Her father scowled, and Tom ducked his head to hide his grin. Clara's flushed face and fluttering fingers betrayed her excitement over the Gladstone party later that day.

Ma reached over and patted Clara's arm. "That's all right, dear. You have a busy day ahead of you."

"Thank you, Ma. Theodore has a surprise for me, and thinking about it makes me both nervous and excited." Clara bowed her head to say a private grace before grabbing for the platter of bacon.

Ma and Pa exchanged knowing looks but said nothing. That meant they must be in on the surprise Theodore Gladstone had planned for Clara. Whatever it was, his parents must approve. He prayed it would bode well for his sister.

"Pass the biscuits, please." Clara turned to Tom and asked, "Do you have any idea what Mrs. Delmont and Faith have planned for refreshments?"

Tom shook his head and handed her the basket of biscuits. "She hasn't shared except that she and her mother had a lot of baking to do. Whatever it is will be delicious, I'm sure."

Alice bounced in her chair, her head bobbing with enthusiasm. "Are you taking Faith to the party? Mrs. Gladstone said it'd be all right if I come. I get to wear the new dress Mrs. Gordon made for me, and I don't have to wear my hair in pigtails. Oh, it's going to be so much fun."

She paused to take a breath and Tom jumped in. "No, I'm not taking Faith to the party because she'll be busy helping her mother, and I'll be busy taking notes for a write-up in the newspaper. Rumor has it that Mayor Gladstone is going to make a big announcement."

Pa buttered a biscuit and peered over his glasses at Tom. "I heard the same thing, and I'm thinking it may have something to do with the train schedule. He's been working on extending the routes since they've built more rails to the west of us."

The twinkle in Pa's eyes told Tom something else might be afoot, but he shrugged it off and helped himself to the scrambled eggs. "I hope so. It'll be nice to be able to go straight on to San Antonio without going to Austin first when I have stories to track down. Sure would save a lot of time for me and money for the newspaper."

Chatter continued around the table and centered mostly on the events for the day. Tom tuned them out and turned his thinking to Joe. Perhaps he would stop by the board-inghouse and check on his new friend. Mrs. Hutchins had warmly welcomed Joe last night, but Tom's curiosity about the man warranted spending more time with him. Perhaps the two of them could meet for a while this after-noon before Tom fulfilled his duties at the Gladstone affair.

His mother spoke to him. He blinked and glanced her way. "Excuse me, what did you say?"

Her laughter rang out. "I asked if you planned to see Joe today."

How did she do that? She always seemed to know what was on his mind. "Um, yes. Thought I'd check on him on my way to the Gladstones' party."

Ma nodded her head and smiled. "That's good. You tell him he's welcome here anytime he has a hankering to stop by."

"I'll do that." He laid his napkin beside his plate. "Now, if you'll excuse me. I have a busy day ahead even though it's a Saturday."

First on his list was finding out more about Joe Fitzgerald.

Later that afternoon, when Tom stopped at the boardinghouse to see Joe, he found that Mrs. Hutchins had Joe busy with carpentry work in her kitchen.

Tom leaned against a counter and crossed his arms. "Looks like you're getting right on to earning your board, Joe."

A broad grin spread across Joe's face. "And it's easy work to repair these cabinets. They're well made, but I'm glad I can be of use around here." He picked up a hammer and a few nails.

The old man had certainly wasted no time in making himself useful, and it also meant Mrs. Hutchins accepted Joe and liked him. That was understandable even though he had no money and his clothes were shabby. Maybe it was the man's smile and his willingness to help that had impressed Mrs. Hutchins.

"I was hoping you'd have some time to visit, but since you're busy, I'll just plan on seeing you tomorrow at church. Services are at nine thirty. Would you like to meet us there?"

Joe nodded. "Sounds good."

"See you then." Tom left the boardinghouse and headed to the town hall, where the party had already started.

Music blared from the building as Tom joined other partygoers and strolled toward the town hall and the Gladstone party. He'd like to chat with Faith, but she'd be so busy helping her ma that there'd be no time for idle talk. When he reached the front steps, tantalizing aromas filled the air and sent Tom's stomach to rumbling. Once inside he headed for the refreshment table first thing.

Faith looked up from placing a platter of pastries on the table and smiled. "Oh, Tom, I'm so glad to see you. People all over have been talking about your friend Joe." She laughed and handed him a peach kolacky. "You wouldn't believe the stories they've concocted about where he comes from and what he's doing here. Some good, and some not so good."

Tom bit into the roll and closed his eyes, savoring the sweetness of the peach filling and the flakiness of the roll. "Hmm. So delicious, as usual." He swallowed the morsel and turned to eye the crowd. "As a newsman I'm not surprised to hear they've been speculating about Joe. Think I'll mingle and see what I can hear. I also need to be jotting down notes for my story for the paper."

"I'm almost through with the things here. Mrs. Gladstone's staff is taking over the serving, but Ma and I wanted the table to look perfect to start out."

"I'll catch up with you later then. Come on over and join us when you do finish here."

"I will. You won't be hard to find." She grinned and headed back to the serving area set up in a side room.

Tom wiped his hands on his handkerchief before heading across the way to greet his family, who stood with the mayor and his wife. He glanced around until he spotted Clara and Theodore over in a corner in an intense discussion by the looks of Clara's face. Then she burst into a huge smile and hugged Theodore's neck.

Tom blinked his eyes and shook his head. Such a display of affection in public didn't reflect Clara's usual polite behavior, but it did match her exuberant personality. He joined his parents as Teddy and Clara rushed over, her face glowing with joy.

She extended her left hand to display a pearl ring in a gold setting. "Mama, Papa, look what Teddy just gave me." Clara beamed up her beau. "This makes our betrothal official."

Tom swallowed a chuckle. So that's why his father and mother had been all smiles this morning. Teddy must have approached them about asking to marry Clara. He reached for Teddy's hand. "Welcome to our family. You've made a great choice in this sister of mine."

"Thank you, Tom. Indeed, I have the most beautiful young lady in the room."

His firm handshake and eye contact assured Tom the young man would take care of Clara.

Pa joined in the congratulations and shook Teddy's hand. "Proud to have you in our family, Son." He turned to the mayor. "I believe it's time for the official announcement."

The two men proceeded to the platform where the band performed. Mayor Gladstone raised his hands to silence the crowd and beckoned his son and Clara to join them. The mayor and Papa grinned like they'd made the most important discovery in all the world. "My fellow citizens and friends in Stoney Creek, it is with great pleasure that Dr. Whiteman and I, along with our wives, announce the engagement and upcoming marriage of our children, Theodore Franklin and Clara Elizabeth." He waved his hand toward the couple as cheers and clapping burst forth in the room.

Tom had to admit they made a striking couple with Clara's fair countenance and Theodore's dark hair and eyes. Tom nudged his mother's arm. "You don't appear surprised. How long have you known about this?"

Heat rose in her face and turned it a bright shade of pink. "After Theodore asked your father's permission to marry Clara, the Gladstones and we decided to have a party to announce it to everyone. When we told Theodore our plan, he decided to ask Clara to marry him right at the party! It's a complete surprise for Clara."

Grinning, Tom shook his head. This put a whole new perspective on the celebration today. He'd been headed the wrong way with his story. Seeing the happy smile and shining eyes of his sister made the change a happy one. Maybe the railroad story would come later. Since social events were not his reporting responsibility, he now had more time for Faith.

He turned and caught her gazing at him. He smiled back and lifted his hand in a brief wave before heading her way. With romance in the air maybe the time had come for him to seriously think about the girl with whom he'd spend the rest of his life. Both Faith and Angela were excellent candidates, but which one would capture his heart?

⋙ CHAPTER 4 ⋘

O N SUNDAY MORNING Tom awakened with conflicting feelings about the day ahead. When Ma had told him to invite Faith to have Sunday dinner out at the ranch with the family, his immediate reaction had been to say he planned to invite Angela instead. He'd really like to get to know her better, but he remembered her aunt had arrived in town on Friday. Angela would most likely prefer to be with her own family today.

As he dressed, remorse for preferring Angela over Faith today ate at his soul. As an old friend of the family, Faith would have a great time at the ranch. He'd enjoy the day with her too, and most likely they would take a ride together on Uncle Micah's horses.

He crossed over to his window and stared out at the cloudless sky assuring a beautiful day for whatever activities were planned. He lifted his eyes toward the blue expanse. "Lord, why did You put two beautiful young ladies in my path? Have I known Faith so long that I've come to take her for granted?"

A sunbeam flashed through the window, and Tom jerked back. If that was a sign from God, maybe he needed to pay more attention to Faith. Still, Angela was a beautiful young woman, and he'd like to get to know her better. "Okay, God, I'll leave it up to You. You'll show me in time which girl is the right one."

He reached for the shaving mug on the bureau near the window. If he didn't hurry, he'd be late for breakfast, and he might end up walking to church. A quick pass over his cheeks and chin with the sharp razor did its job. A few minutes later the enticing scent of cinnamon and sugar floated up from the kitchen. Cinnamon rolls! Now he really had to hurry. He finished buckling his belt as he raced down the stairs.

Pa waited for Tom to slide to a stop on the wood floor leading to the dining room. "Son, is that any way to come down the stairs? You're not eight years old anymore." Although his voice held a stern tone, Pa's eyes twinkled.

"No, sir. I was afraid I'd be late." Tom straightened his tie and strolled to the table where his sisters and Daniel were seated.

Ma entered with a broad grin lighting her face with joy. "About time you men joined us. I figured the aroma of coffee and my cinnamon buns would hurry you along."

After they settled and joined hands, Pa said grace and thanked the good Lord for the beautiful day and the bountiful table.

Ma picked up the basket of fresh cinnamon buns and passed them to Tom. "If Joe is at church, I'm going to invite him to come out to the ranch with us. I'm sure Hannah and Molly will have plenty of food prepared, and he might enjoy being around our family."

"I will ask him, but he may not like crowds." He chose his bun before passing the basket to Juliet. His sisters chatted with Ma and Pa, but Tom's attention centered on Joe. Would he actually come to church this morning? He'd said he would, but he wasn't bound by his words. However, if the ladies at the boardinghouse had their say, he would be there. Although his clothes were worn out, Joe had the shirt and pants Pa had given him. They should suffice as most people didn't pay much attention to men and what they wore.

He downed the last of his breakfast and folded his napkin on the table. "I'll ask Faith if she'd like to ride out to Molly and Stefan's with us after church."

Ma's smile broadened. "Wonderful. Theodore will bring Clara out, so you may use the smaller buggy for you and Faith. Pa and I will take the girls and Daniel in the surrey."

"Aw, Ma, I wanted to ride Dusty out to the ranch today," Daniel pouted.

Pa's laughter rang out in the room. "Ever since Micah gave you that horse for your last birthday you've done nothing but ride him. I suppose it'd be all right today. What do you say, Sallie?"

She rose to remove plates from the table. "Fine with me, but you'll have to stay close to us and not gallop off on your own." She nodded toward Clara and Alice. "Come, girls, let's take care of these dishes so we'll be ready to leave on time."

Daniel, with more energy than he showed for most tasks, hopped up right away to go saddle up his horse. Tom chuckled at his younger brother's enthusiasm and pushed his chair back from the table. Having the buggy for Faith would make their ride much more pleasant. And he wouldn't have to worry about the girls taking up all of Faith's attention with their chatter.

Later when he pulled the buggy into the church yard, he spotted Joe with his fellow boarders, Herb Spooner and Zach Morton. He secured his horse and sauntered over to join them. Several other men had joined the group.

Zach Morton slapped Tom on the back. "Good morning there. We were introducing Joe to some of the other men."

"That's good of you, Zach. How are you this morning, Joe?"

Joe wore the same shirt and pants from last evening but a string tie had been added. Most likely a loan from Herb. He appeared more relaxed this morning too.

"Doing well. That Mrs. Hutchins sure knows how to cook, and the beds ain't so bad either." Joe shook Tom's hand with a firm grip.

Joe's speech patterns this morning sounded nothing like the man who had stepped off the train Friday afternoon. Everything about Joe shouted mystery to Tom. If only he knew where Joe had come from, he could make inquiries about him. Right now he'd have to settle for his own instincts and nose for getting down to the truth of matters. Maybe he should start with Chicago, but Joe hadn't actually said that's where he was from. Another mystery to solve.

"Joe, Ma asked me to invite you to come out to my aunt and sister's ranch for Sunday dinner. She'd like you to meet the rest of the family."

"That's right kind of her, but I promised to finish up a few things 'round the boardin' house and then play a game of horseshoe pitchin' with Zach."

Disappointed, Tom smiled and placed his hand on Joe's shoulder. "Well now, it sounds like you have the afternoon all planned. We can go out to the ranch some other time."

"Thanks, Tom. I got a fascination for horses, and I hear he's got some of the best." He turned back to his conversation with Herb and Zach.

A flurry of color caught Tom's eye. Faith Delmont hurried across the lawn to the church porch. Tom patted Joe's back. "See you tomorrow, Joe. Have to run and catch up to Miss Delmont."

Tom called Faith's name, and she stopped on the bottom step to turn and wait for him. "Glad I caught you before services began. I want to invite you to come out to the ranch with us for Sunday dinner."

Her eyes lit up, and her mouth curved to a smile. "I'd like that. I don't get to see Molly nearly as much as when she lived in town."

"I'm sure she'll be glad to see you as well." He offered his arm to guide her up the remaining steps. "I have Pa's buggy, so we can leave right after the service unless you need to go by your place for something."

⟫⟫⟩⟨⟨⟨

Faith stared at Tom's back two rows in front of her. He sat with his family as he did every Sunday. One day she hoped to be sitting with him in a pew with their own family. Now that was getting ahead of herself, since he'd been paying a lot of attention to Angela Booker lately. Thank goodness Angela didn't attend the same church. Then a smile filled her heart. He'd asked her, not Angela, to go with him to the ranch. Or could she be his second choice? After all, Angela had a visitor today in her aunt. The smile inside her faded.

The preacher spoke of God having a future for all His children, and the good Lord would steer each one person in the right direction if they sought His guidance. Some future for her if it didn't include Tom. She'd be doomed to being the pastry maker for weddings, christenings, and anniversaries...not the bride, mother, or wife. That may be fine for her dear widowed Aunt Ruby, who was happiest with her arms up to her elbows in pastry dough, but it was not what Faith dreamed for her future.

How could she ever compete with someone as beautiful as Angela? Her pale gold curls and intense blue eyes made her the envy of most girls her age, Faith included. Why did Angela have to be as sweet and kind as she was beautiful? Too bad the town didn't teem with young men their age. Of course there were the cowboys and the farmers, but most them were older with only a few young enough for Faith to have even the remotest interest in knowing.

Still, if she was to have a future with Tom, it had to be the Lord's doing and not her scheming and dreaming. Best if she followed the preacher's message.

The service seemed to last for hours but in reality lasted only a little over one. When the final notes of the last hymn faded away, Faith hurried up the aisle to the Whiteman family. She stopped in front of Mrs. Whiteman.

"Thank you so much inviting me to the ranch with your family today. I always enjoy going out there."

"We're glad you can go. That was a lovely table you and your mother set for the party yesterday." She slipped her hand into the crook of Dr. Whiteman's arm.

"Thank you. I'll tell Ma you said so." A hand grasped her elbow. She glanced up at Tom, who now stood beside her.

"The buggy is ready and waiting for us. My breakfast is long gone, and I'm hankering for some good beef and one of Aunt Hannah's pies."

At her nod, Tom placed his hand at her waist and guided her outside to where the buggy sat hitched and waiting. A smile wrapped itself around her heart. At least a half-hour ride with Tom all alone. Now she just needed to make good use of it.

Tom assisted her into the buggy then went around to pick up the hitching weight before climbing in beside her. He snapped the reins, and the horse moved forward.

"This is such a beautiful day to be outdoors." She groaned inwardly. She did not want to talk about the weather.

Tom laughed and his green-tinged blue eyes sparkled. "Yes, it is a beautiful day." He turned a lopsided grin toward her. "What did you think about Theodore's surprise for Clara yesterday?"

Wonderful, a topic other than the weather. "I thought it was so romantic. I don't know how your parents and his kept such a secret. Even we didn't know the true reason for the party. We thought the mayor was going to make some big announcement about the town."

"I think everyone else in town thought the same thing." He laughed again. "I'll never forget the look on Clara's face when she realized what was going on. I don't think she's ever been that surprised about anything."

"Oh, really, don't you think she and Theodore had at least talked about marriage before yesterday? Surely he already knew what her answer would be." It might have been romantic, but she hoped Clara had known his intentions before yesterday. Marriage was something that usually needed to be discussed before making such an important commitment in public. As for herself, she didn't care where, when, or how an actual proposal came as long as it came and Tom did the asking.

"They probably did. I know he came to speak with Ma and Pa while Clara was out with Juliet and Alice. I think he wanted the time and place to be a surprise. It never occurred to me that he would choose the party to do it and that the party would end up being in their honor."

"It's funny how he decided to be Theodore instead of Teddy when he returned from school."

"Oh, I don't know. I was always Tommy until I became a reporter."

True, but Theodore still seemed too formal for the boy she'd known. Faith had been several years ahead of Theodore and Clara in school, and they had been friends until Faith finished and started helping her mother at the bakery full-time. Since then they'd had little time for each other.

Her hands clenched in her lap. Precious minutes had been wasted on the weather and Tom's sister. She had to find a way to turn the conversation in another direction.

Tom spoke again. "I'm glad to see Reverend Booker's church is doing so well. I hope that article I wrote when he first arrived in Stoney Creek had a little something to do that."

Oh, fine, now he wanted to talk about Angela and her family. Then again, maybe she could get more of a sense of what he thought about Angela. "I think that did help. Angela is such a sweet person, and it's nice to have someone around my own age. We're becoming good friends."

Tom's eyebrows shot upward. "You are? Really?" At her nod he shook his head. "I guess it does seem logical since you are close in age. You know she finished four years of college before coming out here with her parents."

Now how did he know so much about Angela? She'd only learned those things when she had been invited by Angela to have dinner with her family. Oh, of course, with Tom at the newspaper, he was bound to know more about everyone in town. Still, that seed of jealousy planted itself deeper into her soul. If she and Angela became rivals for Tom's heart, how could they possibly remain friends? That was something Faith didn't care to experience.

⧽⧽ CHAPTER 5 ⧼⧼

O̲N MONDAY TOM read through his story one more
time before giving it his editor. He enjoyed writing about
the activities of the Texas legislature, and on his last trip
he'd scored an interview with Governor James Stephen
Hogg. Tom liked the man, the first native Texan to serve
as governor. Tom had no doubt Hogg would win a second
term in the upcoming election.

At first they had talked about Hogg's newspaper background, but then the talk had turned to politics. From
what Tom could gather, Hogg planned to support the
Railroad Commission created back in 1861 as well as the
law to regulate alien land ownership, and that was a good
plan. The article Tom held in his hand concerned Hogg's
respect for and defense of law enforcement. Stoney Creek
had a good sheriff and two deputies to help enforce the
law in the town and surrounding areas. If Tom hadn't
loved journalism so much, he might have joined the Texas
Rangers to help keep the law.

At least his real journalistic work had been productive,
but his quest for more information about Joe had hit a
dead end. The man seemed to be avoiding him, and none
of Tom's careful probing had brought about any more
information than what had he had already learned on
Friday. Joe was charming and polite but clearly wanted to
keep everyone at arm's length.

Best to forget about the old man for now and stick to news for the *Stoney Creek Herald*. Satisfied with his completed story, Tom picked it up and strode to Jonas Blake's office. He knocked on the open door and waited for the man to look up. When he did, he smiled then broadened that to a grin.

"Come on in, my boy. Is that your article on Hogg?"

Tom laid the paper on Mr. Blake's desk. "Yes, it is, and I have more notes for an article on his ideas for protecting the welfare of our universities."

"Good, good. Have a seat. I have something I want to run by you."

Curiosity built in Tom as he sat across the desk from his editor, who leaned back in his chair and steepled his fingertips. Mr. Blake wasted no time in stating his thoughts. "What do you think about having a woman doing some reporting around here?"

Tom shrugged and swallowed hard. "It's all right with me, but who do you have in mind?" As far as he knew, no young woman around these parts was interested in newspaper work.

"After covering that party on Saturday, I decided we need a real social events reporter. The two of us won't have time for all that once I take the paper to three editions a week instead of two, and I'm adding a wire service." He tilted his head to one side and smiled.

Tom gasped. Mr. Blake had always said a twice-a-week newspaper had no need for wire, but now he was going to three editions. A wire service would give him the information he needed for the articles he wanted to write about federal and state politics. "Sounds like a good idea to me."

Mr. Blake nodded. "That means you can spend more time on state and national news. I think you can handle the extra work."

"Yes, sir, that would be no problem at all, and I'd enjoy it. But tell me, do you have someone in mind for the social events?" Tom still hadn't come up with any woman from Stoney Creek who would be interested in such a job.

Mr. Blake leaned toward his desk and opened the left-hand drawer. He pulled out a paper and laid it on his desk. "As a matter of fact, I do. A friend of mine has a daughter who graduated from the University of Texas a few years ago. She's been looking for a new position for the past few months. Seems the editor of the paper where she's working now doesn't approve of female reporters. I don't have a problem with it, but I wanted to make sure it set well with you before I send the wire telling her to come."

"It's fine with me."

"I thought it would be. She'll report later this week. Her name is Gretchen O'Neal, and she's about twenty-seven, I believe."

Tom nodded. Four years his senior. Could be interesting, but what sort of woman would like working for a paper? He'd never met such a person, but he looked forward to the experience.

After he left Blake's office, Tom glanced at his pocket watch. Lunchtime already, and he'd have to eat at the hotel today. Normally he'd go home for the noon meal, but today his mother planned to take Alice and Juliet out to Aunt Hannah's and work on some sewing projects. She'd told him to eat big at noon because she planned leftovers for supper.

He grabbed his coat and headed outdoors. They could go without a coat while they worked inside, but Mr. Blake insisted on proper dress when his reporters went out in public. Tom didn't mind it in the cooler months, but sometimes a jacket was too much in the heat.

Tom made his way across the street. At least the temperature hadn't risen much above eighty today, which made the walk to the hotel more pleasant than it would have been in August or even a few weeks ago in September.

Angela and her aunt appeared in the doorway to the mercantile. Tom smiled and removed his hat. "What a pleasant surprise to see you two ladies in town."

Angela's cheeks bloomed pink. "It's such a nice day, we decided to walk into town for a few things we needed. This is my aunt Daisy Booker." She turned to her aunt. "You remember Tom Whiteman from the train."

"Yes, I do remember him. Fine job you're doing with the paper, young man."

Tom nodded toward the older Miss Booker. "Thank you, and I trust you're finding our town friendly."

Although Angela's aunt spoke to him, his eyes were on Angela and how the blue of her dress set off her eyes, as blue as a cloudless sky on a summer day.

"It was nice seeing you, Tom, but Aunt Daisy and I have shopping to do."

Tom's attention snapped back to the conversation. "Of course, I don't want to detain you. It was nice seeing you again, Miss Booker."

Daisy Booker laughed. "Thank you, Tom."

When the ladies departed, Tom blinked. What had happened? He didn't remember one word of the conversation before saying good-bye to the ladies.

The lovely young woman had indeed tied him into knots. Then he glanced up and the Delmont Bakery sign came into view. A twinge of guilt stabbed his heart. Faith. Or Angela? How would he ever make a choice between the two?

⟫⟫⟩⟨⟨⟨

Angela strolled toward home with Aunt Daisy, the meeting with Tom foremost in her mind. He was such a handsome young man and so well liked in the community. Her father had been quite complimentary of him, and her mother hinted more than once that Angela should encourage his friendship.

Aunt Daisy shook Angela's arm. "I must say I'm quite impressed with young Tom Whiteman. I met his parents at the Gladstones' party, and they are a very nice couple. It's a shame they aren't members of your father's congregation. But then again, it's good they are fine Christian people."

"The church Tom's family goes to is the first one organized here in Stoney Creek back in 1867 not long after the war. I believe Tom's family came here several years after that." The churches weren't so different in their beliefs, just their denominational affiliation, and that made not a whit of difference to her.

"I see." Her aunt raised an eyebrow and tilted her head. "Do I detect a note of interest in young Tom?"

Heat rose in Angela's cheeks. "Tom has taken me for tea and dessert at the hotel, but I've been too busy to think about him much." She had been so occupied with unpacking, learning her way around town, and meeting people that she had not had time to think about attracting a suitor and forming a relationship. But once she did, Tom would be at the top of her list.

"Well, I wouldn't let a young man like that get away. He's a fine catch and would make some woman a nice husband."

Angela gasped. "Aunt Daisy! How can you say that? You don't even know Tom Whiteman."

"I know him well enough. He's single, has a good job, is a Christian, and comes from a fine family. What else do you need?"

"How about love? I would want a man I could love with all my heart. And what about him? He would need to love me back."

Her aunt shrugged. "I loved a boy with all my heart, but God saw fit to take him from me before we could be wed. I never married, and now I regret not accepting any of the other proposals that came my way."

Angela bit her tongue to keep from saying anything to hurt Aunt Daisy's feelings. Her sweetheart had drowned the summer they were to be married. Although she'd been sought after by other men, she'd remained single. Which would be worse? To pine away a lifetime for a love that could never be or to marry without love? Angela had no desire to experience either.

If God had a husband planned for her life, He'd show her and give her clear direction as to what she should do. Whatever lay ahead, the Lord would guide her path.

>>>><<<<

Faith dropped the curtain on the window of the bakery. Angela and Tom. They laughed and talked a good three minutes, and the green knife of jealousy sliced Faith's heart. How could her own mousy, drab appearance ever compete with the likes of Angela?

She smoothed the apron over her flower-sprigged cotton dress and reached over to remove the remains of a tea and pastries left by two ladies a few moments ago. Ma's rolls must have been especially good this morning as only a few crumbs remained on the plates.

A few swipes with a damp rag and the little round table sat ready for the next customer. A few patrons who enjoyed light lunches would drop in, but most of the men and families went to the hotel or the café for a solid meal.

After dumping the dishes into the sink in the kitchen, Faith put on a kettle of water to heat so she could wash them. Ma handled the customers as they came in and Aunt Ruby made the sandwiches and filled any orders for lunches, so Faith had a few minutes to herself.

The only problem was that, during any time she had to herself, she thought about Tom. Such a nice day they'd had at the ranch yesterday. She and Tom had ridden two of Mr. Gordon's horses down to the creek that ran across the ranch. They'd talked a lot about their past and the fun they'd had growing up in Stoney Creek. A slight breeze had ruffled his red hair, sending several locks to rest on his forehead. Those blue-green eyes had dazzled her as a young girl, and they continued to do so.

"Faith, if you don't get that kettle of water and pour it over the dishes, it's going to boil away."

Faith jumped and grabbed for a towel to lift the steaming kettle. "Thanks, Aunt Ruby. Guess my mind was elsewhere."

Her aunt grinned, her gray head shaking. "I wouldn't be surprised at all if those thoughts included one Tom Whiteman."

Heat filled Faith's cheeks. "Am I that obvious?"

"Oh, yes, but I can't say that I blame you. He's a fine young man. I've watched you two since you were young'uns, and I've seen the way you look at him lately."

Faith swished soap in the hot water to make a few suds. "I can't help it, but I'm afraid Angela Booker has captured his attention now. He talks about her a lot." Well, that wasn't exactly true, but if he said anything about Angela, it was too much.

"I see." Ruby pursed her lips and peered at Faith. "She's new and shiny like a toy at Christmas, but when it's all over, it's the favorite ones the children come back to and play with."

A toy? Did she want to be an old toy? She sighed and dunked more plates into the water. "I guess an old favorite is better than new and shiny," she said wryly.

"Now, my dear, you have to have faith like your name. If it's to be with Tom, it will be. God will see to it."

"I know, but it sure is hard to sit back and wait. Sometimes God can be just too slow." Faith shook her head and plunged her hands back into the hot water to wash the last of the dishes.

⫸ CHAPTER 6 ⫷

FTER MR. BLAKE made his announcement about the female reporter on Monday morning, the news spread quickly, especially since he told his wife, a noted busybody who spread the news through the recently installed telephone exchange. As he went about his business that afternoon, Tom found himself answering a dozen or more questions about the change.

When Tom sat down to dinner that evening, he had expected even more inquiries from his parents and sisters about the new reporter. However, after his father returned thanks, his siblings appeared more interested in the food than the latest happenings in town.

After dinner that night Tom sat with Clara and their parents in the living room. Clara waited for Theodore to come by for an evening stroll since the weather was still mild.

He glanced now at his sister. She wore the silly grin from Saturday's big announcement of her engagement to Theodore Gladstone. At least he understood why she wouldn't be interested in the new reporter. Clara's only thoughts at the moment were on planning a wedding, not a newspaper.

Finally he could stand it no longer and cleared his throat. "Hmm, I say, what did you think of Mr. Blake's announcement today?"

His mother looked up from her sewing. "I think it's wonderful. If we didn't have to keep our telephone free for calls to your father, I'd have been on it talking to neighbors. As it is, I went into town to Hempstead's, and everyone had something to say."

Pa closed his book and peered over the rim of his glasses. "What do you think about hiring a female reporter?"

"I'm sure it'll be fine, although I don't know what interest a woman might have in reporting news. The wire service is more important. It's going to be a great asset to our town. We'll get the news much more quickly. It'll make my job a lot easier as well. Maybe now I won't have to do quite as much traveling."

Ma nodded in satisfaction. "That's good, but what have you heard about the new reporter?"

"Her name is Gretchen O'Neal, and she's the daughter of a friend of his and is also a graduate of the University of Texas. She's been working on another paper until now."

"I'm glad Mr. Blake is hiring a woman. Women need more jobs like this." Clara grinned and smoothed the front of her skirt.

Ma picked up sewing. "I agree, Clara. Do you know anything else about her, Tom?"

"Not much. She's around twenty-seven, and she lost her job because her previous editor didn't care for female reporters. I agree with your ideas about women as well, dear sister."

Her grin became a broad smile. "Thank you, Tom. This is truly a good thing since men usually don't like to have women around a newspaper office."

Ma stabbed her needle into the pair of socks she darned. "Well, I think Mr. Blake is doing this town a favor. No telling, this state might yet allow women to vote."

When a knock on the door sounded, all conversation about the newspaper and its changes came to a halt. Clara greeted Theodore, and after speaking to her parents, they left. Mama and Papa returned to reading and sewing.

Well, so much for the big news of the day for him. Life went on.

⟫⟫⟫⟪⟪⟪

Joe sat in the parlor with his fellow boarders after dinner. He'd learned this was their custom on weeknights for an hour after the meal when Mrs. Hutchins served coffee or tea. After that the ladies retired to their rooms, and the men sometimes stayed and conversed longer.

Joe listened as the conversation continued from the dinner table. He'd been hearing about the new wire service and the expansion of the newspaper all day. If he hadn't been so determined to keep his identity a secret, the news would have made no difference at all in his life. Now it posed a threat in that young Tom Whiteman would now be able to get news faster, and with his already obvious interest, the world Joe had left behind might be more available to the reporter than it would have before.

Might have been best if he'd never met the young man and his family or let it slip that he'd come from Chicago. However, since Chicago wasn't actually his home, he wouldn't worry about that for now. After only a few days in Stoney Creek, Joe had come to love the good citizens of the town. Most everyone he'd met thus far had been friendly and welcoming to him. All but a few met the criteria he'd set up for his quest for true Christians who accepted people with open arms no matter what their station in life.

Trouble was he hadn't counted on meeting someone like Tom Whiteman. Joe had liked the young man immediately and admired his friendly nature. For now he'd let things go along as they were, but if Tom got too close to the truth, Joe would have a big decision to make. He'd be the one to make the decision as to how much of his past he'd reveal and when he'd do it, and not let Tom press him into any premature revelations.

Mrs. Hutchins brought in the tray with coffee. "I am so glad that the newspaper is going to more editions. Maybe it will draw more people, and the more people we have in Stoney Creek, the better off all our merchants will be."

Herbert Spooner clapped his hands. "Hear, hear, Mrs. Hutchins. I wholeheartedly agree with that. Why, with all the growth we've been experiencing, I would imagine we'll be seeing a bigger school, more businesses, and an extra train route or two. Yes, sir, the town of Stoney Creek is booming."

Miss Simmons said, "You are so right, Mr. Spooner. We have two connecting school buildings now that are already crowded. Families bringing children to our fair town means we'd have to expand and make it larger and maybe even get another teacher."

For the first time since Joe had met her, Josie Rivers actually smiled. "If our town grows, that means the library will too, and that is something I look forward to seeing. I love buying books and stocking our shelves with the latest editions and classics of all kinds."

Joe raised his eyebrows. Her love of books didn't surprise him, but that smile had transformed Josie's face from a sour prune to a ray of sunshine.

Joe made mental notes of what his fellow lodgers said. A desire for bigger schools, a larger library, and expanded businesses revealed a thriving town. The more he heard, the more impressed Joe became. Stoney Creek looked to be a good place to spend some time and employ his talents.

After supper Faith and her mother cleaned up the kitchen while Pa read the paper in the parlor. Faith placed a stack of plates on the shelf in the cupboard. "Clara told me that she and Theodore plan a Christmas wedding. Has Mrs. Whiteman said anything about refreshments for the reception after? I'm sure it's going to be a big wedding what with Theodore being the mayor's son and Clara the daughter of one of our most prominent families."

Mama paused, her hands still in the soapy water. "Yes, she has spoken with me, and we're going to sit down and go over the refreshment list later this week. Ruby is eager to try out some new recipes, so I may propose them to the Gladstones if they turn out."

Faith hid her smile as she reached for the dessert plates to store away. "I imagine Aunt Ruby will be a big help." It would be nice to have her aunt work with them for such an important occasion.

"Yes, I love how she's always trying new things. It keeps our work interesting." She reached for the dish towel. "I hear someone at the front door. Do you want to answer it?"

"Sure." Faith untied her apron and hung it on the hook by the door. Maybe it was Tom, but then he had no reason to drop by. Nevertheless, she smoothed first her hair then her skirt before opening the door. To her delight she found Tom standing there poised to knock again.

"Oh, Tom, I wasn't expecting to see you." She stepped back to welcome him into the parlor.

Tom rolled his hat in his hands. "I'm sorry, I didn't think to check before coming. If it's a bad time, I understand."

"Of course not. You're always welcome in our home." Faith's heart beat double-time. She didn't care what his reason may be, as long as he'd come to see her.

Her father laid down his paper, and Ma strolled in from the kitchen.

"Good evening, Mr. and Mrs. Delmont. I...uh...I hope I'm not interrupting your evening." Tom reached out to shake her father's hand.

"Land sakes, you're not interrupting anything. Mr. Delmont and I were just planning to go into his study and go over our receipts for the day." Mama nudged Papa's arm. "Weren't we, dear?"

Papa scrambled to his feet. "Ah, yes, we were. It's good to see you, Tom, and I'm pleased with the announcement from Mr. Blake today. It'll be good getting more news more often."

"Thank you, sir. It means we'll have more stories to write, and I will always like that."

Faith reached for Tom's hat. "Here, I'll hang that up for you. You'll have to tell me all you'll be doing now with the new wire service and more editions."

Mama grabbed Papa's elbow. "Well, we'll leave you to your visit. There's pie left from supper and coffee still in the pot warming on the stove if you care for any refreshment later."

Papa shrugged his shoulders and grinned as he left the room, guided by Mama's strong hand. Faith swallowed a giggle at her mother's not-so-subtle means of giving her and Tom some time alone. She sat on the sofa, and Tom joined her. "Now tell me what new things you'll be doing at the newspaper."

Tom's face lit up and his eyes sparkled. "Well, it means I'll have more national news as well as state news to cover and write about now. With the new girl coming, Mr. Blake will have the sports scene as his main reporting along with the editorials. That suits him just fine."

Just what this town needed...another woman. "Tell me about this new girl, Gretchen O'Neal. I hear she has a university degree."

"Yes, she does, and her father is a friend of Mr. Blake. She's about four years older than we are."

At least Tom wasn't showing any interest in Miss O'Neal, and that suited Faith just fine. Having Angela as competition was enough for any girl to bear.

Tom furrowed his brow and pursed his lips. "Um, I have another matter I'd like to run past you. What do you think of Joe?"

Faith cocked her head. That was the last question she expected. "What do you mean? I think he's a nice old man, especially since he's cleaned himself up."

"Well, I think that too, but there's something about him that seems a little strange. I mean, I listen to him talk and watch him with other people. His way of speaking and his manners don't match up to a homeless old man with no means of support."

"Oh, I see. I've noticed that sometimes he does speak as though he's quite well educated, but other times he doesn't.

He *is* extremely polite, and his manners are well above average for a tramp." Her hand flew to her mouth. "I'm sorry, that does sound rather snobbish. He may have come from a very nice home and background and simply fallen on hard times."

"I've thought that might be the case. I wish there was some way to find out more about him. He said he's from Chicago, but that's a large city, and unless he committed a crime and is running from the law, I don't see how I can learn any more about him. For all we know, he may not even be using his real name or his real home."

"Sheriff Bolton may be the place to start. Then you can know for sure whether or not he's a wanted man. As for finding out his real name, if Joe isn't it, that will be a real challenge. If he stays in town long enough, he might slip and say something to one of the boarders at Miss Emma's."

"Maybe so, but Mrs. Hutchins isn't about to tell anyone anything about her boarders." He tapped his chin. "But Josie Rivers might. She may not be the friendliest woman in town, but not much gets by her, and she's always curious about other people. Maybe I can interview her for a story about the town library and get her impressions."

Faith reached over and placed her hand on Tom's forearm. "Be careful about that. It would be terrible if she found out you were only doing a story to get information about something else out of her. She may be a little unfriendly, but she does have feelings."

He patted her hand. "I won't hurt her feelings, I promise. I really will do a story on her and the library. It's one of the best things about this town anyway. In the meantime, keep your eyes and ears open whenever you're around him too."

He stood. "Tell your mother I'll take her up on that pie some other time. I need to get back home now and think about how I can go about getting information about Joe. You've been a big help, and I thank you."

"I didn't really do much, Tom." She scurried after him as he headed for the hall tree to retrieve his hat.

At the door he stopped and grinned at her. "You know, we might make a pretty good team. Thanks for the talk." With that he shoved his hands into his pockets and loped down the stairs and off into the night.

Faith stood in the doorway, staring after his departing figure. Yes, they would make a good team, but just not the kind of team he meant. Maybe working with him on the mystery of Joe would draw them closer, and Tom would see her as more than an old friend. She closed the door and leaned against it. Well, a girl could dream, couldn't she?

⟫ CHAPTER 7 ⟪

By THE END of the workweek Tom had made no progress in his pursuit of information about Joe Fitzgerald. Sighing, Tom leaned back in his chair and placed his palms behind his head and his feet on the bookcase nearby. The man had arrived in Stoney Creek a week ago, and he still remained a mystery. Tom had wired the Chicago papers asking about anyone from there with the old man's name, but so far he'd heard nothing. Not that he'd expected any return. With over a million people, who had time to worry about one little man?

Maybe Joe would come to dinner at the Whiteman house this Sunday. It was Ma's day to host the family meal after church. With the weather still being somewhat mild for October, they'd set up tables outdoors. He'd like to get Micah's impressions about Joe. His uncle had an uncanny knack for reading people.

A train whistle blasted, and Tom slammed his feet on the ground and grabbed his jacket. Gretchen O'Neal was due to arrive on the train, and he sure didn't want to miss that.

"I'm glad to see you taking an interest. Mind if I join you in the walk to the station?" Mr. Blake closed his office door and shrugged on his suit coat.

"Don't mind at all. Hope she's as nice as you say she is."

"Oh, she's that and so much more." He strode ahead of Tom to the door and out to the sidewalk. Mr. Blake's grin held more than a simple compliment. "Well, don't dilly-dally. Let's go. Mrs. Blake will be waiting for us."

"Yes, sir." Tom jammed his hat onto his head and followed his boss.

They arrived at the station a minute or so ahead of the train. Tom glanced around at the crowd there on the platform. Either a lot of new people were coming into town, or Miss O'Neal had created a great deal of curiosity among the good people of Stoney Creek. With all the talk during the week, the latter probably prevailed.

The train whistle shrilled its approach and metal ground against metal as the train coasted to a halt. Several people stepped down into the waiting embrace of family or friends. Tom craned his neck to keep an eye on the train steps. The air left his lungs in a gasp when a woman filled the doorway.

Dressed in royal blue from her head to her toes, she stopped with her hand on the door rail and gazed out over the crowd. Mr. Blake called her name, and the blonde vision's eyes lit up and a smile that dazzled like the sun spread across her face. If her brains matched her beauty, the newspaper couldn't help but flourish. Besides that, every eligible male in town would be burning up Mr. Blake's doorstep. Tom swallowed hard when she stepped off the train in one fluid motion as smooth as the silk of her dress.

Mrs. Blake wrapped her arms around Miss O'Neal. "Welcome to Stoney Creek, my dear Gretchen. We've all anticipated your arrival." She then stepped back to allow her husband to speak to the young woman.

"I'd like to introduce you to your fellow reporter." Mr. Blake guided her over to where Tom stood. "Miss O'Neal, this is Tom Whiteman, our state and national news reporter."

She extended her hand toward Tom, and he wrapped it in his. "We're pleased to have you join us, Miss O'Neal."

Her hand, as soft as kitten fur, slipped from his. "Thank you."

Tom breathed deeply of the faintly sweet scent of rose water emanating from Miss O'Neal.

She continued. "I'm pleased to meet you, and do call me Gretchen. Since we'll be working together, I see no need to be so formal."

Her smile revealed perfect white teeth and created a sparkle in her deep blue eyes.

Tom shook his head to clear it. "Yes, I...I suppose that would be easier."

She laughed and turned to Mrs. Blake. They locked arms and headed toward the Blake carriage. Tom stared after the two women. How had a beauty like Gretchen managed to escape marriage or at least being spoken for? Most likely her career came before any thoughts of court-ship or marriage. Just as well, because from the admiring glances directed her way, Miss O'Neal had already made an impression on the town. But to Tom she was too old and almost too beautiful. He found himself somewhat intimidated.

Mr. Blake chuckled beside Tom. "Gretchen is a beau-tiful girl who is just as beautiful on the inside. She'll be a great asset to our news staff."

"I believe you're right, Mr. Blake. I'm sure everyone will welcome her to Stoney Creek." However, it remained to be seen whether Tom would welcome her presence on the staff of the newspaper. Working with a woman, especially a beautiful woman, would be different indeed.

>>><<<

Faith stopped on the sidewalk across the street from the train station. A very attractive young woman accompanied Mrs. Blake as they walked away from the station platform. This must be the new reporter everyone had been talking about. Faith shook her head and blew out her breath. Just what this town needed—another other beautiful woman to vie for the attentions of the male population of Stoney Creek.

Then a grin spread across her face as Deputy Sheriff Jeb Cooper all but ran up to the two women as they neared the Blakes' carriage. He swept off his hat and nodded to the ladies. His greeting carried across to where Faith stood.

"Good afternoon, Mrs. Blake, and welcome to Stoney Creek, Miss O'Neal."

Mrs. Blake laughed. "Good afternoon to you too, Deputy Cooper." Then she turned to the girl. "Gretchen, dear, this is Jeb Cooper, deputy for our Sheriff Bolton."

"Thank you, Deputy Cooper. Everyone has been so warm in welcoming me to your town."

He reached for her elbow. "Here, let me assist you up into the carriage."

A figure emerged from around the corner and sped to the carriage. Herbert Spooner slid to a stop and frowned at the deputy. Faith clutched her stomach to keep from laughing. Competition already for the fair lady's hand.

Both men glared at one another, but since Jeb already held her arm, he assisted Miss O'Neal into the carriage. Not to be outdone, Herbert Spooner did the same for Mrs.

Blake, who appeared to be working her mouth to keep from laughing as well. When the ladies were seated, the deputy hastened to untie the harness from the rail, and Mrs. Blake picked up the reins.

"Thank you both, and a good day to you." She clicked her tongue and flipped the reins to urge the horses forward.

The two men stood in the middle of the street still glaring at one another. Finally Jeb Cooper turned on his heel and headed back to the sheriff's office. Mr. Spooner turned the opposite direction to the bank.

Faith spotted Tom and waved. He grinned and waved back, and then made his way across the street. When he stood next to her, he chuckled. "Well, it seems Miss O'Neal has made quite an impression on our town in only a few minutes."

"I don't blame Jeb and Mr. Spooner for their interest. She's quite a beautiful woman." Faith narrowed her eyes and tilted her head. "You didn't show any interest, or are you just biding your time?"

Tom leaned his head back and all but bellowed in laughter. "Now why would I do that when I already have the prettiest gal in town to escort about? Besides, she's too old."

Heat filled her face. She hadn't been fishing for a compliment, but it sure was nice to hear one. Then a new thought sent her nerves into a tizzy. What if he meant Angela Booker as the prettiest girl? Before she had time to ponder that idea, Tom stepped into the street.

"I have to get back to the office and finish my story, but one of those berry tarts your Aunt Ruby makes would sure taste good about now. Are you headed that way? I'll walk with you if you are."

Well, even if she wasn't headed back to the bakery, there was no way she'd miss an opportunity like this. A trip to the mercantile could wait. "I'd be delighted for your company." She allowed him to grasp her elbow and assist her off the sidewalk and across to the bakery.

"Have you learned any more in your search for information about Joe Fitzgerald?" The touch of Tom's hand on her arm sent rivers of warmth through her arm and straight to her heart. This is the way she'd like it to be all the time with him.

"Not a thing. Of course I didn't really expect an answer. Who really cares about one man in a large city? Have you heard anyone in town talk about him?"

Faith shook her head. "Not anything other than the usual curiosity like where he came from, what is he doing here, and if that's his real name."

"Seems like he hasn't given anyone information about his past. He answers questions, but his answers are usually vague. He did say he'd done carpentry work, but that's about it. Sure would be nice to get an answer from my inquiry."

"Maybe you will soon."

"I doubt it. I'll have to come up another plan." He opened the door to the bakery, and they stepped inside. Tom sniffed the air and grinned. "Hmm, I smell chocolate and cinnamon."

"Mama is experimenting with chocolate and mixing it in cookie dough and cake batter. I must say the cake results are quite good, even without icing."

"Sounds delicious to me. A slice of cake and cup of coffee just might get me through the afternoon."

He sat back and grinned while she went behind the counter to retrieve the cake and pour a cup of coffee. A few minutes later she returned with a tray and set the cup and plate on the table. She had poured a cup of tea for herself and sat down across from him.

"Don't you need to get back to work?" She didn't want him to go, but then she didn't want him to anger Mr. Blake with his absence.

"Not right away. I've finished my news stories for the day. I'll go back over them before turning them in to go to press for Saturday's edition." Tom shoved a bit of chocolate cake into his mouth and sat back with a satisfied smile across his face. "Outstanding cake, even better than a tart."

Faith shook her head. Tom would have said that about whatever Ma or Aunt Ruby cooked up. Those two women had more recipes stashed away than most people would believe, but then that's what made their bakery such a success.

When he finished, Tom pushed his plate away. "Now that was the best thing I've had all day." He waved to Faith's mother behind the counter. "Excellent as usual, Mrs. Delmont." Then he stood and dropped some coins on the table. "It's time to get back to the paper. Thanks for the visit. Remember to keep your eyes and ears open for anything new about Joe."

"I will, although I don't think I'll hear anything unless he offers the information himself."

"Most likely not, but it won't hurt to be alert." He picked up his hat and headed for the door and back to his work.

Faith gathered the cups and plate to return to the kitchen. The bakery cases were all but empty now after the last of the lunch patrons and those who wanted baked goods for their suppers had left. She glanced at the watch pinned to her shoulder. Time to close for the day and prepare for tomorrow.

At the door she turned the sign over and the key in the lock. She stood there for a few more minutes simply staring down the street toward the newspaper office. In the past few months every minute she spent with Tom had become precious to her. She sucked in her breath and shook her head. She could do nothing to keep him from choosing Angela over her, but she certainly could do something to make the choice a little more difficult. In the next few days she'd concentrate on finding out more about Joe Fitzgerald and helping Tom unravel the mystery surrounding the old man.

⫸ CHAPTER 8 ⫷

*T*OM SEARCHED FOR Joe on the church grounds, hoping to find him before they went inside for services. He'd agreed to have dinner with the Whiteman family after church, and Tom wanted to make sure Joe had come this morning.

Faith caught up to him. "If you're looking for Joe, he's around at the side talking with a few of the men."

"Thanks. I want to make sure he doesn't forget he said he'd have dinner with us today." He started that way then stopped. "Um, it might be a good idea for you to join us since I've asked you to help with unraveling this mystery."

Her face lit up with her smile. "Thank you, I'd love to join you. I'll check with your mother to see if she needs help." With that, she picked up the hem of her skirt and climbed the steps to the church.

He'd intended to ask Angela since Faith had come along last week, but he had sought her help, so it was only right to include her today. With a shake of his head he hurried to the side of the building to look for Joe. There would always be other times to ask Angela to join him.

Joe spotted Tom right off and waved. "Hi there, young man. These here men have been telling me about some carpentry needs around town. Appears I'll be busy the next few weeks or so."

"That's good news. Means you'll be staying around for a while." The longer, the better as far as he was concerned. Now he would have more time for research. "You haven't forgotten about today, have you?"

"Not when it comes to your ma's cookin'. She's one of the best around."

"Wonderful. Just come on to the house after church. With the nice weather, we'll have tables and chairs sitting in the yard behind the house so we can eat outside today." He shook Joe's hand and nodded to the other men. "Good to see you gentlemen. Glad you're going to keep Joe busy."

Tom then hurried back to the front entrance and bounded up the stairs. He slowed to a sedate walk to enter the building and mosey down the aisle to the family pew. He slid in beside his mother. "Joe will be there today. He didn't forget."

"I should hope not." She cut her gaze to his but didn't turn her head. "Faith let me know she'd be there as well. Since I didn't have time to bake cookies for the children, she's going to bring some new chocolate cookies her mother is trying out."

Tom's stomach rumbled with that news. "If they're anywhere near as good as her chocolate cake was on Friday, I may eat more of them than the children do."

An amused smile accompanied a nod. "I'm sure you could." She poked his arm. "Now hush and make room for your father."

He stood and inched his way past his sisters to sit on the far end of the pew. Pa filled in the vacant space beside Ma. The pianist struck a chord, and everyone picked up their hymnbooks.

After what seemed like hours, the preacher raised his hands for the final benediction. His anxiousness to talk more with Joe around his family and get Micah's take on the old man accounted for Tom's impatience this morning. The hard bench hadn't helped either.

Tom followed his parents and siblings up the aisle and out to an afternoon filled with sunshine. Faith joined him at the bottom of the steps.

"Will you go with me down to the bakery to pick up the cookies? Ma is likely to talk with Mrs. Gladstone another half hour, and I don't want to wait that long."

Tom hooked her hand onto his forearm. "Sure. It's a pleasant day for a walk. Besides, maybe if I'm good, you'll give me one of those cookies a little ahead of time."

Faith slapped at his hand. "No, you'll have to wait just like the others."

"A man can try, can't he?" He grinned down at her, but she merely nodded and looked straight ahead.

Tom mused. "I suppose Gretchen O'Neal went to Reverend Booker's church this morning with Mr. and Mrs. Blake. She sure created a stir when she went into town yesterday to shop with Mrs. Blake. Even Daniel made a comment about her looks."

Faith laughed. "I can imagine so. She turned more than a few heads when they came into the bakery to pick up Mrs. Blake's order for the weekend."

After unlocking the door, Faith retrieved a box from under the counter and filled it with cookies. Even when closed the place smelled of cinnamon, sugar, and chocolate. Tom breathed in the aroma and eyed the box in Faith's hands. How could he entice her into letting him have one early?

She locked the door and laughed. "I see that 'poor little me' look in your eyes." She lifted the lid and extracted one cookie. "You may have one now, but the rest are for the children. If we have any left, you can fight your brother over them."

Tom grabbed it from her hand and almost shoved it into his mouth, but stopped at his lips. If this was to be the only one, he needed to savor it. One tiny bite confirmed what he expected. Delicious. "Wow, you'll sell a lot of these."

"Mama hopes so. Maybe then we can get that new stove we need so badly. The one we have is getting old and unreliable. She's seen one in a catalog she'd like to have because it's bigger with an extra oven."

Tom nodded, but cookstoves were the last thing that interested him right now. The cookies, yes, but how they were made, no. Faith rattled on for a few more minutes then stopped on the sidewalk.

"You're not the least bit interested in our kitchen, and here I've been running on like Stoney Creek. Best we get on over to your house with these cookies." She stepped up her pace and went ahead of him.

"Wait, Faith, I want to remind you to keep an ear out around Joe. We still want to find out more about him."

She didn't stop but turned her head to call back, "All right. I won't forget, but you'd better hurry on now."

Tom didn't waste any more time getting back to the Whiteman house. Faith went on inside, but Tom sought out his uncle Micah. He found him in the back helping set up tables. Tom caught up with him between trips to the storage shed.

"Micah, may I have a few words with you?"

His uncle stopped and looked back to the men with the tables. "Sure. I think we're about done here. Hannah's spreading the tablecloths, and all the benches and chairs are in place. What can I do for you?"

"You remember the old man I met on the train and brought home with me?"

"Yes, I do. I hear he's helping with odd jobs around town. What about him?"

"I need your help. You're pretty good at reading people, so I'd like for you to talk with him and give me your impression of him."

"Any particular reason?"

"Well, some things just don't add up. He was a smelly, dirty mess when I found him. Looked like he didn't have anywhere to go or anywhere to live."

Micah shoved back his hat. "So, he's just another old bum looking for handouts."

"I don't think so. For one thing, he has almost perfect teeth. When he talks, he sometimes uses really poor grammar, and other times it's perfect. His manners are often contradictory as well. I've seen him use the right utensils, say the right words to people, then at other times he acts like he's never been around folks in a social setting before."

"That does sound a bit odd." Micah scrubbed his chin with his fingers. "I tell you what I'll do. I'll engage him in a little talk and see what he knows about various subjects. Maybe I can get a feel for him from that."

Tom expelled his breath in a whoosh. "Thanks. I hoped that's what you'd say." He glanced over his uncle's shoulder. "Looks like the womenfolk are coming out with

69

the food. I'm going to make sure I get to it before some of my cousins do. I'll see you after dinner."

With Micah doing a little snooping, they might start unraveling the mystery of Joe Fitzgerald…if that was his real name.

⟫⟫⟫⟪⟪⟪

Joe kept an eye on Micah and Tom while he finished helping set up tables. Micah had introduced himself as the husband of Mrs. Whiteman's sister, Hannah. They had several young'uns running about the yard. He sensed right away the shrewdness in the man's character. There'd be no fooling that man on a horse or cattle trade. He'd have to be on his toes around the cowboy.

He'd already met Hannah and realized right away she carried one leg much shorter than the other. Her bright personality more than made up for the flaw in her physical being, however. She reminded him so much of the daughter he'd lost in a boating accident on Lake Michigan. Hannah even had the same red hair as his Rebecca.

Joe shook off the memory and reached out to assist Mrs. Whiteman with the large platter of meat she carried.

"Oh, thank you, Joe. Molly's carrying the second one. Can't have too much meat around this family of men. Have you met everyone yet?"

"Most of them, I think. I met Molly and Stefan and Micah and Hannah, but haven't had the pleasure of all their children as yet."

Sallie Whiteman wiped her hands on her apron and laughed. "There's a passel of them for sure." She glanced around at the group then raised her hands above her head and began clapping.

It didn't take long for all the clan to quit whatever they were doing and gather around. Joe's stomach growled in anticipation of the food now spread on the main table. If the others were as good a cook as Sallie, they were all in for a treat.

Sallie quieted the crowd and pointed to her husband. "Manfred, if you'll do the honors."

They all held hands and Joe found himself between Micah and Tom. He stifled a grin at how the two of them had maneuvered themselves to either side of him. After the prayer, plates were filled, and the families sat around to eat and visit. The food was just as good as Joe expected it to be, but the fact that neither Tom nor Micah asked many questions put Joe on edge. Those two had something up their sleeves besides their arms.

Sure enough, after the dessert of warm pie and cream, the two men asked Joe to walk with them to help digest the huge meal they'd just consumed.

Micah guided them toward the barn at the back of the property saying he wanted to take a look at Daniel's horse to make sure the lad took good care of him. Once there he did inspect the horse, but that didn't take long.

When he straightened up from checking the horse's shoes, Joe steeled himself for the questions sure to come.

Tom didn't disappoint. "You've been mighty busy this week, and we haven't had much chance to talk. How are you liking Stoney Creek?"

Innocent enough, and a question he had no trouble answering. "It's a nice town, and so far the people have been a mite friendlier than some other stops I've made along the way."

Micah brushed straw from his pants leg and raised an eyebrow. "Oh, and you've visited a lot of towns like ours?"

Telling the truth without revealing too much about himself should satisfy their curiosity. "Yep, I've been crossing this great country of ours for a spell now. Decided I wanted to see more of it before I die."

"I get to do that across Texas with my reporting. Must be nice to see other states. Wish I could, but a reporter's salary wouldn't allow it. How do you do it?"

Now was the time for only a bit of the truth, but no lies. "Well, you see, I visit a town long enough to do some odd jobs to earn money for the next stop along the rails. After being in Illinois and Missouri, I decided to come to Texas, and it sure is a big state to cover. Taken me longer than the others so far."

Micah sauntered out of the barn beckoning Joe to follow. "We do have a big state. So you plan on leaving us soon as you make enough money to buy train fare to the next town?"

Now how could he answer this question? Leaving had been part of his plan in the beginning, but he liked this town and what he'd seen so far. "Not sure about that. Might decide to stay a while longer. The ladies in this here town are mighty fine cooks, and the room at Miss Emma's is mighty comfortable."

Before either Micah or Tom could respond, a swarm of arms and legs surrounded them with shouts and pulled Micah toward the house.

"Come on, Pa. We got the ball and bat out and we need you to play with us."

"Okay, okay." Micah grinned and allowed the boys to pull him away. "We'll talk again later, Joe. Nice meeting you."

Joe breathed deeply and let it out. He'd dodged that bullet. Then he realized Tom still stood there. He grabbed the boy's arm. "C'mon. I heard Faith say she'd brought some cookies from the bakery. Like to see if there's any left."

He headed for the house, but Tom didn't follow right away. Joe turned to see why and found Tom standing in the yard, his arms folded across his chest with a look that said he wasn't done with his questions.

Avoiding that young man had grown harder with each day, but this was the type of town he'd been looking for these past months. He'd just have to be more careful about where and when he spent time with Tom.

Chapter 9

*E*ARLY MONDAY MORNING Tom glanced through the notes he'd written about Joe after Micah had talked with the man. His uncle's observations were the same as Tom's. The man was an enigma and had something in his background he didn't want others to know. With a sigh Tom shoved the notes to the side and picked up the papers he needed for his trip to Austin.

The door to the offices creaked open, and Gretchen O'Neal walked in. She wore a plain black skirt and white shirtwaist over which she wore a black jacket. Her hair had been pulled back in a bun at the nape of her neck with a black felt hat sporting a single black feather sitting on top. Tom nodded his approval. This young woman was ready to work, but even with such a stark change from her clothing on Friday, she was a very attractive woman and still rather intimidating with her self-confident air.

Tom extended his hand toward Gretchen. "Welcome to our office, Miss O'Neal."

She glanced around the space. "Thank you, Mr. Whiteman. It's much bigger than I thought it would be." She smiled and grasped Tom's hand in hers.

He led her to a new desk by the window. "This is where you'll be working. If I'm supposed to address you as Gretchen, then please call me Tom."

One thing became evident; life around the newspaper office would be most interesting in the coming weeks.

"Of course. That will be much easier, Tom."

"I see you're getting acquainted with our office." Mr. Blake emerged from his office to add his greetings. "I'm sorry I had to leave before you came down to breakfast, but I had some things to do here."

"That was quite all right. Mrs. Blake explained it to me. I didn't mind the walk at all this morning. The fall air is crisp and invigorating." She turned to Tom. "Don't you think so, Mr. White...er...Tom?"

Words caught themselves in Tom's throat, and he all but stammered. "Er...uh...yes...it is. Fall is a nice time of year." Heat filled his face. He held no attraction to the woman, but she could sure make a mess of his mind without any trouble. She exuded a boldness and self-confidence he hadn't seen in many women.

Mr. Blake beckoned to Gretchen. "Come to my office. I can bring you up to date with our stories and give you your assignments." He turned to Tom. "I believe you have yours already." With that they disappeared into the office, but the door was left open.

Tom grinned. Mr. Blake was taking no chances being alone with a woman as attractive as Miss O'Neal. Angela Booker and Faith Delmont were just as pretty as Gretchen, but he had the feeling Gretchen cared more about her career than any man.

Tom pushed the new reporter from his mind and set about jotting down a list of the research he'd need to do in Austin to make his time there more profitable. While in Austin he planned to sit in on a session of the legislature in order to let the people in Stoney Creek know what their elected officials were doing. Not much might be on the agenda, but it was Tom's job to keep up with it all. He'd be glad to get the wire service installed and cut down on some of these out-of-town trips.

Tom was deep into research when Gretchen returned from Mr. Blake's office. She stopped at his desk. "Looks like you're working on an important story."

He jerked his head upward. "Oh, uh…um…yes. I'm preparing for my trip to Austin later this week. Did you get your assignment?"

"Yes, he wants me to interview some man named Joe Fitzgerald and see what I can learn about him."

Tom erupted into laughter. "Good luck with that." If she got a real story, he'd eat his hat.

Gretchen's eyebrows rose to an arch. "Really? Isn't he some old man you met on the train?"

Getting her view of Joe would be interesting, especially since it was now her assignment. "I did meet him on the train. He said he'd come from Chicago. I sent off for some information from the paper there but so far haven't heard anything from them."

She hung her jacket on the coat rack. "Of course you wouldn't. Perhaps I can come up with some questions that will get him to tell me more about himself."

If she was able to do that, her reputation as a reporter would shoot up in his estimation. Joe had been so wary around everyone, however, that Tom sincerely doubted she'd have any success. But he kept his thoughts to himself.

"I'm leaving this afternoon for Austin and won't be back until Thursday evening. I'd be quite interested to hear what you find out."

"I'll be glad to share what I learn…you can read it in the Wednesday edition of the *Herald*." A wide grin turned up the corners of her mouth and her eyes sparkled.

Ah, yes. The newspaper office would see a lot of changes in the days ahead, and from the looks of Miss O'Neal, they wouldn't be bad at all. As she settled at her desk and inserted a sheet of paper into her typewriter, the telegraph operator from next door pushed open the front door and headed for Tom's desk.

"Mr. Whiteman, got a message for you." He held out a sheet of paper.

"Thanks, Andy." Tom grabbed it and began reading. He groaned and flopped back in his chair.

"Problems, Tom?" Gretchen spun her chair to face Tom.

"Not really." He handed the message to her. "The Chicago paper says no information on anyone by that name. He suggests trying some of the smaller towns around Chicago. This doesn't surprise me, but it was a long shot I had to take. Guess we're on our own trying to figure out who he is."

Gretchen handed the paper back to him. "What a disappointment. But since Joe Fitzgerald is on my story list, I think I'll go hunt him down now and see what I can learn." Gretchen rose from her desk and shrugged on her jacket. After placing her hat back on her head, she picked up pencil and pad and marched out the door, her skirt swishing about her ankles.

Tom returned to the work before him and muttered, "I wish you good fortune with that, Miss O'Neal."

>>>\<<<

Down the block Joe spotted Miss O'Neal exiting the newspaper office. His first impulse was to turn around and head the opposite direction. Then, deciding she couldn't be avoided forever, he stood in the doorway of the mercantile and waited for her to see him. If she did and came his way, he'd answer her questions. If not, he'd be spared this time and could go on about his business.

Miss O'Neal noticed him right away. Her face lit up with a smile as she waved and called, "Mr. Fitzgerald, you're just the person I'm looking for."

He smiled in return and observed her with a keen eye as she approached. More than a few male heads turned to follow her path, and rightly so. Despite the severe clothing, her comely figure was one to be admired.

Her footsteps ended by his side. "I'm glad I found you so quickly. I wasn't sure where you'd be."

"It's a small town; you wouldn't have had any trouble. Now what can I do for you, young lady?" As if the pen and paper in her hand weren't clue enough.

"I'd be delighted if you'd sit and answer some questions for me. Mr. Blake has assigned me to write an article about you for the *Herald*'s next edition. Is there someplace we can go and be more comfortable?"

Joe surveyed the town before him. The bakery shop held temptation, but they'd have too many interruptions from curious townspeople coming in on the pretense of buying a muffin or a few cookies. The hotel wasn't good for the same reasons, and of course the saloon was out of the question.

"Why don't we go back to the boardinghouse and sit a spell on the porch?"

"That sounds fine to me. It's only a few blocks away."

As they made their way down the street, more heads turned. Most likely their being together whetted the curiosity of a lot of the good people of Stoney Creek. When they turned the corner to cross over to the boardinghouse, Mrs. Rivers waved from the door of the library and hurried toward them. No doubt she'd seen them through the plate glass window by the door.

"Wait up a moment, you two." She caught up to them, her breath coming in short gasps. He'd never seen the widowed woman move quite that fast.

"Miss O'Neal, I was coming down to the news office to see you. I wanted to ask if you could possibly do a piece on our town library. Tom said he would, but he hasn't yet."

Miss O'Neal smiled and grasped Mrs. Rivers's hand. "I'll check into that, Mrs. Rivers. I've heard from Mrs. Blake that you have a fine library."

Pink tinged Mrs. Rivers's cheeks, and her shoulders lifted with pride. "We certainly do, and if more people know about it, then the more likely they are to visit us and possibly make donations for its support."

Joe made a mental note to visit the library. He'd neglected to do that in his walks to the downtown area of Stoney Creek. Miss O'Neal appeared very interested in what Josie Rivers had to say, and that spoke more to him about the young woman's character than anything she may say to him. Mr. Blake had made a wise choice in bringing her to town. Mrs. Rivers had become more animated than he'd ever seen her, and that certainly altered his first impression of her.

The two women finished their conversation, and the librarian headed back to the library. Miss O'Neal flashed her smile again and nodded toward the boardinghouse. "Shall we continue on to our destination?"

He walked beside her up the front steps and to the wicker table and chairs Mrs. Hutchins had for guests on her porch. They settled in their seats, and Joe leaned back, his elbows on the armrests and his fingertips touching. "Now what I can I do for you, Miss O'Neal?"

She paused with pencil in one hand and tablet in the other. "Seems you haven't been in Stony Creek much longer than I have, but more people talk about you than they do about me."

"And that is important because?"

Her hand fluttered the pencil, and she cleared her throat. "No reason, just an observation." Her shoulders lifted, and her back straightened. "Now, let me see. Tom Whiteman said that you come from Chicago. Is that correct?"

"When I met him on the train, I was coming down from Chicago." Let's see how she handled this interview. If she was as astute as her fellow reporters, he'd have to hedge with his answers, but he would not lie.

"But you have been to Chicago. Did you live there?"

"Yes, I've been to Chicago, and I've lived a number of places."

"I see. Well then, what brought you to Texas? I know Tom invited you to stop at Stoney Creek, but why were you in Texas to begin with?"

Before Joe answered, Mrs. Hutchins appeared at the door. "Oh, I didn't know you had company, Joe. Hello, Miss O'Neal. May I bring you something to drink like sweet tea?"

"Yes, Mrs. Hutchins, I'm sure Miss O'Neal would appreciate it as I would."

"I'll be back in a moment." She disappeared back into the house, and Miss O'Neal leaned forward.

"You were about to tell me why you are in Texas."

"Oh, yes. I simply decided I wanted to see this great country of ours and took out across the states. As I told Mr. Gordon recently, I stop in a town long enough to make a little money, then I buy a ticket for the next town on my route. The trip through Texas is by far the longest to this point."

At her raised eyebrows, Joe realized he had been speaking with the voice he used back home and not the one of an old, beggar man down on his luck, riding the rails. He couldn't go into that dialect now though, or her suspicions would shoot to the sky.

After Mrs. Hutchins set the tea glasses on the table, Miss O'Neal's probing continued, but he kept to simple words, short answers, and as little information as he could divulge without a falsehood. After a few questions about his carpentry skills and his odd jobs around town, Miss O'Neal quit writing and closed her notebook.

"I guess that will do it for now. I think I may be able to write a story about our new town handyman. I do hope you'll decide to stay in Stoney Creek a little longer than you have other places. I'm finding it to be a very friendly town."

She stood and held out her hand. "No need for you to walk back with me. I'm sure you have other things you need to do. I've enjoyed our chat and hope to see you more often now that we've met."

"It's been a pleasure, Miss O'Neal." He grasped her hand and grinned. "I'm sure we'll see each other about town."

A minute later she hurried down the walk and across the way to the main street. Joe stood, his hands resting on the porch railing. At least she hadn't learned any more about him than most of the people in town already knew. He reached into his pocket for the list he'd started in his room last night. Tomorrow he'd finish what he'd set out to do before Miss O'Neal interrupted his plan.

CHAPTER 10

OE TRUDGED UP the stairs to his room after lunch. At the top of the stairs he stopped and breathed in deeply. Not bad for a man his age with a death sentence hanging over his head; climbing steps would grow harder as the days progressed.

The good people of Stoney Creek had kept him so busy the past few days that he'd never completed the errand he'd set out to do on Monday. Now that he'd finished the bookshelves for Miss Simmons at the school, he had some time to himself. With Tom Whiteman out of town for a few days, this was his chance to work on his plan.

He changed to clean trousers and shirt. They were getting a little threadbare, but they suited the image he wanted to convey. He sat at the table he used as a desk, his pencil poised above the paper. Before going to the bank, he'd stroll about town and take note of a few more businesses. One person he wanted to have a chat with was Sheriff Bolton. The security of the town and especially the bank held particular interest to Joe. He added that to the list he had begun over the weekend.

Perhaps a stop by the livery should be on the list. He'd heard about the blacksmith there, but he wanted to meet the man for himself.

Satisfied with what he had to do in the next few hours, Joe sauntered downstairs and pushed open the kitchen door. He poked his head around the edge. His landlady stood at the sink scraping carrots. "Mrs. Hutchins, I have a few errands to run in town. Will supper be at the usual time tonight?"

"Sure and it will, Mr. Fitzgerald. Have a hen roasting with vegetables. I bought one of those new chocolate cakes Mrs. Delmont cooked up, so we'll have a fine dessert tonight."

"I've heard her chocolate concoctions are really good. Missed out on her cookies last Sunday. I'll be sure to be on time tonight."

A few minutes later he crossed over to the street leading to the main part of Stoney Creek. Most of the buildings were of board, but a few newer ones were of brick and stone. Mrs. Rivers waved to him from the library now housed in the former land office. That establishment had moved to the new courthouse.

Joe chuckled and waved back. From the way Josie Rivers stationed herself at the plate glass window, she must know when everyone in Stoney Creek came into town. She knew a lot about the good citizens of Stoney Creek, but he didn't dare start asking her questions. She'd tell him all right, but then she'd tell everyone else that he'd asked.

By far the finest building on Main Street belonged to the theater. Tom had said the place had been open only a few years, but they'd had some of the finest entertainment available to perform there, and a new play was scheduled to open there tonight according to the colorful posters adorning the outside wall.

Across the street a number of women entered the bakery, where tantalizing aromas of bread baking wafted out to the street to entice patrons to come inside. The ladies must be ready for afternoon tea and pastries.

To most folks up north any town in Texas sounded wild and untamed, befitting the tales of the Wild West they heard. But in Stoney Creek he'd found crime to be all but nonexistent and the citizens law-abiding and friendly. Even the saloon was tame in comparison to some he'd seen.

People nodded and spoke a few words to Joe as he made his way through town. To them he was a grungy old man Tom Whiteman had met on a train and invited to town, and who happened to be a good carpenter. Hadn't taken long for that word to spread. If time and circumstances had been different, he wouldn't mind settling here for his old age. Since both his wife and daughter had gone on to be with the Lord, he had nothing to hold him back home, but he did plan to go back there to die.

His steps became more urgent. If the doctors he'd gone to back home were right, he had precious little time to do what he'd set out to do. Willy Brunson waved to him from the livery. Now would be as good a time as any to visit the old man and meet the blacksmith.

"Good afternoon, Willy."

"Hey there, Joe. You in need of a horse this afternoon?"

"No, I'm simply taking a walk around Stoney Creek since I didn't have any work and have a little free time."

"Yep, I hear tell how people are keeping you busy building stuff. Nice of you to help out the school." Willy removed his hat and ran his palm over his bald head.

"It's been my pleasure. I've been told you have a fine blacksmith here. I'd like to meet him."

"Sure, come on back. Burt's finishing up some new shoes for Doc Whiteman's horse. Can't have one of his horses going lame."

Joe followed Willy through the stable area and through a door near the back. On a cool day like today the open fire from the pit warmed the area. Burt held a pair of tongs holding a shoe in one hand and a solid hammer in the other. Joe stared at the man's bulging biceps straining the homespun shirt. A black leather apron circled his ample chest and midsection, and his hands held firm on his tools.

Willy waited until Burt stopped banging and pounding the horseshoe before speaking. "Burt, Joe here sez he's wantin' to meet you. He's the one came in with Tom on the train. And Joe, this here is Burt, the best blacksmith in the whole county."

Well over six feet tall, Burt towered over Joe. When their hands clasped, Burt's was strong but not hurtful. "You're the one Miss Sallie told my Lettie about. Pleasure to meet you."

Joe's curiosity rose another notch at the man's clear speech. It bore none of the dialect and mannerisms of most folks like Burt he'd met in the South. Strong white teeth filled the man's mouth and shone against the black skin surrounding it when he smiled. "Nice to meet you too. Mind if we talk a bit?"

"I have a little time. These shoes are ready for Doc's horse, so I need to get them on soon."

Willy stepped back. "Well, you two get on with your jawin'. I got to get the buggy ready for young Mr. Gladstone. He's takin' his gal Miss Clara to the openin' of that new play at the theater tonight." He turned and headed back to the stables.

Burt leaned on the handle of his hammer with the head of it braced on the anvil. "Now, what would you like to talk about?"

Joe hadn't really given that much thought to it, but curiosity about the man brought on a question or two. "How have you liked living here?"

Once again a huge grin spread across his face. "Right nice. We came here with Doc and Miss Sallie. My wife, Lettie, grew up with Miss Sallie back in Louisiana. She wouldn't have it any other way but for us to come here with them."

"I don't detect the kind of speech I've heard from most of your race in the South."

Burt's laugh filled the room. "I 'spect most of you northerners would be surprised to learn I had schooling under one of the finest lawyers in Louisiana. His daughter is the one who taught my Lettie to read and cipher along with Miss Sallie. The Dyers were fine people."

"Hmm. That dispels some of the horrible stories I've heard."

"Don't get me wrong, Mr. Fitzgerald. There were some dark, dark times, and there still are, but some of us had people like the Dyer and Whiteman families taking care of us. Stoney Creek has been good to us as well. We were the only Negro family for a year, and then others began drifting in."

Joe had guessed that by the number of other families like Burt's he'd seen. "Where do you and Lettie live?"

"We have a house a little ways out of town. Other families like us live out there in our own little community. We have our own church and school there now. Miss Molly taught our boy, Yancy, and daughter, Dorie, until Yancy grew too old. He's about as big and strong as I am now."

The more Burt told him, the more interested Joe became. "So you don't come into town and attend one of the churches here."

Again Burt's laughter rang out. "Well, it's like this." He leaned both forearms on his hammer. "We darkies, as some call us, have our own ways to worship that are a little different from what you white folks are accustomed to. We sing a lot, preach some, sing some more, and then preach again. Early afternoon we stop and have dinner on the grounds with all the food prepared by our women, and then we might have more preaching at night."

Joe shook his head and chuckled. "I can see how one of our church meetings might be boring after that, but don't you feel isolated and discriminated against?"

"No, because the people in town are friendly, and we have no problems buying supplies. I know it's not like that in most other towns, but Mayor Gladstone is different. He takes his Christian and civic duties very seriously."

Joe's appreciation and admiration of Stoney Creek grew another notch. He'd seen enough abuse and persecution of former slaves to last a lifetime. After a few more questions about Burt's family Joe glanced down to see the newly forged horseshoes and realized he'd kept Burt from his work. He extended his hand toward the blacksmith. "It's been nice talking to you, and I look forward to meeting your family, especially that son, Yancy, if he's like you say he is."

Once again Burt grasped Joe's hand in a firm hand-shake. "Oh, he is."

Joe left Burt to his work and contemplated the man and his lifestyle. So many places he'd been had far too much racial strife, although he could understand why. Carpetbaggers had come down and ruined much of what the Southern people had managed to save. Finding peace between the two races wouldn't come easy and would take more years than he liked to think about unless the good Lord came first.

He exited the livery and stopped on the boardwalk to decide his next destination. The courthouse loomed to his left. Here again red brick and native stone comprised a two-story building with a tower in the middle that housed a clock. Mayor Gladstone had every right to be proud of his town, which grew larger every week. Two new streets had been added on the east side with houses being built as new families arrived and sought places to live.

Even with its growth the feel of family still pervaded, and once again the desire for a place to really call home rose in his chest. Impossible. Best get rid of those thoughts and get about business.

The sheriff's office sat across the corner from the courthouse. Joe made his way there. He found Sheriff Bolton seated behind his desk perusing wanted posters.

"Good afternoon, Sheriff. Mind if I sit a spell and ask a few questions?"

Sheriff Bolton didn't rise from his seat but did wave his hand toward a chair next to the desk. "I have a few minutes to spare. What can I do for you?"

"I hear there was a bank robbery in town several years ago. How safe is your bank now?"

"And why do you need to know that?" Bolton leaned back in his chair, elbows on the arms and fingertips pressed together. His eyes narrowed, and he stared at Joe.

Not much was likely to get by this man. "I'm considering an account at the bank, and I want to be sure my money is safe."

"I see. We did have a robbery. Micah Gordon's father was shot and died at the infirmary, and Miss Swenson was injured. We did finally catch the thieves, and we have new security measures in place. Your money is safe with us."

"No known outlaw gangs roaming the hills or hiding out?"

"None that I know of." He tapped the papers on his desk. "There are fewer wanted posters because more of the thieves are being caught and brought to justice or are hightailing it farther west to less tamed lands."

Joe had his answers and decided not to arouse any more suspicions on the part of the sheriff. Mrs. Hutchins had told him earlier that except for a few drunks getting into fights, the jail cells sat empty most of the time. That suited Joe fine.

"I appreciate your telling me this. Looks like my money will be safe." He stood and extended his hand.

The sheriff shook Joe's hand. "Guess that means you might be staying a little longer in town."

"Yes, it does. The people are friendly, and I enjoy doing a little carpentry work here and there. Thank you for your time."

Joe stepped through the doorway but sensed the sheriff's eyes still glued to his back. A good visit, but it may have aroused more than a little curiosity and certainly suspicion if he was any judge of the wary look in Bolton's eyes.

He glanced down the street and realized evening shadows had begun to fall. Where had the time gone? Stoney Creek was a town that closed up early. Only the hotel, café, and saloon stayed open past dark. Even now the twang of the Texas Star Saloon piano rang on the evening air.

All the displays from the front of Hempstead's Mercantile had been taken inside. Up the block the bakery and bank both sported signs to let customers know they were closed. One wouldn't find such peacefulness in the early evening in any of the larger cities he'd visited. The horsecars, people milling about, and lights and noise from all the places open in the evenings made for a very busy and restless life in those places. He much preferred the simple pleasures of a small town.

A few yards from the tailor shop he spotted Zachariah locking up. When the tailor spotted Joe, he waved and called out, "Come on, my friend. We don't want to be late for Mrs. Hutchin's supper. I saw her stop in at the bakery, so we'll have a fine dessert tonight."

Joe stepped up his pace. No, he didn't want to miss that meal either and certainly not if she indeed had purchased one of Mrs. Delmont's chocolate concoctions. A trip to the bank and visit with Mr. Swenson would have to wait until another day.

CHAPTER 11

AITH FILLED THE glass display cases with pastries and buns fresh from the oven. She loved the smells of spices all blended together with the aroma of fresh yeast bread. Mama and Aunt Ruby brought two more trays from the kitchen.

Two pies and two cinnamon cakes completed the array for those who liked to drop in early in the day for coffee or tea and a sweet treat. Mama closed the door on the case. "Mrs. Booker has ordered two dozen pastries for the Ladies' Altar Guild meeting at their church this morning. I'd like for you to deliver them there at nine o'clock. The meeting starts at nine thirty."

"Yes, ma'am, I will." Faith flipped the sign on the door to show the bakery was now open for business, and the first one in was Tom.

"Can't get past this place in the mornings without stopping in."

The grin on his face sent Faith's heart into a tailspin. He'd left town Monday, arrived back from Austin on the Thursday late train, and gone straight home, so she hadn't seen him since the Whiteman family dinner on Sunday.

"What can I get for you?" Faith hurried behind the counter to hide her trembling hands. The day brightened whenever he came into the shop, and these few days had been quite dull in his absence. If all he came in for was to buy a pastry or two, she'd be happy just being near him.

"Hmm, I think I'll have one of the jelly-filled rolls, kolacky, I believe it is."

Using a clean sheet of parchment, she selected a bun and placed it in a paper sack. Tom placed a few coins on the counter and grinned. "Couldn't find any this good in Austin."

"Oh, and how was your stay in our fair capital?" She rang up his purchase and handed him a few pennies in change.

"Quite informative. I have a lot of news to report in my next story about the governor. I still haven't learned anything more about Joe Fitzgerald, though. Even Gretchen didn't really learn anything we didn't already know. What about you? Have you had any opportunity to visit with him while I was gone?"

"No, he's been busy with carpentry work, although I did see him strolling about town earlier this week. He went into the livery and then down to Sheriff Bolton's office."

Tom frowned and pinched his bottom lip. He snapped his fingers. "I bet he's seeing if there's a wanted poster with his name on it. I should have remembered to speak to the sheriff. Thanks for letting me know."

He grabbed up the sack and headed for the door. "I'm sure this will go well with my morning coffee."

Faith nodded and sighed. If only she could capture Tom's heart like her ma's cooking did his stomach. Some days he treated her like she was the only one in the world, but on others he hardly seemed to notice she was around. This morning he'd been more interested in his kolacky and what she'd heard from Joe than he was in her.

"Faith, I have more tarts ready. Come get them, please."

"Yes, Ma, I'm on my way."

When she entered the kitchen, Aunt Ruby turned from the counter where she prepared bread for the lunchtime menu. Her spectacles slipped down her nose as she peered at Faith. "Was that Tom Whiteman's voice I heard out front a few minutes ago?"

"Yes, it was. He came in for one of Ma's kolacky." Faith picked up the tray of fruit tarts. "I hear the bell, so I'll take these and put them in the boxes as soon as I take care of whoever just came in."

After her errand Faith spent a busy morning serving customers. Even with the café down the street, some people still came into the bakery for a light meal at midday. With Stoney Creek growing like it was, the bakery and the town café stayed busy.

Finally the last customer left. Faith wiped away crumbs from a table by the front window and glanced out to see Joe entering the bank. Now why would Joe be going to the bank? She grabbed a piece of paper and pencil from her apron pocket and scribbled on it the time and Joe's destination.

⟫⟫⟩⟨⟨⟨

Joe paused before the bank doors. Once he took the next few steps and talked with Mr. Swenson, there would be no turning back. He'd be settling for the next few months in Stoney Creek. Still, he'd have to leave before Christmas and return home.

Drawing a deep breath, he grabbed the door handle and pulled. When he stepped into the building, he had to pause again to let his eyes adjust to the dimmer light. Herbert Spooner called to him.

"Hi there, Joe. How can I help you today?"

"Is Mr. Swenson in his office?"

"He sure is. Let me get him for you."

Herbert left the teller's cage and headed for the president's office. Herbert might be curious as to Joe's purpose in the bank, but he wasn't the sort to be nosy.

Mr. Swenson exited his office with hand extended in greeting to Joe. "Good afternoon, Joe. What may I do for you?"

"May we step into your office where it's more private?"

The banker raised his eyebrows but opened the gate separating the office from the bank lobby and gestured for Joe to enter. Mr. Swenson followed Joe into the office and closed the door. He walked around to the chair behind his desk and sat, nodding for Joe to be seated across from him.

"How can I help you, Joe? Do you need a loan?"

"No, no, nothing like that. I've come to open an account."

"I see. You've been making a little money with your carpentry jobs, so you want to keep it safe. I'm happy to assist you with whatever you need." Then he grinned. "Guess that means you plan to stay awhile."

"It does." Joe leaned forward with arms resting on the chair and his hands clasped in front of him. "I plan to leave my account here when I do leave, if that's all right."

Again Mr. Swenson's eyebrows rose. His mouth puckered as he contemplated Joe's request for a moment. Finally he nodded his head. "Certainly. We can hold your funds as long as you like."

"Thank you." He pulled an envelope from his pants pocket and handed it to Mr. Swenson.

"This is the money I've made so far from my carpentry work. It's not much, but it's a start. I trust you will keep this information to yourself."

"Of course. We do not discuss our depositors with anyone." He reached into a drawer and pulled out a paper. "Fill this out and we'll set up the account right away."

Joe picked up the pen and begin filling out the paper. "It's been easy to make friends with people here. How was it when you came?"

"The town was a little smaller then, but we made new friends who thought it a good idea to be friends with a bank president. When Mrs. Swenson passed and again when the bank was robbed, we learned who our true friends were."

"And I imagine most of them were from your church with Doc Whiteman and his family leading the rest."

"You're exactly right. Mrs. Whiteman and Mrs. Weatherby organized the ladies of the church to make things easier for Camilla and me. And it didn't stop after the first few weeks either. Those two ladies continued to make sure we were all right. They took care of Camilla when she was shot during the robbery. A lot of people stormed the bank and wanted their money, but Doc Whiteman talked some sense into them."

"That doesn't surprise me at all. I've been impressed by the Whiteman clan. I've never seen such friendly, caring people anywhere I've traveled. They took me in, helped me get on my feet, and made sure I had whatever I needed."

"I for one am delighted that you're staying. We haven't had this much curiosity and excitement in town since Micah Gordon returned home after his absence of five years."

Joe chuckled. Yes, he had created a lot of curiosity, but would they feel the same about him when they learned the truth?

⇶⫘

Tom read over his article about Governor Hogg and his ideas on education one more time. Satisfied he had all the information correct, Tom laid it on his desk and leaned back in his chair. The only other sound in the room came from the clacking of Gretchen's typewriter keys as she worked on a story for Saturday's edition of the *Herald*. Now that the paper came out on Mondays, Wednesdays, and Saturdays, circulation had picked up even more.

Gretchen's chair squeaked as she backed away from her desk. "For a small town, Stoney Creek sure has its share of social events. The Ladies' Altar Guild at your church, Tom, and the Women's Missionary Society at the other are planning to have a special fund-raising activity next week."

Tom laid down his pen. "I've heard Ma, Mrs. Weatherby, and Hannah discussing the Box Supper Auction. They're raising money to build an addition to the church."

"The Missionary Society wants to raise money for an orphanage in Dallas. Mrs. Booker told me they need equipment and furnishings for the children's rooms. They're adding a new dorm section that should be ready in time for Christmas. Both are excellent causes, and it's good to see the two churches working together on this."

"What's the name the mission ladies are calling their event?"

"It's the Fall Fantasy of Fun and Frolic. Rather a secular title for a church group, don't you think?"

Tom shrugged. "Not really. Sounds like fun to me."

"Have you asked anyone to go with you? Deputy Cooper asked me, but I told him I'd be working."

Tom wanted to smack himself. With the election coming up and the business with Joe, he'd clean forgotten about the festival and box supper a week from tomorrow. He'd planned to ask Angela if he could escort her but then thought of asking Faith. Now he hadn't asked either one of them, and it was rather late to do that. Better if he waited and took his chances with the box supper. "No, I haven't asked anyone. I haven't had time to think about it."

He reached over for a copy of Wednesday's paper. Time to change the subject. "Read your article about Joe. Good writing, but it doesn't have much we didn't already know."

"Strange, but while we were talking, it sounded like he was giving me a lot more information than that." She paused and tapped her chin with her index finger. "You know, Tom, there is some mystery about him. I noticed that his speech and use of language is very good. He's well-mannered too. I'm wondering if that penniless old man routine is some kind of disguise."

That exact thought had crossed Tom's mind more than once since Joe had come to town. He had nothing to go on but a hunch, but if another reporter believed the same, then there might be something to the idea.

"It's only been a few weeks, but he usually leaves town after he makes enough money for a ticket to his next destination. I say we leave him alone for a bit. Maybe he'll let his guard down and reveal something to us unintentionally."

Gretchen bit her lip, but her head bobbed in agreement. "I'm thinking you're right. We can keep our ears open and our eyes on him for however long he might decide to stay."

"Faith Delmont is helping too. She sees a lot in town through that big plate glass window, and she hears a lot too when the ladies come into the bakery." Even if Joe stayed for only a few more days or weeks, Tom wanted to know more about him, especially who he really was, where he had come from, and his purpose for staying in Stoney Creek. With three of them using their powers of observation and two reporters employing their skills for nosing out news, they might uncover Joe's secret after all.

CHAPTER 12

HE DAY OF the fund-raiser for the churches arrived with disappointment staring Faith in the face. Over the last week Tom had stopped by the bakery almost daily to buy a pastry and chat, but he had not asked to escort her to the festival. But then he hadn't asked Angela either—at least that's what Angela had told her. The only bright spot was the hope that Tom would select her basket for the auction this afternoon.

The smell of smoke and something burning wafted up the stairway and sent Faith running down to the kitchen to find the cause. When she met her mother in the bakery downstairs, she was fanning the air with a towel over a tray of cookies.

"Mama! What happened?" Faith scurried to help fan the air to rid it of smoke.

"That oven is what happened. It's even more unpredictable today than usual. Thank the good Lord that this is the last batch, so we still have plenty to sell at our booth."

She slid the cookies off the tray and pushed them into the garbage bin. "And that reminds me. You better get on over there with the last of these boxes. Aunt Ruby just left with a wagon full. You can meet her over there."

Faith loaded her arms with the boxes she could carry and headed for the festival grounds at Reverend Booker's church. When she reached her destination, Aunt Ruby had the tables covered and the signs with prices tacked up. Good thing Tom hadn't asked to accompany her because now she most likely wouldn't have time to spend with him anyway.

"Where do you want these, Aunt Ruby?"

"Set them over on that back table. I'm setting the pies here. We can sell them whole or by the slice."

Faith stacked the boxes before she opened one to put on display. After arranging the cookies on different plates and by flavor, she covered them with wax-coated paper to keep them fresh. One sample cookie sat atop the paper to identify the contents beneath.

Aunt Ruby had used glass covers from the bakery over the cakes that were to be sold whole. Several others were ready to be sliced for individual sales. Vases of asters and chrysanthemums decorated the tables, as well as pumpkins, apples, and gourds supplied by a local farmer. He had a booth where he would sell the same items for others to enjoy.

Various aromas mingled in the fall air and whetted Faith's appetite. Sausages, smoked meats, and hot cooking oil dominated with hints of the great food to be served later. The sounds of hammering and sawing came from those finishing up their booths this morning.

Mama joined them just before the booths were to open. "I finally got the burned smell from the kitchen and cleaned up the mess." She stoked the wood in a small wood stove at the back of the tent. Milk warmed in a pan on top, ready for the hot cocoa mixture she'd brought with her.

Aunt Ruby set tin cups on one counter of the booth. Joe had helped make this one for them and had made sure it fit all Mama's specifications. Aunt Ruby opened the tin of cocoa. "There's just enough hint of a chill in the air to make hot chocolate and apple cider a nice treat."

Faith set out the till box. "I might have to have a cup before too long." The weather had cooperated this mid-fall morning, which meant a lot of people would be out and about taking advantage of mild temperatures before a cold spell blew in.

One advantage of living deeper to the south in Texas was the late arrival of winter. In the past they'd even enjoyed mild weather up until Thanksgiving. Faith discarded her shawl and folded it. She placed it on a chair and smiled at Mayor Gladstone, who had just stepped up to their table.

"Good morning, Mayor. Looks like a fine day for a festival."

"Indeed it does. Sheriff Bolton guarantees there won't be any shenanigans to spoil things."

Even though the robbery at the livery occurred during the festival several years ago, he and the sheriff still worried something else like that may happen.

As soon as the open sign went up, customers began stopping by. As usual, Mama's cinnamon buns and Aunt Ruby's scones were a hit. Faith counted up the money in the box. So far the first hour brought a good sum. Papa had decided to donate half of the earnings to the mission offering for the Dallas orphanage. If all the booths showed such success, then the ladies would have a tidy sum by evening.

Thinking of the evening reminded her of the box social. She untied her apron and laid it over the back counter. "Mama, I'm going back home to fix up my box for the auction."

Mama nodded as she helped another customer. On her way to the house Faith met her father. "The booth is doing well, Papa. I'm sure the mission ladies will appreciate your donation."

"Yes, yes, I'm sure they will." He muttered and hurried on past toward the town park and all the booths.

Something about his demeanor niggled at Faith as she reached home. The faint odor of burned cookies reminded her of this morning's mishap and was likely the cause of her father's distraction. He was concerned about their old stove and how poorly it was performing. If only there were some way they could get a new stove before Clara's wedding. If they did, all the baked goods would be the best they'd ever made.

Once she reached home, Faith headed for the upstairs kitchen. Too bad it wasn't large enough to do the kind of baking they'd be doing for the holidays ahead. She added more wood to the stove and got out the black iron skillet. Fried chicken always sold well in box lunches.

An hour later she had a box filled with the chicken, homemade pickles, two slices of dried apple pie, Mama's special potato salad, home-canned green beans, and homemade bread. She wrapped the box in brown paper from Hempstead's store and decorated it with her favorite fall colors of orange, yellow, and gold.

On her way to the church with her box, she spotted Tom down the street. She turned the corner and hurried down to the next block where she could get to the church without seeing him. Rules said they weren't supposed to let any of the men see the boxes until bidding time, and she hadn't counted on seeing Tom or she would have covered hers with a piece of cloth.

After depositing the box at the church, Faith made her way back to where she had seen Tom earlier. When he came into view, she stopped short and caught her breath. Angela was with him. With tears in her eyes, Faith scurried her way around where the two stood and ran back to the booth. Surely Angela hadn't lied to her. Maybe they had just happened to meet.

Now Tom would most certainly not bid on her box. He intended to have supper with Angela. How could she ever compete with the blonde hair, blue eyes, and sweet disposition of Angela Booker?

>>><<<

From the corner of her eye Angela spotted Faith down the street. Now Faith would think Angela had lied about not going to the festival with Tom. She'd have to explain the first chance she had. She turned her attention back to Tom, who had been asking her about the orphanage in Dallas. He had just asked her how large the orphanage was.

"The orphanage has several hundred children now, and they need furnishings. We hope to collect enough money to pay for six beds and six chairs."

"How generous and thoughtful of your church to undertake such a project. Are you happy with the story Gretchen published about the festival earlier this week?"

"Yes, it was perfect. We're happy the newspaper was so willing to help us publicize the event."

"We're always open to anything for the good of Stoney Creek." He smiled and offered her his forearm. "Would you like to take a walk down to the Delmont booth for a cup of hot cocoa? Mr. Hempstead special orders the cocoa for Mrs. Delmont to use in her cooking."

She glanced down at her hand on his arm and started to pull it back, but what harm would there be if they were simply going for a stroll? "That sounds delightful. It'll help to ward off the little chill I feel."

They ambled down to the next block, and Angela breathed deeply of the delicious aromas coming from the food booths.

Tom stopped and sniffed the air. "Mr. Dietrich is making his funnel cakes again. He pours batter through a funnel into hot oil, and the dough fries up good and crunchy. He has syrup, sugar, or homemade preserves to top them."

"Ooh, that sounds delicious. Do let's get one."

"Of course, I'd be delighted to share one with you. He makes them really big." They approached the booth and Mr. Dietrich greeted them with his characteristic German brogue.

"*Gut* mornin', Tom. Here for one of my cakes, are ya?'

"Yes, sir, I am." He placed a coin on the counter as Mr. Dietrich lifted the cake from the hot oil and drained it. He placed it on a clean piece of parchment and laid it on the counter.

"Now, what shall I put on top?"

Tom glanced at Angela. "What shall it be?"

"Just the sugar. Syrup and preserves may be too messy."

After sprinkling the top with a cinnamon sugar mixture, Mr. Dietrich handed over the concoction. "Here ya go. Enjoy."

Tom pinched off a generous portion and gave it to Angela. When her lips closed around the bite she'd taken, the sweet crunchy goodness delighted her taste buds. "Oh, my, this is even better than it smells. I have to tell Mother and Aunt Daisy about them."

"Looks like Mr. Dietrich has won over another customer." Tom grinned and popped a morsel into his mouth.

When they had finished the delicacy, Angela dusted her hands together. "I think I'm ready for that hot chocolate now."

"Um, before we do that, would you consider going for a ride tomorrow afternoon after lunch? We could ride down by the creek. That is, if the weather stays this nice."

Her heart skipped a beat. Tom was inviting her for a ride and a picnic. This could be a chance to really get to know him better. "I'd be delighted to spend the afternoon with you. Thank you for asking."

"Good. I'll pick you up at two o'clock at the parsonage." Angela again grasped his arm, and they made their way to the Delmont stand for hot cocoa. When they stepped up to the counter, Faith turned her back on the two and busied herself with a plate of cookies in the back. Mrs. Delmont scowled at her daughter before turning to Tom and Angela.

"What will it be for you?"

"Two hot cocoas if you please."

Angela stared at Faith's back, and guilt stole into her heart. Faith had welcomed her to town and been nothing but cordial and friendly. Now here she was with Tom, for whom Faith apparently had feelings. Doubt clouded her mind about tomorrow's ride. She'd have to find out more about Faith and Tom's relationship and make sure she wasn't muddying the waters between them.

Mrs. Delmont handed them the two cups, and Tom plunked down the coins for the drinks. When Tom led her toward a bench where they could sit and drink their chocolate, Angela glanced back, but Faith still had her back to them. Definitely not a good sign.

After the cocoa Angela excused herself by telling Tom she'd meet him later after she helped her mother in their church's booth, where the ladies were selling quilts and needlework.

When she reached the booth, a number of customers browsed among the items for sale. Aunt Daisy welcomed her and set Angela about collecting money from the buyers.

Even as she smiled at people and wrote receipts for purchases, her thoughts were on what happened at the Delmont booth. Faith had completely ignored their presence. This was so unusual for the usually sunny and friendly Faith. What if Faith cared for Tom as more than a friend? Angela couldn't come between them. Somehow she'd have to make amends even though she truly enjoyed Tom's company.

When time came for the box supper auction, Angela hurried to the First Church's grounds. All the boxes had been placed on a table for display. Angela spotted hers right off. She joined the other women who waited on the sidelines for the bidding to begin.

Clara grabbed Angela's arm. "Isn't this exciting? I do hope Theodore understood my hint about my box. Even though that may be cheating, I don't want to share it with anyone else."

Angela laughed. "I'm sure he'll know which one is yours. I don't really care. I think it would be fun to have someone new win my box."

"Well, I've seen plenty of the cowboys in town, so they'll be bidding good and high to get a box from one of the single girls."

The bidding began, and the first boxes went quickly. Jeb Cooper had the highest bid on Miss O'Neal's box, and a cowboy bid highest on Miss Simmons's box, with Theodore Gladstone winning Clara's.

When one decorated in the colors of fall came up and Tom bid on it, Angela realized that it must be Faith's box. Angela bit her lip. If Tom won the box, maybe it would soothe Faith's feelings, and she would not think so poorly of Angela.

When the bidding finally ended, two cowboys had outbid Tom on both Faith's and Angela's boxes. A flash of compassion for Faith stabbed Angela's heart. Her face registered disappointment, but then Faith smiled and wandered off with the young man who won the bid.

"Miss Booker, I believe this is your box."

Angela glanced up to find a clean-shaven, nicely dressed cowboy holding her box. "Yes, it is." She extended her hand. "I'm pleased to meet you, and I do hope you enjoy the meal I prepared."

"Anything prepared by hands pretty as yours will be tasty." He offered her his arm and led her to one of the tables set up for eating.

She had wanted to meet more people, so here was her chance. After all, she did have a picnic planned with Tom tomorrow, and then she'd have her chance to get to know him better. But should she have agreed to meet him? If anything happened between Tom and her, how would Faith react?

Angela drove the thought from her mind and concentrated on the cowboy seated across from her. One step at a time...

≫ CHAPTER 13 ≪

$\mathcal{T}$OM HITCHED HIS pa's horse to the buggy. The weather had cooperated with sunshine for his afternoon ride with Angela Booker. The time had come for him to get to know her better. He had known Faith his whole life, but Angela only a few months. Still, he'd known Angela long enough to know that, like Faith, she was a beautiful Christian woman who shared his faith and reliance on God.

He'd prayed about which young woman should be a part of his future, but so far the Lord had been silent on Tom's love life. This afternoon's ride down to the creek should shed some light on his predicament. He'd even had Ma fix up a basket of cookies and lemonade for refreshment.

The week hadn't revealed any new truths about Joe either. Faith had told him about seeing Joe going into the bank, and Tom drew the conclusion that Joe had opened an account and would stay in Stoney Creek longer than he had originally planned. This meant Tom would now have more time to dig into Joe's past. Although he hadn't come up with a way to do so, Tom's confidence in his investigative skills assured him he would find more information.

Tom stowed the basket in the buggy and drove the few blocks to the parsonage behind Reverend Booker's church. After dropping the hitching stone, Tom made his way to the front door. The church and parsonage had been here only a short time, but they blended in with the town so well they didn't look quite so new.

He lifted his hand to knock, but the door opened before he could do so. He poised with his hand in the air as Angela grinned at him.

"I was watching for you from the window. My parents have a couple from church visiting, and Aunt Daisy is taking a little rest, so I hurried to meet you."

A chuckle escaped Tom. "And you almost had a rap on the nose."

"I'm sorry about that, but now that you're here, shall we be going? I've already said good-bye to Mama and Papa." She wrapped her shawl about her shoulders and pulled the door closed behind her.

"Of course, and our carriage awaits." He held her elbow and walked beside her to the buggy.

A few minutes later he turned the buggy down the road leading to the creek. "I hope you don't mind riding down by Stoney Creek. It's nice this time of year. The trees have all turned to their fall colors and offer a beautiful setting."

"I don't mind at all. I love this time of the year. The weather here is perfect. We lived in the northwest part of the state, and November usually meant cold weather and getting ready for winter."

"Here in the lower part of Texas it doesn't start getting colder until later in the month, maybe around Thanksgiving." Tom groaned inside. Couldn't he come up with a better topic than the weather?

Angela, though, continued the conversation. "I've really grown to love the people and the town. Everyone has been very friendly, and there has been no rivalry or competition between our new church and your old, established one."

A wave of relief washed over Tom. This was a much better topic. "I believe that's because there is always room for another church to fill with people who love God and want to worship. Any place growing in population needs more than one church to meet their needs."

Angela cut her gaze toward him. "Those are my father's sentiments. When a few people from town decided to build another church, they came to Father with the news that the town was growing and needed another church. Since he's a man of vision, he accepted the challenge to come here and begin the new church."

"And it looks like it's doing well. I may have to come over and visit just to see what's going on." He pulled the horse to a stop. "Here we are at one of my favorite spots."

He stepped down from the buggy then went around to help Angela down from her seat. He reached behind her for the basket and a blanket. "I have lemonade and cookies and a blanket to sit on. Ma thought we might enjoy these as we talked."

"How very sweet of her. I've only seen your mother at the store and in the bakery, but she's always been very friendly, and she did call on Aunt Daisy to welcome her to Stoney Creek. I've heard she's a very good cook."

"You heard right about that. Ma loves to cook." He spread the blanket on the ground under one of the oak trees and set the basket near the edge. This was going even better than he had imagined, but he preferred some topic instead of his family and his mother's cooking.

>>>><<<<

Angela sat beside Tom, and they gazed out at the creek. "Have you lived anywhere else but Stoney Creek, Tom?"

"No, not really. My folks came here when I was a young child, so it's the only home I remember. Pa came to replace the doctor who was retiring. He had a big family as well, so his house and offices fit our family perfectly."

"I think I've met most of your family, but my goodness, they are a large group. What with the Whiteman and Gordon families merged and all the relatives, you could fill a church all by yourselves."

"And there's more in the future what with Clara marrying the mayor's son and then Daniel, Alice, and Juliet coming up as well."

Angela removed her hat and let the ribbons trail through her fingers. "And what are your plans, Tom? Do you want to keep working for the newspaper?"

"I'm not sure at this point. I like working for Mr. Blake, and this is my hometown, but I've thought about what it would be like to work for a larger newspaper in Dallas or Houston."

He leaned back on one elbow and grinned up at Angela. "That's enough about me. Tell me more about yourself."

"We've lived in three towns since I was a little girl and now Stoney Creek. When Father feels God leading him to another church who offers a call, he'll move. I don't mind though. I love getting to know different parts of the country and making new friends."

"I can't imagine moving so much." He broke off a piece of grass and rolled it between his fingers. "Have you thought about your own future and what you might do?"

Angela pulled her legs up under her skirt and rested her chin on her knees. "I've been reading about a woman named Lottie Moon, who is a missionary in China. Her work sounds fascinating. It's a wonderful way to serve the Lord."

Tom sat up straight. "Sure, but it's on the other side of the world. There should be plenty to do right here in America and most certainly Texas."

"Yes, my father says Texas is a great mission field. I'll serve God wherever He calls me to go." If it happened to be here with Tom, that might not be so bad. Time would tell where their relationship was headed. "Have you given much thought to where God might want you to serve?"

"I agree it's important to pray about what God wants us to do with our life. Unless God leads me in a dramatically different direction, I think I'd be content to stay right here in Stoney Creek for the rest of my life."

"It's good to be content with the life God has given you." Angela wished she had that same emotion. Ever since she'd read about Lottie Moon, she'd felt a stirring inside. As much as she was interested in Tom and as much as she liked Stoney Creek, she cared more about what the Lord wanted for her future. Would He ask her to stay, marry, and have children? Or would He ask her to go to a strange place and experience a life she couldn't even imagine?

With her thoughts and emotions in a jumble, Angela decided she needed to spend more time with the Lord in deciding which direction to go. But for now she would enjoy this time with Tom.

⤜⤜⤜

Faith stood beside her horse in a grove of trees up creek from where Tom and Angela sat. How could he have brought her to their favorite spot? Of course it wasn't private or anything, but it had been special. Tears blurred her eyes, and she blinked them back.

After seeing them together yesterday at the festival, she'd hoped that maybe Tom would bid on her box for the auction. She'd been delighted when he did, but then one of Micah Gordon's cowhands had outbid him. The dinner had been pleasant enough, but it hadn't been Tom.

Now here Angela and Tom were here on what looked like a picnic. They appeared to be in a serious conversation under her favorite tree. Were they making a commitment to each other? They hadn't known each other long enough for that. Still, the idea rolled around in her head and caused her stomach to tie itself in knots.

Faith leaned her head against her horse's flank. Tom had only greeted her in passing at church this morning. She should have known he had other plans for a Sunday afternoon as nice as this one. Why had she decided to ride out to the creek today? The stately trees, rolling meadow, and gurgling creek all faded to the background. All that occupied her senses was the sight of the couple now seated under a tree...one of her favorite trees.

Jealously rose like bile and threatened to cut off Faith's breath. She bit her lip and breathed deeply to bring some calm back to her body. It had been bad enough when they had come to the booth yesterday, and now they were here together again.

Faith didn't want to see anymore. She swung her leg up over her horse and turned back toward town taking care she wouldn't be seen by Tom or Angela.

After leaving her horse with Willy at the livery, Faith walked back up Main Street. Not ready to go home, she strolled past the bakery and down to Pecan Lane, her heart filled with jealousy. When she reached the boardinghouse, Joe stood at the edge of the path in front of the house.

Maybe if she got him to talk with her, she'd have more information for Tom, and he would take more notice of her. "Hi, Joe, are you out for a walk?"

"Just getting back. I saw you coming down from town and decided to wait for you." He opened the gate in the fence lining the front lawn. "If you're not going anywhere in particular, come sit a spell with me."

That was one invitation she wasn't about to refuse. "Thank you, I believe I will. Lead the way."

Joe settled in one chair on the wide porch and Faith in the other. Joe said nothing for a minute or two, and Faith searched her mind for a question to ask or anything to start a conversation.

"Is something troubling you, dear girl?"

Faith jerked back and her eyes opened wide. "Why...why would you ask that?"

"I see it in your eyes. Have anything to do with Tom and Miss Booker? I saw them together at the festival yesterday and then again leaving in the buggy when I came out of the boardinghouse earlier."

Heat filled Faith's cheeks. "I guess. Angela's a wonderfully sweet girl. I can see why Tom would want to get to know her."

"So you like her, but not the idea of her being with Tom."

How did this old man see and know so much? No one else knew of her pangs of jealousy whenever she saw Tom and Angela together. Or did they?

"I'd rather not talk about that right now if you don't mind."

"Don't mind at all, but I'm here if you need to."

His smile softened her heart, but what could a stranger say to help this situation? "Thank you, Joe. I'll remember that."

A lot of questions filled her head, but they were not the ones she wanted to be asking while sitting with Joe. She cleared her throat and was seeking another topic for conversation when he spoke up again.

"I really like your town, Miss Delmont. It's a thriving community, but still has that hometown, family feel to it that makes a person feel welcome. Even the ones who doubted me a bit have been friendly the past week or so."

This was more like it. Faith leaned forward. "I noticed you've been busy doing carpentry work. From what I've seen, you're good at it too. Where did you learn the trade?"

"My pa taught me everything I know. He made most of the furniture and things for our home." He held out gnarled hands spotted with the signs of old age. "Can't do as much with 'em as I once did, but I'm getting by."

"What about your family? I imagine your parents are both gone by now, but what about brothers and sisters?"

A faraway look came into his eyes and Joe stared into space. Faith waited, and after a moment he jerked his head then shook it. "Don't have brothers and sisters and no children of my own either."

"I'm sorry to hear that, Joe. I have only one brother, but I miss him terribly. He married and moved to New Orleans to be a doctor there." Questions flooded Faith's mind, but good sense bade her think before she jumped in and appeared nosy.

"Tell me some more about your family, Faith. I take it you've lived here most of your life."

"Yes, I have. In fact, the doctor who was here before Doc Whiteman delivered me in our home above the bakery." A smile tickled her lips. How clever to direct the questions back to her.

"Tell me, if Mayor Gladstone could do anything he wanted for this town, what do you think it would be?"

Where had that question come from? And how would she know what Mayor Gladstone wanted for this town? "Um...I suppose it would be for the railroad to hurry up and complete the new line through here that will take a train up toward the northern part of the state. It's supposed to be completed by next spring, and then we'll have a direct route to Colorado."

"And what would you want most, Miss Faith Delmont?"

She laughed. "That's easy. Aside from Tom, we need a new stove for Mama in the kitchen and a bigger place to serve our baked goods."

"Business is good then?"

"Well, yes and no. We spend a lot of money on repairs, and Mama does a lot of cooking for people who can't do it for themselves. Like when Mrs. Olson had her twin boys to add to four other young'uns and had to stay in bed. Mama took a meal over to their house every night until Mrs. Olson was on her feet again."

Faith glanced toward the street and sucked in her breath. The buggy carrying Tom and Angela had turned onto Pecan Lane in the direction of the parsonage. A stab of jealousy pierced her heart.

Joe turned to stare in the direction her gaze pointed and shook his head. Faith stood and held out her hand. "Thank you, Joe. I've enjoyed talking with you, but I best get back home. Mama will most likely start worrying about me."

"I've enjoyed it too, Miss Delmont. Tell your ma I sure liked that pecan pie Mrs. Hutchins bought for our Sunday dinner."

"I will. Hope we can talk again sometime. Bye now." Faith hurried down the sidewalk to the street. One thing for sure, she didn't want Tom to see her out this time of day. She had news for him, but it could wait until tomorrow or even the next day. Tears once again threatened, but she blinked them back. She was not going to cry over Tom Whiteman.

⋙ CHAPTER 14 ⋘

OE SIGNED HIS name on the letter he planned to send back to his lawyer. This should take care of all the business he'd left behind when he'd begun his journey. As soon as he heard back from Stanley Baxter, he could begin dealings with the lawyer here in town.

Satisfaction at making the right choice filled Joe's heart. The Lord had been good to him in so many ways and had blessed his life even with the tragedies that had happened along the way. The Lord had been on every step of this journey begun last summer and would continue to walk with Joe the remainder of the way, however long that might be.

He sauntered down the stairs at the boardinghouse. The only sounds in the house came from the kitchen where Emma Hutchins prepared something for dinner. This time he didn't stop to tell her he was leaving but strolled out to the front sidewalk and opened the gate.

He inhaled the brisk fall air, and a hint of cold weather to come filled his lungs. Tom had said they didn't get much snow in this area, but freezing temperatures and ice were common. Joe hoped he'd enjoy decent weather for the remainder of his time here, as he'd be going home to ice and snow soon enough.

Not many people filled the streets of Stoney Creek this afternoon. Mondays were normally slow days anyway after a busy Saturday when one could barely walk or ride in town. Soon the fall decorations would give way to Christmas and truly signal the end of Joe's stay in Stoney Creek. He had come to love the town, and his only wish for now was to be here long enough to see some of his desires for the town come to pass.

He stopped in at the bank to see Mr. Swenson. The bank president stood in the lobby conversing with another patron. Joe waited until he had ended his conversation then approached. "Mr. Swenson, do you have a moment?"

"Certainly." The bank president waved Joe toward his office in the back.

Once behind closed doors, Mr. Swenson asked, "What can I do for you, Joe?"

"I'm impressed with your discretion, Mr. Swenson, and wondered if I could ask you a favor. I need to send a letter home, but I'd rather not have the whole town chattering about it. Would you consent to send this letter for me using the bank's return address? I would compensate the bank, of course."

"Certainly. I will insert it into an envelope with the bank's return address. No questions about it will arise. We can trust James Hempstead, but no telling who might be at the general store when I post it. Until we actually get that post office for Stoney Creek, our mail isn't all that private."

Just as Joe had anticipated, Mr. Swenson asked no questions and readily agreed to Joe's unusual request. Just one more indication that Joe could trust the banker with the rest of his plan when the time came to put it into action.

Joe stood and extended his hand. "Thank you. I appreciate your discretion."

"I'm happy to be of service."

Joe appreciated the firm grip of the banker's hand. Everything in his dealings with Mr. Swenson had proven him to be reliable and trustworthy, and he looked forward to more dealings with the man.

After leaving the bank, Joe stood on the boardwalk. Parts of Main Street had been laid with bricks and stone and made for less mud in the rains, but it also made for more noise from wagon and buggy wheels and the clip-clop of horseshoes. Several people greeted Joe as he made his way back to the boardinghouse.

He needed to make one more stop, however. When the Whiteman house came into view, he stepped up his pace. On the street in front of the house he stopped and gazed at the structure. He well remembered his first night in town spent at the Whiteman home. The welcome, the food, and the fellowship with the family had been like none he'd experienced on his cross-country trip. Truly, he felt like he'd come home.

He entered the center reception room of the clinic to be greeted by Hannah Gordon. "Good afternoon, Joe. Are you here to see the doctor?"

"If he isn't busy, I'd like to have a few minutes of his time."

"He isn't busy. I'll let him know you're here." She disappeared through a door.

A few minutes later, Doc Whiteman waved Joe into his office. "What's on your mind this afternoon, Joe?"

"Nothing much." He followed the doctor into his office. "Nice to see Hannah in her nursing duties."

"She's a real blessing. Comes in on Tuesdays, Wednesdays, and Fridays. Mrs. Gordon cares for her children in the summer. In the winter months Hannah brings them into school then works with me until they get out. A real nice arrangement." He sat behind his desk and nodded toward a chair. "Have a seat, and tell me what I can do for you."

With the doctor's well-known reputation for integrity, anything said in this room would be kept in strict confidentiality. "I've run out of some medication I've been taking. My doctor at home gave me a good supply, but I've been gone longer than I expected. He gave me the prescription order, but I didn't want to raise questions with the apothecary in town or let word get out about my illness."

Dr. Whiteman leaned forward with his forearms resting on his desk. "What type of medication are you taking?"

"It's for the pain that sometimes comes with my condition. The doctor says it's cancer and I don't have much longer here on this earth."

The doctor didn't change expression. He simply nodded and asked, "Where is this cancer located?"

"In my colon. Had surgery earlier in the summer, but the doctor couldn't get it all. He gave me about six months, and that six months will up around the first of the year."

"I'm sorry to hear that, real sorry. From what I've seen, cancer can be quite painful. I can understand your need for pain medication. Let me have your prescription, and I'll take care of it for you."

"I do appreciate it. Hasn't been a very bad pain up until now, but the bouts with it are coming closer together."

"I imagine they are." Dr. Whiteman's eyes narrowed, and he pursed his lips. "Don't you have family back home wondering about you and where you are?"

Joe grinned. "I figured you'd be asking that. I think a lot of people would like to know more about me if their questions are any indication."

That brought a chuckle from the good doctor. "Yes, they would. My wife and son are among those I know who are curious. I'm surprised you've been able to keep the information hidden from Tom or Miss O'Neal."

"Oh, that's been tough, for certain. Those two are very good at their jobs, and I believe Faith Delmont is on the hunt for the truth herself, but I've become an expert at evading their questions. As to your question, no, I don't have any family worrying about me. My wife and I were only children. We had one daughter who would be about Miss Hannah's age now and even had beautiful red hair, but she died in a tragic accident ten years ago, and then my wife passed on three years ago."

"That's sad news, and I'm sorry for your loss." He leaned back in his chair. "I know you say your doctor gave you six months, but he can't be sure. According to our Lord, your days were numbered before you were born, and only He knows the time you are to die."

"That's true, but I'm weaker now than I was back in June, and I think the good Lord is preparing me for what lies ahead. At least I know where I'm going, and I'll see my beloved Mary Ann and Rebecca. Until then, I have things I want to get done. I believe I can trust you not to reveal any of this, even to Mrs. Whiteman."

"Patient and doctor relationship confidentiality forbids me to do so."

"That's what I counted on." Joe pulled a slip of paper from his pocket and handed it to the doctor.

Dr. Whiteman studied the prescription before placing it on his desk. "Let me know if your pain becomes worse, and I'll make sure you get a stronger dosage."

Joe stood and extended his hand to a confidante for the second time that day. Each one knew only half his secret, and that's the way he wanted it to stay. "Thank you for your time, and I'll drop back in when you have the prescription ready."

After shaking hands with the doctor, Joe waved good-bye to Hannah and strolled back out to the street. His body ached as weariness settled in his bones. Time for some rest before dinner. He'd accomplished the two major tasks on his list for today, and that filled him with joy and satisfaction. Two men he trusted knew two different parts of his secret, and because of their honesty and adhering to the rules of their professions, the secrets would remain exactly that.

≫≫≪≪

Tom studied the schedule before him. Mr. Blake had given him another out-of-town assignment. He'd be gone for a few days covering Governor Hogg's bid for reelection. Even with the new wire Mr. Blake wanted firsthand information from Tom of his impressions of the race.

He tucked the schedule away in his satchel. His bag sat packed and ready to go on tomorrow's train, but first he wanted to see Faith and let her know he'd be gone a few days. He also wanted to see whether she'd learned anything more about Joe.

After bidding good-bye to his parents, Tom grabbed his hat from the hall tree and squared it on his head. As he walked toward the Delmont house, he envied the close relationship between his mother and father. They had married as soon as Pa returned from the war in 1865 and had celebrated twenty-seven years of marriage this past June. Theirs was the kind of love he wanted with a woman, but so far his heart hadn't given him a clue, and God had been silent as well. He liked Angela, and he wanted to know her better. He'd known Faith so long she'd become like one of his sisters.

Tom hesitated at the top of the stairs to the Delmont home above the bakery. Faith might be helping her mother with preparations for the next day at the bakery. Maybe this wasn't a good time.

His hand lifted to knock. He'd come this far and might as well finish and take his chances. After the second rap Faith opened the door. A bibbed white apron covered her greenish-blue dress, and her brown eyes opened wide in surprise. Tom's heart skipped a beat. For some reason this time her beauty hit him full force. He swallowed hard as she smiled.

Tom snatched off his hat. "Hello, Faith. Am I interrupting, or do you have a few minutes for a visit?" His fingers clutched the hat brim. Since when had Faith's presence made him this nervous?

Faith stepped back and pulled at the strings of her apron. "I always have time for you, Tom. Come in. Mama and I were just finishing the pies for tomorrow." She lifted the apron over her head and wadded it over her arm.

Mrs. Delmont appeared behind Faith. "Good evening, Tom. Faith and I are done, so you two go on and visit a spell. Would you like anything to drink or eat?"

Much as Tom would have loved a few of Mrs. Delmont's cookies, he shook his head. "No, I'm fine, thank you."

She nodded, smiled, and then left them alone.

"It's a nice evening. Could we sit on your balcony and talk?"

"Of course." Faith reached for a shawl on a peg by the door and wrapped it around her shoulders. Then she stepped around Tom and out onto the balcony, which ran across the back of the building. She lit a lantern and set it in the middle of a small table, and then she sat down and waited for Tom to join her.

The evening had cooled but not so much as to be uncomfortable. Hanging baskets of Boston fern hung from the eaves of the balcony, and pots of bright yellow and bronze flowers sat along the railing. Tom pulled up a chair and sat. Before too many more days the white wicker furniture would be stored away until warmer weather next spring, but tonight the two chairs and table offered a pleasant place to chat.

For some reason he couldn't fathom, Tom's hands shook as he clasped them between his knees. "Mr. Blake is sending me on another trip to cover the state election campaign, so I'll be gone until Saturday."

Faith's eyebrows raised and her head tilted. "Oh, that should be interesting with all the candidates who want to oust Hogg."

"It will be, but I'll also have a chance to hear more about the presidential election as well. With Mr. Cleveland determined to serve a second term and Harrison just as determined to stay in office, I should have lots of information to write about." Why in the world was he discussing politics? Get to the real purpose of the visit.

"Faith, the important thing is that while I'm gone, I want you to be eyes and ears for me and watch Joe carefully. For some reason I have a feeling he's up to something, but I can't quite put my finger on what it might be."

"Couldn't Miss O'Neal do that for you?"

"Not really. She's a reporter, and Joe doesn't seem to trust her any more than he does me. You've become a friend, so he might open up to you." Besides, he didn't want Gretchen nosing around and come up with a story before he did.

"I see. If that's what you need me to do, I will, but have you ever considered he might really be just an old man who wants to travel around and see the country before he dies?"

"Maybe, but I feel it in my bones. There's a lot more to his story than he's revealed since he's been here."

Faith bit her lip and appeared hesitant about something. Tom sat back in his chair and peered at her. What went on in that pretty head of hers? "What are you not telling me?"

"I had a visit with Joe Sunday afternoon."

"And you didn't tell me? What did he say? What did you find out?"

"I...I'm sorry. I didn't think about it until now. He told me he learned carpentry from his father and that he had no family." She paused a moment. "Funny thing is, he had me talking about my family and the town before I could ask more about him."

"He's good at that, but at least we know more than we did. Don't know that it helps much, but it's something."

A comfortable silence developed as he studied her. A few tendrils of hair had escaped from their pins and trailed down her neck. Heat from the kitchen had given her cheeks a rosy glow that enhanced her natural beauty, and her brown eyes glowed in the lamplight. What would it be like to caress those cheeks and run his fingers through her dark hair?

Heat began in Tom's neck and ran up to his face. He jumped from his chair. "I...um...I better be going. Have some work to do before leaving tomorrow." He didn't really, but something had changed, and he had no idea what to do about it.

"All right. I probably won't be able to see you off at the station tomorrow. We're usually pretty busy that time of day." She stood and moved to stand beside him on the top step. Her face turned up to his.

"I understand, and thanks for the information about Joe. We make a good team." His hand rose and his fingers slid across her cheek. Before he had his wits about him, he leaned down and brushed her lips with his. "You're a beautiful woman, Faith Delmont." Before she could react, he pulled away, shook his head, and raced down the steps.

His heart pounded.

What in the world had possessed him to kiss Faith?

CHAPTER 15

AITH LEANED AGAINST the balcony rail and stared after Tom until he disappeared into the night. Her fingertips brushed her lips. What had just happened? That was the first time Tom had ever come even close to doing anything romantic. And now not only had he said she was beautiful, he'd kissed her!

Her heart pounded in her chest. Whatever it meant, she had thoroughly enjoyed the touch of his lips on hers. She fanned her face with her hand as the heat rose in her cheeks. This was much more than a simple kiss, or at least it was to her. Tom had left so suddenly. Maybe it'd been a mistake and he'd regretted it immediately.

Those thoughts would get her nowhere. She shook them off and doused the lamp. She stepped inside the house and closed the door behind her. Tears filled her eyes. She loved Tom with all her heart. If this was an indication he might return that love, she'd be the happiest girl in Stoney Creek.

Her mother appeared in the hallway. "Oh, is Tom gone already?"

"Yes. He's leaving town tomorrow and wanted to say good-bye." And to ask her to keep an eye on Joe, but Mama didn't need to know that.

"That was nice of him." She stopped in front of Faith and touched her cheek. "You're blushing, my sweet. What happened?"

Faith flung her arms about her mother's neck. "Oh, Mama, I'm so confused." Tears began to fall, and she sobbed.

Mama patted her back and held her close. "What has you confused, my dear?"

"I…I don't know what to do about Tom." She released her mother and stepped back to swipe the tears from her cheeks. "I love him, but I'm not sure how he feels about me."

"I see. Let's go into the parlor where we can talk." She held Faith's hand and led her to the sofa. "Now tell me all about it," she said as they sat down together.

"I've known Tom practically all my life. He's always been so nice to me and paid some attention to me as well, like those times when Mrs. Whiteman's friends from Louisiana came to visit and we would go to the theater and parties together. Then he was off to school, and I was so afraid he'd find a pretty girl there and bring her back to Stoney Creek as a bride. But he didn't, so I still had hopes for us."

"Have things changed between the two of you?" Mama reached over and held Faith's hands.

"I don't know. Since Angela Booker came to town, he's been with her a lot. They even went for a buggy ride together last Sunday, and he took her to our favorite place."

"I imagine that hurt you." She squeezed Faith's hands. "I've seen him with her a time or two, but I had no idea you felt anything more than friendship toward Tom. You two are always laughing and having such fun together. Although I had hoped you two would be together some day, you seemed more like a sister to him."

"That's part of the problem. We've known each other so long and done so many things together that I *have* felt more like his sister, but now my heart says otherwise."

Tears trickled from the corners of her eyes and stained her cheeks. "He kissed me tonight…just a quick one, but I liked it and wanted him to do it again. Instead, he jumped like he'd been shot and ran off down the stairs like the sheriff was after him."

Mama smiled and pulled Faith close to her side. "Honey, I'm sure he was just as surprised by what he did as you were, and he had to get away to think about it."

"I guess that may be it, but why would he even do it in the first place?"

"I think he cares more about you than he realized. It may have been a spur-of-the-moment type of kiss, but I believe it came from his heart."

Faith bit her lip and remembered his words about her being beautiful. He'd never said anything like that before. She turned and hugged her mother. "Oh, Mama, I do hope it did."

"Remember that God has a plan for all three of you. Be patient, and He'll reveal that plan to you, Tom, and Angela in His timing."

Mama was right as usual, but patience was one virtue Faith sorely lacked. She rested her head on her mother's shoulder. "May I take time tomorrow to see him off at the train?"

"Of course you can. Aunt Ruby and I can handle things."

"Thank you." She wiped her cheeks and faced her mother. "Tell me your impression of Joe Fitzgerald."

"And why would that be of any importance to you?"

"It's a long story, but essentially Tom asked me to keep an ear open to learn what I can about Joe. Tom is suspicious of the old man and who he says he is."

"Why, Faith Delmont, I can't believe you're probing into a man's private life. Joe is a nice old man down on his luck, and it's none of your business who he really might be or where he comes from."

Faith swallowed hard. She should never have said anything about Joe, but it had spurted forth from her mouth before she even had time to think about it. "I'm sorry, but he is mysterious, sort of, and I don't really know anything."

Mama lifted Faith's chin and peered at her. "All right, but promise me that you won't get too nosy and cause Joe any harm."

"I do promise, Mama." And she'd keep it, but that didn't mean she'd stop asking questions and trying to find out more about him, for Tom's sake.

Mama patted Faith's shoulder and stood. "I'll hold you to it. Now, it's time to get to bed. We have an early morning."

Faith continued to sit as Mama left the room. She'd go to bed in a minute, but she wanted to savor the moment when Tom kissed her.

A few minutes later she sighed and made her way to her room. After undressing and pulling her gown over her head, she sat on the edge of the bed. She'd keep her promise to Mama, but the identity of the old man did whet her curiosity. She pulled the covers back and crawled beneath them with a vow to be even more observant of Joe in the future.

Her fingers caressed her lips again. Tom had kissed her.

>>><<<

Despite the dark of the evening Tom sat on the porch at home. The memory of the kiss with Faith lingered in his thoughts. He'd never had any romantic notions like that toward her before even though he had considered courting her. Then tonight she'd looked so beautiful in the lamplight with her eyes so full of life and sparkle that he'd been overcome with emotion.

A groan escaped into the night air. What if he'd ruined their friendship? What if she had no such feelings toward him? If only he could see her tomorrow and get an idea of what she might be thinking now, but she'd said they'd be too busy at the bakery for her to see him off on his trip.

The glow from the lamplight revealed a figure on the walk in front of the house. He peered out into the dim light. "Joe, is that you?"

"Why, yes, it is. I didn't expect anyone to be up so late. It's a nice fall evening for a walk about town." He took a step away. "Good evening, Tom. Have a nice night."

"Joe, wait, I need to talk with you a minute." He had an inexplicable urge to talk to him about Faith. Now why would that be? How could Joe know what he should do about Faith?

Joe stopped and turned back to Tom. "Can't it wait until tomorrow?"

"No, it can't. I really need some advice. Ma and Pa are already in bed, so I don't want to disturb them."

Joe hesitated a moment before answering. "I see. I suppose I can spare you some time." He walked up to the porch and joined Tom.

"Now what's on your mind, young man? What's so urgent it can't wait until tomorrow?"

"I'm not sure where to begin. It's about Faith Delmont." Tom clasped his hands between his knees and leaned forward, thankful Joe couldn't see so well with just the light from the lamp at the street.

"Ah, an affair of the heart, is it?"

Even though Joe's face wasn't clear, Tom sensed the old man's smile. "I guess it is," Tom admitted. "We've been friends all our lives, and we've done all kinds of things together and with each other's families. She and my sister Clara have been good friends for as long as I can remember, and I guess Faith has been like a sister to me."

"And things have changed?"

How could this man be so discerning? "I'm not sure, but I think they have."

"May I ask your feelings for Miss Booker?"

Angela? How did Joe know about Angela? "Why do you ask that?"

Joe leaned toward Tom. "I saw you take her in your buggy for a ride last Sunday, and most times that means a young man may be courting a young woman. Is that not the case?"

"No, yes, oh, I don't know. I do admit I had a notion to court her, but now this with Faith makes me stop and think. She's more what I would want in a wife." Tom's heart leaped in his chest. Where had those words come from? He'd had too many unexpected thoughts and actions for one night.

"Interesting. Have you said anything to Miss Delmont?"

"Um, no, I didn't want to spoil our friendship, but I... I... sorta... kissed her good night." Another groan. How dumb did that statement sound? Good thing he hadn't added the bit about telling her she was beautiful.

Joe chuckled. "I think maybe you gave her a hint of your feelings tonight. How did she respond?"

Heat filled Tom's face once again. "Well, I'm not sure. You see, I ran off soon as it happened."

This time Joe laughed out loud. "My boy, you have a thing or two to learn about young women."

"Yeah, I guess I do. I sure hope I didn't ruin our friendship with that kiss, and it wasn't a real kiss. I kinda brushed her lips with mine." Could this be any more humiliating?

Even in the darkness Joe's head shaking was obvious. "Son, I'm sure Miss Delmont is just as confused as you are at this point."

Before Tom could respond, a man ran up the sidewalk yelling, "I need to see the doctor right now!"

Tom stood and grabbed the man by the arms. The man shook and tears streamed down his cheeks. "Slow down, Mr. Kirk. My pa's asleep. What's the emergency?"

"It's my wife, the new baby's coming, and it's too soon. Please get your pa. I need him to come help her."

The fear in the man's eyes gripped Tom's heart. "I'll go get him. Joe, get him some water while I wake up Pa."

He left the two men, raced up the stairs, and pounded on his father's door. "Pa, Pa, Mr. Kirk is here, and he says his wife needs you. He says the baby's coming early."

The sound of the bed creaking and then his pa's voice filtered through the closed door. "I'm up, Tom. I'll be dressed and down in a minute."

"Okay."

Clara emerged from her room and punched him on the arm. "What's all the racket? You could wake the dead with that yelling."

Tom glanced over her shoulder to find Alice and Juliet standing in their doorway, rubbing their eyes. "Mrs. Kirk's baby is coming, and Pa's going out to help her. Go on back to bed."

He pushed past Clara and jumped down the stairs. Mr. Kirk set down the glass he'd been holding when Tom burst through the door to the porch. "Pa's on his way. How did you get here?"

"My horse is out at the street."

"Then I'll run out and saddle Pa's. It'll be done by the time he gets down here." Tom ran to the barn and snagged the saddle from its perch and carried it to Midnight's stall. "Sorry to disturb you, old boy, but Pa needs you."

After making sure the saddle was on securely and the bit was positioned correctly in the horse's mouth, Tom led him out of the barn and toward the house. His pa came running across the yard.

"Thanks, Tom." He swung up onto the saddle and secured his bag. He called back as he sped away. "Don't know how long I'll be. Hope to be back in time to say good-bye, but if I'm not, have a safe trip."

Tom stared after the departing figures until they and the lantern Mr. Kirk had brought disappeared into the night.

He returned to the porch to find Joe still sitting there. "I thought you'd be gone by now."

"No, I wanted to talk more with you." He waved toward his chair. "Sit and tell me about this man and his family."

⫸ CHAPTER 16 ⫷

ARLY TUESDAY MORNING as soon as she'd finished breakfast, Angela hurried down the street toward the Delmont Bakery. She had planned to come on Monday, but her mother had kept her busy all day with one chore after another. After what had occurred over the weekend, she simply *had* to talk with Faith about Tom Whiteman. Angela was attracted to the man, but Faith was a genuinely lovely person, and Angela didn't want to spoil any relationship Faith and Tom may have. She'd noticed the look of dismay on Faith's face just before Tom stepped up to the Delmont booth, and she had seen how Faith turned away and didn't greet them at all. That told Angela more than words.

Tom and Faith had known each other almost all their lives, so it seemed that, if they were interested in each other, they would have made it known by now since they both were past the age so many young couples married. Although her own age was three years younger than Faith, Aunt Daisy and Mama thought Angela should be betrothed if not already married.

What they didn't understand was that she believed God had a plan for her life, and she wanted to follow wherever He might lead her. She'd been praying about her relationship with both Faith and Tom, and she prayed this morning that she might find a definitive answer today that would help her determine a future path.

A woman exited the bake shop. Angela stepped back, swallowed hard, and then entered the bakery. Although she'd had a full breakfast, the warm sugar and spice aroma of the shop set her mouth to watering for a hot cinnamon roll and a cup of tea.

"Good morning. What brings you out this early? Can I seat you at a table?" Faith came to greet her, but her eyes held a wariness that belied her cordial greeting.

"Yes, that would be fine. I'm out early because I wanted to speak with you about something." Butterflies danced in her stomach, but a cup of hot herbal tea would settle those...she hoped.

Faith shrugged. "This is as good a time as any. We won't be really busy again until around noon when people start coming in for lunch." She led Angela to a table against the back wall.

Angela placed her purse on the table and sat. "This will do nicely. Before you join me, could I order a cup of herbal tea? I don't care for coffee."

"I'll be right back with a fresh cup." Faith disappeared through the door to the kitchen area.

Angela clasped and unclasped her hands. Why did she have to be so nervous? Faith had become a friend, and they had talked about so many things in the past few months. True, they had never discussed anything too deep, as they were still getting to know each other. But now the one thing they both had avoided talking about had to be discussed today. The last thing she wanted was to lose the good will of a person she respected and wanted as a friend.

But how could that happen if they both were attracted to the same man?

Faith returned with a tray holding two cups and a plate of plain sugar cookies. She set it on the table, but no smile accompanied it as in the past. "I thought this might be a little welcome for us both."

"Thank you." Everything she'd planned to say disappeared and left her mind blank as a new slate board. She sipped her tea, letting the warmth slide down her throat to soothe the nervous chill running down her spine.

"Has your father said anything else about having one Christmas Eve service at our church?" Faith lifted her cup to her mouth and peered at Angela over the edge.

That was a good a topic as any for the moment. "Yes, he and Reverend Weatherby decided it would be a good idea. Your church is large enough to take care of everyone who might come for the service. The children at the school have been rehearsing a play Miss Simmons wrote for them, and Papa asked her if she'd do it as part of the Christmas program rather than a separate one. She agreed, so it looks like we'll have one large gathering instead of three." Angela stopped and sipped her tea. Here she rattled on while what she really wanted to say buried itself deep in her mind.

"Now that makes sense to me. Christmas is such a busy season, and with Clara and Theodore getting married as well, this will make the holidays easier for everyone. I hope my aunt Hannah will be the one to play the piano for the program. She plays better than anyone else in Stoney Creek."

"So I understand. I'm sure Papa and the others will work it all out to make a grand celebration." Angela set her cup down and stared at it. "I imagine you're doing the refreshments for the wedding." Why couldn't she get to the real point of her visit?

"Yes, we are. It's a big order, and Mama is delighted. Aunt Ruby is too, and they've been poring over recipes and ideas all week." Faith sat back and tilted her head to the side as a frown furrowed her brow. "What's the real purpose of your visit, Angela? You didn't come here to talk about Christmas and the wedding."

Angela bit her lip. Now she had to speak up and seek her answers. "I have a question for you, and I do want you to be honest."

At Faith's curt nod Angela plunged ahead. "You and Tom have known each other for so many years, yet you are both still unmarried. Does that mean you don't have that kind of feelings for each other?"

Faith's eyes opened wide, and she gulped. She set her cup down and leaned forward. "I don't know about him because he's always treated me like his sister, but I think I've been in love with him since we were in first grade and he helped me up after I fell on the playground."

Angela's heart fell, but then she'd had her suspicions. "That sounds like something Tom would do. I think he's a very handsome and nice man, but I don't want to encourage him if you are truly in love with him. We weren't really together on Saturday. We happened to run into each other and shared a funnel cake."

Again that frown appeared, and Faith narrowed her eyes. "I saw the two of you down by the creek Sunday. I had gone riding and happened to be down the way from where you stopped."

Angela detected a slight tremor in Faith's voice as she spoke. "We had a nice visit and talked about our plans for the future." She reached across for Faith's hand. "I really don't know if my future is here in Stoney Creek. I've been praying for God's direction in my life, and I want to wait and see where He leads me. I need to decide where I can be of service, and what I should do with my life."

Faith gasped. "Angela, if Tom is interested in you, don't you think should give him a chance to say so? I don't think it really matters how I feel. I certainly don't want to get in the way of his happiness."

"That is so like you, Faith. You would rather see Tom be happy and be miserable yourself than pursue him if he liked someone else. I do think he's a wonderful person, but I believe it's best to trust in the Lord and let Him guide any relationship."

"Yes, I feel the same. God has a plan for our lives, and we have to trust Him to do what is best."

Angela reached across and squeezed Faith's hand. "I respect you deeply, and no matter what happens, that will not change." She pushed back her chair. "I've got to go. I left some things undone at home, and Aunt Daisy and Mama will be expecting my help. Thank you for being honest, and don't you give up on Tom. Promise me."

"I won't. I promise."

"Good. I know he will pray about what God wants him to do, and he'll make the right choice."

Faith walked with her to the door, and Angela squeezed her arm in farewell. It was time to go. Not only did she have chores to do, but she also had some powerful praying time ahead.

>>>≫≪<<<

After Angela left, Faith sat back at the table. That had been the strangest conversation she'd ever had. Angela was certainly a better woman than Faith with her honesty and her desire to serve the Lord. Faith hadn't been exactly honest when she had said she wouldn't stand in the way if Tom decided he wanted to court Angela. On the contrary, Faith would do whatever it took to get Tom to pay more attention to her. She hadn't admitted her jealousy either, but then that was for no one else to know except maybe Joe, and somehow that man seemed to know everything anyway.

Tom's kiss confused her even more now. It hadn't been more than a touch, and it hadn't been romantic or passionate. She drew in her breath then exhaled sharply. The kiss meant nothing until Tom could clarify its meaning for himself.

The train whistle sounded, and Faith jumped up from her chair. Tom was leaving on that train, and if she didn't hurry, she'd miss the chance to tell him good-bye. Pulling off her apron, she called to her mother, "I'm going to the station."

She dropped her apron on the counter, flew out the door, and raced down the street. When she rounded the corner to the station, Tom stood with his valise in hand waiting for all the incoming passengers to disembark. "Tom, Tom, wait, please."

He turned, and a grin spread across his face. "Faith, I wasn't expecting to see you. I thought you said you'd be too busy at the bake shop."

"We had a lull, and I couldn't let you leave without saying good-bye. Besides, I remembered something about Joe I forgot to tell you last night."

"Then tell me now. I have to be on board in a minute or two."

At least he wasn't running away from her. Like him, she could ignore last night's kiss for now and focus only on their friendship. So Faith told him what she'd learned and what she'd seen. "First, I was cleaning tables by the window, and he was dressed in his Sunday clothes and went into the bank."

"That is interesting. I found out he's been to visit Sheriff Bolton as well. Now what kind of business would he have with a banker and a sheriff? I'll have to do a bit of investigating into that."

Her heart did a double flip when Tom's face lit up and his eyes sparkled at her news. He grabbed Faith's shoulders and kissed her cheek. "Thanks for sharing. Now I'll have something else to occupy my mind while I'm traveling."

Faith's eyes opened wide. Oh, my, he'd kissed her again. Only on the cheek, but it had been out in public. Her fingers touched the spot where his lips had grazed her face.

The train whistle blew again, and Tom picked up his valise. "I have to go now, but thanks again, and I'll see you when I get back on Friday."

He hopped aboard the train but stood in the doorway to wave good-bye to Faith as the train began rolling toward its next destination.

When the train disappeared around the bend, Faith shook herself. What a difference a day could make. After last weekend she'd truly believed he had no interest in her. Then he'd kissed her last night, Angela had come to visit today, and he'd kissed Faith again. No matter what the kisses might mean, she had to set her mind to allowing God to show her His plan for her life. As much as she wanted Tom to be a part of her future, if he wasn't what God wanted for her, she'd accept His will and find some other direction for her life.

❧ CHAPTER 17 ❧

ARLY FRIDAY AFTERNOON Joe sat by the window
in his room and gazed out over the town of Stoney Creek.
This window was the best thing about his room in the
boardinghouse. As it was one of only two rooms on the
front side, he'd been lucky it had been vacant when he
arrived.

From his vantage point he saw a lot of what went on
in town. Although Main Street was a block over, a lot of
traffic used the street in front of the boardinghouse to get
to town since it was the main thoroughfare east and west.
He could even see the tower of the courthouse over the
rooftops of stores and businesses. He had come to love
this town and its people.

The one he contemplated now needed his attention and
soon. Tom had told him of the Kirk family situation, and
he hadn't painted a pretty picture. The baby born into the
family on Monday night was number six in birth order,
but number four in surviving children. The family had
moved here almost two years ago and started farming on
a plot of land south of town. A bad hailstorm last year and
a very dry summer had all but wiped out their crops for
two years. Others had suffered damage too, of course, but
none were in as much debt as the Kirk family.

Joe had also learned that the family faithfully attended
church. In addition, Mr. Kirk often volunteered to help

others in need, using his carpentry skills to repair homes damaged by the hail. No matter his own needs, he tried to help others, as did Mrs. Kirk.

Joe admired such an unselfish attitude and wished there could be more men like Mr. Kirk. Satisfied with the impressions he had of Stoney Creek and its citizens, Joe headed out for his day. First stop, the bank, and then over to the good doctor to pick up his medication.

When he reached the bank, Mr. Swenson hurried to greet him. With lowered voice he said, "Come into my office. I have some news for you."

Once inside, Mr. Swenson closed the door, and Joe sat down. "Thank you for being discreet. I'm sure we raised some curiosity, but at least they don't know what you want to see me about."

Mr. Swenson eased into his chair before handing a piece of paper to Joe. "This came this morning to the telegraph office. You've had a reply to the letter I sent out for you on Monday."

Joe held the paper and read, "Received letter this morning. Pleased to hear from you. Request noted. Stop. Will be taken care of immediately. Stop. You'll be hearing from me soon. Stanley Baxter."

Joe laid the telegram back on the desk and grinned. "Good man, Mr. Baxter. I knew he'd take care of things for me."

"Is there anything more I can do for you, Joe?"

Even Mr. Swenson, trained professional that he was, could barely disguise his curiosity. Good thing it was time to reveal his plan. Reaching into his pocket, Joe pulled out a paper and spread it in front of the bank president.

"Yes, Mr. Swenson. I could definitely use your help. Now this is where I'd like to start, if you would be so kind..."

⇢⇢⇢✦⇠⇠⇠

As soon as Tom stepped off the train on Friday evening, he made plans to see Faith. The information she'd given him about Joe had been put aside while Tom covered the last few stops of Governor Hogg before the election next Tuesday. The man had made some very good campaign promises regarding education in the state of Texas, and thus Mr. Blake had given the paper's support to Governor Hogg.

Now that he had his articles written, he was ready to again turn his attention to Joe and his visits to the bank and to the sheriff's office. It had been a month since Joe arrived in town, and still he remained a mystery. Tom wanted to clear up the story about Joe and find out his real name and purpose before the man decided to pick up and take off for the next town.

After going home to greet his family and freshen up from his trip, Tom headed for the Delmont home.

Faith answered the door after the first knock. Her eyes opened wide when she found Tom standing on the balcony. "You're back, but I didn't expect to see you tonight. I thought you'd be with your family."

"I've seen them already. We need to talk a little. May I come in?"

She pulled the door back and stepped aside. "Of course, I'm sorry. Guess I was more than a little surprised to see you."

Tom's conscience pricked him. He'd have to do a little explaining about that kiss the other night, but he wasn't even sure himself what it meant. If it ruined his friendship with Faith, he'd be sorely regretful. Then her smile reassured him.

"I'm glad you stopped by. A lot happened while you were gone."

Mrs. Delmont stopped by the parlor entry. "Good evening, Tom. How nice to have you back. Could I get you something to drink or eat?"

"No, I'm fine. I came by to see Faith. I have a few questions for her." And he'd rather ask and discuss them in private.

A smile lit up Mrs. Delmont's face. "I see." She nodded toward Faith. "Your father and I will be in his office if you need anything."

After she left, Tom fingered the brim of his hat and gazed about the room.

Faith grabbed his hat. "Goodness me, I'm a ninny tonight. Let me hang this up and you have a seat. Mama and Papa are going over the books for the end of the week, so they'll be busy for a while."

A few minutes later they sat next to each other on the sofa. Tom decided to start with the easier subject. "Have you found out anything else about Joe while I was gone this week?"

"Not really. I did see him go by your place after you left that day. Seems he's been visiting a lot of different places this week. I know he was at the library and even checked out a few books, but Mrs. Rivers wouldn't tell me what kind of books he checked out. He went back to the bank today and visited your father too."

"That's a lot. Of course he would have reason to visit every one of those places. I believe he opened an account at the bank for the earnings he's made doing odd carpentry jobs. Most likely he simply went in to visit with my father. The two seem to have become friends. You know

Pa won't tell me anything Joe says to him whether he's a patient or not."

"Your observations sound logical to me. I must agree that he's a very interesting old man with some unusual habits, but I think he's simply enjoying our town more than some of the others he's visited."

"You're probably right. I guess he'll let us know only what he wants us to know." The palms of his hands became moist, and he rubbed them together. How could he approach the subject of his feelings and that kiss without sounding dumb?

Faith moistened her lips and tilted her head. "I had a most interesting visit this week with Angela."

Tom's head jerked up, and his blood pumped furiously through his veins. "You had what? A visit from Angela?"

"Yes, you know we've worked on several projects together."

Tom's pulse slowed. Oh, yes, they had done projects together. "So what are the two of you working on now?"

Faith's eyes sparkled with that teasing look he had seen so often in the past. What was it about this girl that now had him tied up in knots?

"We talked about the Christmas program and your sister's upcoming wedding among other things. Angela is a delightful person, and I can understand if you have feelings for her."

Tom's palms grew slick with more moisture, and he rubbed them across his knees. "I...uh...I...well, I did take her for a buggy ride." Then his brows knit together. "Why, did she say something else about me?"

"Tom! You know I wouldn't betray a confidence."

This was not going like he'd planned at all. Maybe it would be better to leave and let the topic of their kiss come up another day. If Angela did have feelings for him, he'd have to figure out a way to let her know he wasn't interested. After the other night, Faith had been the one girl to dominate his thoughts and his heart.

"I'm sorry. You wouldn't do that to a friend." He stood to leave, but Faith still sat. "I'll see you at church Sunday." He strode to the entryway and retrieved his hat. He turned to say good-bye and found Faith behind him.

His heart pounded, and his eyes focused on her lips. He lifted a hand to her cheek. "Faith, you are the best friend a guy could ever have, and I don't want to lose that."

She blinked her eyes and gazed up at him, the sparkle no longer there and a question within their depths. He stepped back and jammed his hat on his head. "I think I'd better be going right now." He pushed through the door and bolted down the stairs.

Once around the corner he stopped to lean against the building. Now what was he supposed to do? He didn't want to hurt Angela, and he didn't want to lose Faith as a friend. He'd have to be less attentive to Angela, and somehow make Faith see him as more than a friend. If he'd read her eyes right tonight, perhaps she already did.

He slapped his forehead, almost knocking off his hat. Rats, he should have kissed her a few moments ago and declared his intentions right then and there. He shoved off the wall and headed home. All he could do now was to take every opportunity to woo Faith properly, once he could get up the nerve to do so.

>>>><<<<

Faith sank down onto the sofa after Tom left. What had come over him tonight? She'd never seen him quite like that. And what he said made no sense. If he wanted to be with Angela, why didn't he come right out and say so? True, she and Tom had been friends forever, but why did he say he didn't want to lose that friendship? Nothing made any sense.

She heaved a big sigh and headed to her bedroom. The door to the office was open, so Faith peeked in at her parents. They were huddled over the desk and spoke in low voices. Faith knocked and waited until her mother turned around.

"Oh, Faith, is Tom gone already? He didn't stay long."

"I think he must have been tired from his trip." No sense telling her all that had been said. She entered the room and went to her mother's side. "Is everything all right?"

Pa glanced up from the columns of figures he'd been studying. "Yes, but we still don't have enough to purchase that new stove and remodel the kitchen for the bakery." He removed his glasses and ran his hand down his beard. A sure sign to Faith that all wasn't as he said.

She bent to kiss his forehead. "Then I'm sure we'll be all right until we can. Mama does wonders."

"Yes, she does, but I'm planning on finding someone to clean out the stove pipe and check the stove to make sure it's safe. After all, we do have the wedding coming up."

"That sounds like a good idea." Faith yawned and covered her mouth. "Ooh, I'm more tired than I thought. I'm going to bed."

Mama hugged her and planted a kiss on her cheek. "Have sweet dreams, my dear. We'll see you in the morning. Don't forget, you have that planning meeting in the morning for the Christmas services."

That reminded Faith once again of her visit with Angela. This business with Tom and Angela gave her a headache. Why did life have to be so complicated?

She undressed then pulled a heavy cotton gown over her head. After buttoning the top around her neck, she crawled between the covers and lay back. Visions of Tom and her growing up danced through her mind in a kaleidoscope of memories. Not much had happened in either of their lives that the other didn't know. They didn't have any secrets, or at least she had no secrets from him. Except maybe not letting him know how much she loved him was keeping a secret.

She flopped over to her side and pulled her knees up. Life had become so involved since becoming an adult. The wonderful days of childhood and school and just being together were only a distant memory now. Proper etiquette for young men and women of courting age had taken over. Why did there have to be rules? Why couldn't she simply come out and tell Tom she loved him and wanted him to kiss her again?

Her eyes opened wide, and she turned back over to stare at the ceiling. The one thing she'd forgotten to do in these past weeks was pray. The Lord had plans for her as well as Angela, and it was up to both of them to find out what those plans might be and then follow.

She scrambled from the bed and to her knees, her head resting on the coverlet and her hands clasped.

Dear Lord, please forgive me for leaving You out of my daily life these past few weeks. I've been self-centered and concerned only about my feelings and doing everything Tom asked me to do regarding Joe Fitzgerald. I'm so confused about my feelings for Tom. I really do believe I love him and want to spend the rest of my life as his wife, but I have no idea how he looks at me except as a friend or a sister. His words were sweet, but that kiss was more like one of friendship. I should have seen it as that and not let my hopes get all raised thinking he'd want to court me.

I know You have plans for both our futures, but it sure would be nice to know a little in advance exactly what those plans may be. I pray those plans for me will include Tom, but if they don't, please, Lord, let me understand and accept that. Show me Your truths and the way You want me to go. I pray in Your precious, holy name. Amen.

Peace filled her heart in the darkened room. She crawled back between the covers, ready to let the events of the future unfold with God's own timing and methods. She was His daughter, and fathers always wanted only the best for their children. With a contented sigh, she pulled the covers to her chin and closed her eyes.

≫ CHAPTER 18 ≪

HEN TOM INVITED him out to his sister's ranch for their Sunday dinner, Joe accepted with anticipation of seeing Molly and her husband, Stefan. She'd been at the center of an attempted theft of prize horses from the livery. Micah and Sheriff Bolton had been instrumental in breaking up the ring of horse thieves because of her.

For an apparently quiet town, Stoney Creek had had its share of excitement in the past. If things went the way Joe planned, there would be much more excitement in the future, especially in the weeks ahead before Christmas.

Just to be sure he'd have no pain today, Joe had taken one of the pills the doctor had procured. The bouts with his illness were coming closer together but were still manageable with the medication.

Sitting in church now a few rows behind the Whiteman and Gordon families, he once again envied the closeness they had. His one regret in life centered on the fact he'd not had a larger family. As he and Mary Ann were only children, they'd wanted a larger family, but that had not come to pass. Now he had come to feel a part of these two families as they had welcomed him with open arms.

Molly and Stefan had not been into town for church the past two Sundays. He looked forward to time at their ranch today and getting better acquainted with Stefan Elliot, whom he had met briefly at the Whiteman dinner three weeks ago. Stefan had been disfigured while serving in the cavalry in Arizona, and his acceptance of the scars intrigued Joe. Molly had stood by him and helped nurse him back to health.

The service ended, and Joe gathered with other congregants on the lawn. Mrs. Whiteman invited Joe to ride with her family as they were taking a larger surrey to carry everyone. Dr. Whiteman unhitched the horses while the younger girls scrambled aboard with Clara. Joe glanced around for Tom then spotted him on his horse alongside Daniel. Joe shook his head. If Tom was riding, then that must mean Faith would not be coming to the ranch today.

He'd not seen two young people more in love than those two were with each other, but neither one seemed aware of how much the other cared. He only hoped he'd be in town long enough for them to finally see the light and decide to marry.

The drive to the ranch ate up almost an hour, but with pleasant weather today, and the company, the time had gone by rather quickly. As they approached the Elliot ranch house, Sallie Whiteman spoke to him.

"Thank you for accepting Stefan and being so nice to him. So many times people cringe and don't know what to say or how to act around him."

"I admire his courage, but he most likely would say it was his duty and what he'd been trained to do. I've heard that many a time from soldiers I have met in the past."

Dr. Whiteman pulled the surrey to a stop near the house. "Yes, Stefan would say that. He loved the military, but I tell you, I've never seen a man who has a way with horses like Stefan does. Micah and Levi are good, but even Micah saw the potential in Stefan and urged him to come to Texas and go into partnership with him and Levi. Stefan has charge of all the horse trading and training."

When the young couple welcomed everyone to the ranch, Joe studied Stefan from afar. The scars were bad, but even so one could tell he'd been a handsome man. However, Joe had never been concerned with outward appearance. God had taught him to look at a man's heart first, and that's exactly what he did.

Stefan finally reached out to grasp Joe's hand. "Welcome to our home. I'm glad you've decided to stay in Stoney Creek a bit longer. Micah and Levi have told me even more about you since we met a few weeks ago."

Joe removed his hat and nodded to Molly, who stood beside her husband. "It's indeed a pleasure to be here, Mrs. Elliot."

Pink rose in her cheeks. "Please call me Molly. Everyone else does, and it's much friendlier."

"Then I will do so as well. Thank you."

Sallie Whiteman wrapped her arm about Molly's shoulders and leaned close to whisper something in her ear as the two walked into the house. Once again a blush rose in Molly's face. A smile formed in Joe's heart. If he guessed right from the smile on Sallie's face and the blush on Molly's, Molly would soon be adding a grandchild to the Whiteman family.

Tom stood back and marveled once again at Joe's demeanor. His manner of speaking with both Stefan and Molly belied his initial attempt to appear as a shabby, homeless drifter. Everything about this man brought confusion and question. One thing Tom had noticed in the past two weeks, however, was that Joe no longer attempted to hide his manners or correct speech. Perhaps he was feeling comfortable enough now to drop some of his pretenses and reveal bits of who he really was, or maybe he was planning to leave so they'd never know.

Tom followed Micah and Stefan into the stables to take care of the horses. "Stefan, what do you think of Joe?"

"My impression is that he's not just a bum traveling the rails. I see intelligence and breeding in his eyes."

Trust Stefan to give a straightforward answer. "I've come to that conclusion myself, but he's avoided all mentions of his background with the skill of a born businessman, maybe even a salesman."

Stefan stroked his chin and nodded. "That tells me he doesn't want his past known and he's not going to reveal any more of it than he wants others to know. I suggest you let it go. If you haven't found out about an evil, unlawful background, then simply treat him as you would any other visitor to Stoney Creek."

Micah slapped them both on the shoulders. "That's what I've been telling him. Now that's out of the way, let's get into the house. My stomach's been grumbling long enough. It's time for some good cooking from our womenfolk."

Tom couldn't agree more. From the aromas wafting in the air from the open door, a spread to fill the belly awaited them. All the children were seated, and Tom stifled a laugh at Grace's insistence that at age fourteen she should be sitting with the adults at the big table. Hannah wrapped her arms about Grace's shoulders and leaned her forehead against her daughter's.

A few seconds later Grace smiled and nodded before heading over to join her younger cousins and brother. With a family this size, it wouldn't be long before they'd be adding to the adult table.

After everyone was seated, the family grasped hands, but Molly stood up before Papa could offer a prayer. A faint blush bloomed on her cheeks. "Stefan and I have an announcement to make. We haven't been to church the past few weeks because I felt poorly in the mornings. Looks like we'll be adding a new little Elliot to our family come spring. We wanted all of you to know."

She sat back down but not before everyone began offering congratulations. Tom shook his head. His sister did like the spotlight, and this was one way to get it, especially since they'd been waiting for over three years for this moment. After everyone settled back down, they joined hands once again, and his father asked the blessing for the food and for the new baby to join them in about six months.

As his father prayed, Tom breathed a prayer for his relationship with Faith. He needed guidance as to whether or not to tell Faith his feelings and risk the chance of ruining their friendship.

After dinner all of the women but Molly went to the kitchen to help clean up and of course to discuss the latest family news. His sister grasped his forearm.

"Little brother, I sense something is going on. Care to tell me about it?"

One thing hadn't changed since her marriage. Molly could still read him as easily as ever. There'd be no escaping her until he told her everything. "We need to go somewhere else. I'd ask you to take a ride with me, but that may not be best right now."

"Oh, pooh, I can still ride if I want to, but let's walk out to the garden in the back. It's not that cold yet, so a walk would be nice."

Tom followed her outside and around to the back where Molly had planted a flower garden with a fountain and a bench in the center. Fall blooms of chrysanthemums and asters filled the area with color. She led him to the bench and patted the seat beside her.

After he sat down, he swallowed hard. Where to begin? Might as well state it right out. "It's Faith. We've been friends forever, but I'm not sure where things are right now."

"Hmm, something tells me you are beginning to see her as more than a friend."

"Yes, I suppose I am." He gazed toward the house before turning back to his sister. "You and Stefan had known each other as children, so how did you know when you loved him?"

Molly's features softened with the smile she directed at Tom. "I looked up to him and adored him when we were children, and I really cared a great deal for him while he and Clarissa visited that summer. It wasn't until he was injured and tried to turn me away that I knew I couldn't bear the thought of not spending the rest of my life with him. He said he loved me, but the injuries to his hand and face made it impossible for him to return to military duty, and he didn't want to tie me down with a disfigured husband."

"Oh, yes, that was when we went back to Louisiana for Grandma Dyer's funeral."

"It was, and it's also the time Uncle Micah talked some sense into him and convinced Stefan he'd be a wonderful horse trainer and breeder. Once that was determined, I told Stefan I'd never leave him and I'd pester him until he loved me back."

A faraway gleam filled her eyes as though remembering that time back in St. Francisville. He waited a moment to let her memory settle. "Must not have taken long for that to happen."

Molly's laughter filled the air, and her shoulders shook. "That was the funniest thing. Once I'd made my declaration, he made his and grabbed me and kissed me in front of everyone there. I thought Papa was going to burst open his seams the way his chest puffed out."

"Wish I'd been there. I remember how worried Ma was when they came to fetch Pa because you'd been hurt."

"Stefan was so brave coming after me when my horse ran away. If he hadn't been there with his father to get me when the buggy overturned, I could have died." Another smile played about her lips. "Maybe that's when Stefan decided he loved me."

She shook herself and patted his arm. "That's enough about me and Stefan. Have you said anything to Faith?"

"No, not really." Not told her, but his kiss should have been a clue.

"And?"

There she went again, reading between the words. "I...um...well...I kissed her."

Once again Molly's laughter rang out. "And you think she doesn't know something from that?"

Heat crept up from Tom's neck. "Maybe, but I don't want to lose her as a friend."

Her demeanor sobered as she leaned toward him. "Tom, if you really care about her, the friendship will only be better. Stefan and I are not only husband and wife, but we're also friends. Marriage is friendship as well. You'll see what I mean as your relationship with Faith grows."

"I hope you're right."

Molly slapped him on the arm and stood. "I am most definitely right. Now, let's get back inside and see if we can find any leftover pie. Mama's are the best."

She was right about the pie, so maybe she was about Faith as well. The next few weeks were going to be the best and worst of his life. The best because of his love for Faith and worst because he'd have to find a way to let her know about it. And then he'd need to pray she returned his love and didn't end their friendship.

➤ CHAPTER 19 ≪

O N Wednesday morning Tom read the news coming over the wire and gasped. Cleveland had done it! He had beat out the incumbent Benjamin Harrison and accomplished something no other president had done in the history of the United States. Cleveland had served as president as a result of the 1884 election then lost to Harrison in 1888 by the electoral vote. Now Cleveland had won a second term, this time collecting both the popular vote and the electoral vote.

Gretchen stood behind Tom reading the same news. "Wow! Can you believe that? It's history in the making."

"It sure is, and I can't help but wonder if the twenty-two electoral votes the Populist Party garnered might have had something to do with it." Tom dropped the news tape and returned to his desk. He had a story to write.

He placed a pad and pen on the desk. "I guess we'll never know how those votes might have gone without the third party."

Gretchen pulled a sheet of paper from her typewriter. "You men and your political ideas. Just wait until we women have the right to vote. You'll see a big difference then."

"That day will be a long time coming, you can count on it." Tom leaned toward Gretchen's desk. "What story have you done? More about the great festival we had?"

"No, it's nothing social. Have you ever heard of Isadore Miner Calloway?"

Tom shook his head. "Can't say that I have. Is she another one of your women's suffrage advocates?"

"Perhaps then you've heard of Pauline Periwinkle."

Tom slapped his knee and laughed. At Gretchen's frown Tom stopped snickering and said, "She's that woman who writes a column for the *Dallas News*. She's always up to something promoting suffrage and women's clubs and protesting injustices to women. Pretty radical, if you ask me."

"Humph, she's one of the smartest women I know, and her columns tell the truth. She's trying to organize an association for women in the press, and when she does, I plan to join."

The last thing Tom needed was to get into a discussion of women's rights. Besides, despite the silly name, Pauline Periwinkle was a good writer. "Good for you. I do believe more women will be hired by our newspapers to report on a lot of things and not just society news."

Gretchen beamed at him. "Thank you, Tom. I'm glad you're not entirely against women."

Tom hid a grin and turned to his own work. Gretchen all but marched into Mr. Blake's office. Tom sincerely hoped Mr. Blake would print her story. Gretchen had proved to be a good reporter.

After completing the news article on Cleveland, Tom started on his Hogg story. After a hard-fought campaign through Texas, Hogg won a decisive victory over his opponents, George Clark and Thomas Nugent. With all the talk about the railroads dividing the parties, the farm and ranch vote brought in the decisive victory. In the three-way contest, the final results gave Hogg 43 percent of the votes, with Clark receiving 30 percent and Nugent coming in third.

He added more about the campaign before ending it and pulling the paper from his machine. He sat back, satisfaction at a job well done filling him.

Gretchen stopped at his side. "I'm glad the election is over." She pulled her chair over from her desk. "Look, my father is editor of a newspaper much larger than this. I'm going to write to him about Joe Fitzgerald. Maybe he can use his influence to nose around and get some information for us. He not only has newspaper connections, but he's made many friends in the business world. This is just the type of thing he loves to do. "

"That sounds like a really good idea. All we know is he's from somewhere north and his name, if that's his real name. I have a feeling he's not going to be around here much longer. He should have plenty now to buy a ticket to wherever his next stop might be."

"I agree, so as soon as I finish my latest assignment, I'll send a wire to Father." She scooted her chair back to her desk and went to work on her next story.

Tom turned in his articles and accepted Mr. Blake's praise for a job well done. Since the time approached noon, he decided to head home for some of Ma's leftovers from last night's meal. A ham sandwich with Ma's homemade pickles would be just right.

As he walked home, he noticed a nip in the air. What little winter this part of Texas got would be coming in soon. What they needed was a good, strong, cold wind to blow in from the north. His mother may not care for it, but Tom loved the colder weather of the winter months.

At the house he found his mother and Clara in the dining room eating and talking. His mother jumped up when he entered. "Oh, Tom, I didn't expect you home for lunch. Can I fix you something?"

"No, you and Clara go on with your business. I'm hankering for a ham sandwich, but I'll fix it." He continued on into the kitchen. There he cut slices of his mother's fresh-baked bread and stacked some ham on top. After filling his plate and pouring a glass of milk, he sauntered back to the dining room to join Ma and Clara.

"What has you two so engrossed this time of day, as if I didn't know?" He grinned and bit into his sandwich.

Clara raised her eyebrows and winked at Ma. "Don't forget you have to wear one of the new dress sack suits Teddy has ordered from New York. All the men in the wedding will be wearing them."

"Well, I can wear anything for a few hours to please my sister."

Clara laughed out loud. "Now that's a good one. I remember how you fussed about having to wear a suit to Molly's wedding four years ago."

Heat flooded Tom's face. "I suppose I did make a ruckus then, but I'm older now and know how to be proper."

That brought on more laughter from both his mother and sister. He pushed his chair back from the table. "I say, if you're going to laugh at me, I shall retire to my room." After picking up his plate and glass, he headed upstairs for solitude. Their laughter and giggles followed him until he closed his door and sat at his desk. Women and their ideas about fashion and proper attire.

A huge bite of ham filled his mouth, but new thoughts of the wedding filled his head. Faith was to be his partner in the wedding party. If he married her, would she make as big a fuss about the clothes? Probably not. She was much too practical. At that thought he almost choked on his bite of sandwich. Why was he thinking that far ahead? He had to establish a relationship with her first, and that seemed to grow harder every day.

⟫⟩⟪⟨

Joe stepped back to eye the counter cabinet he'd just installed for Josie Rivers at the library. It wasn't as large as he would have liked it to be, but he had worked with the materials given him. Mrs. Rivers now had a place to check out books and take them back in. Before she'd been using a small table set up by the door with file boxes to store the library cards she'd made for each book.

"It really looks nice, Joe, and has so much more room than the table." Mrs. Rivers came up beside Joe and ran her hands over the smooth top. "I'm going to set things up right now." She grinned and opened the first drawer.

While she transferred cards and papers from the boxes to the cabinet drawers, Joe strolled through the library once more. She had a good selection of books, but it wouldn't be long before those shelves would be filled with the books he and Mrs. Rivers had discussed last week.

A few patrons came in, so Joe bid Josie good-bye and strolled back to town. The library had been one job he'd done for free, but because he wanted to keep his reputation as a homeless man saving up money for a ticket to the town, he accepted small fees for other jobs.

At the town hall he met Mayor Gladstone coming out of the building. "Good afternoon, Mayor."

"Good afternoon to you too. I hear you like our town and are extending your stay."

"You heard right. Stoney Creek is a right nice place to spend time. The people here are mighty friendly. You can be proud of them and the way your town is growing."

"Ah, yes, we are growing fast, and therein lies a problem."

Joe raised his eyebrows. "And what would that problem be?" He had guessed some things the town might need, but to hear it from the mayor would give Joe more insight into what he could do for Stoney Creek.

The mayor hooked his thumbs in his vest pockets and rocked back and forth. "That railroad business is one thing. They're supposed to start work on it soon so we'll have more direct routes west and north. Another thing is electricity. I'm hoping we can get the electric lines from Dallas to come down this way. I haven't heard from the commission yet as to when we can expect such service."

"Both of those would be good." But they were not the kind of things Joe could help accomplish. "Any special needs you see?"

The mayor stroked his chin. "Well now, there are always things we need. I don't want to raise taxes, but we may have to. Main Street and the streets one block on either side of it are in need of repair, and we need better, safer sidewalks because they're not in as good a condition as they need to be. The center of town may be on a bit of a hill, but we still had some flooding years ago."

"How often does Stoney Creek flood?" No one had mentioned that possibility to him.

"Oh, maybe once a year if we have a really heavy storm come through or a hurricane comes up from the coast. It has to be a real corker of a rainstorm to flood the middle of town, but some of the homes get water in them from time to time. We tried to build a dam using sandbags and other stuff, but we didn't have enough to really do any good."

Not much Joe could do about a dam, but people most likely would need some help after their homes flooded or a hurricane caused any damage. Tornadoes had been known to blow through this part of the state as well. He'd have to think more on that one.

The mayor spoke again. "One thing I'm proud of is being able to get a generator in time for this year's tree lighting ceremony at Thanksgiving. My wife showed me some electric light bulbs that would be safer and prettier on the tree than candles. I ordered some of them as well. It's going to be the best tree we've ever had in town." The mayor stopped and grinned at Joe. "You planning to stick around for that festivity?"

"Think I just might do that, Mayor Gladstone. Sounds like it'd be a pretty sight to see, and I like Christmas trees."

"I do believe we'll have the best, with Mrs. Gladstone's help of course." He touched the brim of his hat. "I must be off about other business in town. You take care, Joe." Mayor Gladstone strode down the street toward the county courthouse and his office.

Joe scratched his head. Stoney Creek sounded like it was in good hands. The mayor was maybe a little pompous, but the man did have a right to be proud of his town. Joe would have to do some praying and thinking on what he could do to make the town even better and keep it on the road to progress.

CHAPTER 20

AITH MADE HER way into Hempstead's Mercantile with a list in hand. New orders came in every day, and Papa had said if they kept up this pace along with the extra holiday baking and the Whiteman-Gladstone wedding, they'd soon have enough for a new commercial-style stove in the bakery.

The town still buzzed from the election results posted at the newspaper office this morning. She supposed it was important, but politics didn't play much into her life at this time. Maybe if she could vote it would make a difference. No matter about that now, the supply list took precedence over anything else.

Mrs. Weatherby met Faith coming from Hempstead's. "Oh, Faith, I'm so glad to see you. The ladies of our church have decided to give a wedding party for Clara. You know, like the one Gretchen told us she'd read about in Dallas and Houston."

Faith vaguely remembered the conversation, but she'd been busy with taking care of customers and hadn't heard the full discussion. "I seem to recall that."

"Well, we're having it at the church hall two weeks from Saturday. The five ladies who are hostesses are providing the food, but we'd like to know if your mother could make those delicious little pecan pies she makes for special occasions."

"She and Aunt Ruby are at the bakery now, so why not go on over and speak with her? We've had a good crop of pecans this year, so she will most likely agree to make the tassies."

"Oh, is that what they're called? Funny little name." She grinned and patted Faith's hand. "I'll hurry on over there now and visit with your mother." With a wave of her hand she hurried down the steps and practically ran over to the bakery.

Faith shook her head. Those pecan tassies would be perfect for the occasion, and everyone in town claimed no one made flakier pie crusts than Irene Delmont. Faith was getting better, but she still had a ways to go to match Mama's baking.

The bell over the door jangled when she entered the store. Mr. Hempstead stood at the counter speaking with Mr. Kirk. From the look on the farmer's face, something good had happened.

James Hempstead, the owner's son, hailed her. "Good afternoon, Faith. How can I help you?"

"I have a list of things Mama needs for the bakery." She handed him the list and glanced over to where the two men still talked. The grin on Mr. Kirk's face had changed to one of surprise and amazement.

"I don't want to be nosy, but what has Mr. Kirk smiling so?"

"You're not being nosy, and I suppose it'll be all over town soon as he leaves here anyway. Seems someone paid his bill in full and set aside another amount of credit for him to buy whatever he needs for his family."

"Oh my, that is wonderful. I heard what a difficult time his wife had with their last baby not long ago. He's had a hard time with his crops too."

"Yes, and Pa was helping him out as much as possible by not collecting what Mr. Kirk owed, but now he's being taken care of. And before you ask that question I see coming in your eyes, we don't have any idea who paid for everything."

Faith glanced back to Mr. Kirk again as he left the store with an armload of food and other items. "I'm really happy for them. Owing money can really make a person depressed."

With a nod to the older Mr. Hempstead, she picked up a tin of baking powder. While she shopped, her thoughts meandered back to the Kirk family. Several times her mother had placed extra bread and other items in a basket to take to the Kirk farm. Mama, knowing the family wouldn't take straight-out charity, made the excuse that day-old bread and baked goods didn't sell well, so she was giving them away to whoever wanted them. Faith imagined Mrs. Kirk knew the truth but accepted the offering anyway.

While Mr. Hempstead totaled up the amount of her purchase, Faith brought up Mr. Kirk's situation. "James told me about Mr. Kirk. That's amazing. I can't think of anyone here in town who would do something like that."

"It's a puzzlement for sure, but all I can do is what I was told. Mr. Swenson made the arrangements, and I'll carry them out."

The bell jangled again, and Mrs. Rivers from the library dashed in. "Oh, Mr. Hempstead, the man at the station sent a note that a crate had arrived for me and it was here at the store. I haven't ordered anything."

"It sure is, Mrs. Rivers, and it's from a store in Dallas. James, go get it and bring it out here for Mrs. Rivers."

Faith stood by with a little more than curiosity flowing through her. What kind of goods would Mrs. Rivers be getting from Dallas? Well, she'd know soon enough as James hauled the crate in from the back storeroom.

Margaret Hempstead, James's wife, descended the stairs from their home above the store. "What's all the commotion down here?" She eyed the large crate. "Oh, my, what is that?"

Mrs. Rivers ran her hands over the rough surface. "That's what I'd like to know." She stepped back with hands on her hips. "James, find something and get this here crate open so we can see what's inside."

By now a few other customers had entered the store. Faith hid a grin. Wouldn't take long for this news to be all over town. Tom should be here to take notes. She detected a story in the making.

James pried off the lid and brushed away some of the straw covering the contents. Mrs. Rivers's sharp intake of breath broke through the murmurs of those gathered.

She stepped back with one hand on her cheek and the other over her heart. "Books! Where did they come from? I didn't order them."

James pulled out a sheet of paper. "This looks like an invoice and it says the bill is paid in full."

She fanned her face. "Oh my, oh my...I can't believe this." Then she peered at the heavy crate. "How am I ever going to get this back to the library?"

"James and one or two of these other men will load it onto our wagon and bring it down. They'll unload it inside for you." At his father's nod James and two men dragged the crate back to the storeroom.

Red flushed Mrs. Rivers's cheeks. "I don't know what to think. Joe finished up my new checkout counter today, and I was just wishing for some more books. Now here they are, just like that." She swiped her hands on her skirt. "I'm mighty grateful for whoever did this, and now I'm getting on back to the library so I can put those books where they belong."

She marched from the store, leaving everyone behind to ask where the books had come from. Mr. Hempstead finished tallying her order, and Faith picked up her bundle, hoping she'd run into Tom soon. Something was going on here, and she wanted to be sure he heard about it.

>>>><<<<

Tom knocked on the bakery window and peered inside. Faith laid her cleaning cloth on a table and hurried to open the door.

"You're just the person I wanted to see." She grabbed his arm and pulled him inside.

"I know you're closed, but I wanted to ask you about something."

"Come over here and sit down. I want to tell you what happened a while ago at Hempstead's store."

Tom's eyebrows shot up. That was what he'd come to ask her about. On his way back to the office after lunch at home, he'd heard all kinds of tales on the street from Mr. Kirk becoming a rich man to Mrs. Rivers getting a box from a secret admirer in Dallas.

He sat down, and she grabbed his hands. Warmth from her touch shot up his arms and straight to his heart. Her face held such an earnest expression that he pushed aside his feelings and waited for her to tell him her news.

A few minutes later she finished her tale and sat back, still holding his hands. "Now isn't that the strangest thing you ever heard of in your life?"

"It is rather odd, I must agree." Indeed, nothing like this had ever happened before. He was happy for Mrs. Rivers and the Kirk family, but it sure would be nice to know who the benefactor might be.

"Tom, do you think it could be your uncle Micah? You know how he always wants to do things to make Stoney Creek a better town."

He chewed on that for a few minutes and let it roll around in his head. Finally he shook his head. "No, I don't think so. He helped out with the generator for the tree lighting, but I don't think he is wealthy enough to do more than that."

"Hmm. Then who could it be? Some even asked if it could be your father because he's always going without pay to take care of folks."

"Which means he doesn't have the extra money to do something like this." Still, with his father's kindness toward his patients, he could understand why people might think he'd be that generous.

They sat in silence a few seconds before Faith sat up straight, her eyes open wide with a new thought. "Joe was with Mrs. Rivers at the library this morning. He made a new counter space for her to check out books and keep records. You don't think maybe..." Her voice trailed off.

Tom's news-sniffing brain went into high gear. Could it be possible? No, the man was penniless, or at least he said he was. "I don't know. He was so dirty, smelly, and shaggy when I first met him on the train. True, he cleaned up rather well, but his own clothes are still ragged and old. The only decent ones he has were given to him."

He jumped up from the table. "Look, I have to get back to the office. Gretchen asked her father to put out word he's trying to get information about a Joe Fitzgerald. I want to mull over this information with her and see if we can come up with anything."

He reached out and squeezed Faith's hands between his. "Thanks for taking the time to go over this with me. You'd make a fine reporter, Miss Faith Delmont." He kissed her cheek again and raced out the door. He'd have to wait until another day to learn what her feelings for him might be, but right now he had a story to track down.

⫸ CHAPTER 21 ⫷

OE RELISHED THE attention Mrs. Rivers and Mr. Kirk had received for their unexpected gifts. Nothing delighted him more than to see people grateful for what they were given. Since the books arrived on Wednesday, Mrs. Rivers hadn't stopped talking about them during meals at the boardinghouse.

This morning he planned to pay a visit to Alex Hightower, the only lawyer in town since, as he'd heard, Mr. Murphy had retired last year because of poor health. He needed to set things up so Mr. Hightower and Mr. Baxter could work out details and make sure every necessary step for what Joe planned kept to the law.

As he left the boardinghouse and headed to town, the overcast skies cast a pall over the landscape. The once-bright colors of autumn had fallen away, and the trees appeared dull and lifeless. Despite the roiling clouds toward the north, the air remained still. If Joe wasn't mistaken, a big storm was headed this way. He'd better get his business taken care and get back to his room before the skies darkened further.

He reached town and passed by the tailor shop. Zachariah Morton hailed him from the doorway. "Joe, I have something for you. Come on inside."

Joe glanced back to the threatening sky but decided he'd have time for a quick stop. When he entered the showroom, Zachariah wore a huge grin as he held out a suit toward Joe.

"Made this for you in appreciation of the work you did for me in building the new display cases."

The black suit was tailored in the latest single-breast, straight-hemmed jacket style for men. Joe shrugged his arms into the sleeves of the jacket. Zachariah had done an excellent job. He ran his hand over the fine wool the tailor had used. Almost as fine as the ones he'd had made years ago in the city. "Thank you, Zachariah. It's very nice and it fits extremely well."

A tinge of red flushed the tailor's cheeks. "I consider myself to be a master tailor and can pretty much figure the size of a man from observing him."

Joe removed the jacket and handed it back to Zachariah. "I'm honored to accept such a gift from you. Thank you." He didn't need the suit, but if he refused the offer, the man would be hurt more than if Joe had slapped him in the face.

"Good, good. I'm glad you're pleased. I'll box it up, and you can take it with you."

"Yes, there looks to be a storm brewing and coming in from the north, so I'll take it back to the boardinghouse now."

By the time Zachariah had the suit boxed, the sky had darkened more. When Joe stepped outside, the wind had picked up. If he hurried, he could make it back to the boardinghouse before the rains came. Others in town had the same idea of finding cover as they scurried into businesses or urged their horses and carriages homeward.

Joe reached the boardinghouse steps with the first large raindrops hitting his head. Time to settle in for a rainy afternoon. His business with Hightower could wait.

Delightful aromas filled the air inside the boarding-house. He stopped by the kitchen to greet Mrs. Hutchins.

"From the delightful smells here, we must be in for a special supper tonight."

Mrs. Hutchins wiped her hands with a towel. "Since it looks like a storm is heading this way and most likely bringing some cooler temperatures with it, I put on a pot of stew. And I baked an apple pie as well."

"Ah, then we'll eat hearty tonight. I'll be up in my room if you need me for anything." He ambled from the kitchen but stopped in the parlor before heading upstairs. Now the sky had turned even darker, and the tree branches swayed about the street.

Joe shuddered. He'd heard the talk of Stoney Creek's previous floods and sent up a silent prayer for the Lord to protect the town this day.

⤜⤜⤜◆⤛⤛⤛

Despite Gretchen's father's efforts, Tom still had nothing new on Joe Fitzgerald. He had even tried to talk with Mr. Swenson, but the man stood his ground concerning privileged bank account and client information. This Tom had expected, and the banker's refusal only served to increase his respect for the man, but it led to more curiosity about Joe.

Joe had been to the sheriff simply to ask about the security of the town, and no wanted posters with Joe's likeness appeared in the stack the sheriff had received.

With the elections over, things had quieted down in the news world for the moment. He'd written a few feature articles, but nothing really whetted his appetite like the mystery surrounding Joe Fitzgerald.

Gretchen burst through the door and shoved it closed against the wind. "Looks like we're in for a big storm. The sky is really dark." She untied the ribbons on her hat and laughed. "Good thing Mrs. Blake made me wear this one with ties today or I'd be minus a hat. The wind nearly captured this one."

Mr. Blake stepped out of his office. "The weather is looking worse by the minute. I say we shut down and head for home, or we might be stuck here for the evening."

Tom and Gretchen wasted no time gathering their belongings. Tom handed in his latest feature article. "Here's my latest story, and it looks like this weather may rustle up a story or two. I'll be on the lookout."

"Good, you do that. I'm sure we're in for a rainstorm like we had a few years back. Meanwhile, I'll take this home with me and look it over." He added it to the satchel he carried. "Now get on out of here. If this is as bad as it looks, the creek might flood."

"Yes, sir, Mr. Blake." Tom shrugged on his coat. "See you tomorrow." He decided against wearing his hat. No sense in losing it to that wind.

He strode across to the livery. Early this morning Tom had smelled rain in the air and elected to ride into town. Now he was glad he had, for he'd be home much more quickly than walking the eight or so blocks to his home.

The horse must have sensed the building storm because he headed straight for the Whiteman stable and barn behind the infirmary and house. Tom slid off the horse and took care of the saddle and trappings. After making sure everything was secure in the barn and the horses had oats, he ran toward the house as huge drops of rain fell from the sky and the lightning flashed.

He all but fell into the kitchen and pulled hard to close the door behind him. "It's going to be a mess out there." He shrugged out of his damp jacket.

His mother reached for it. "Your pa and some of the other men headed to the creek right away to put up the sand barrier. From the looks of the sky, I don't think they have near enough to keep that creek from coming to town."

When the makeshift dam hadn't held the last storm, the townspeople had ordered loads of sand and filled bags to use for the next storm. They'd been stored in an empty warehouse donated by one of the townspeople.

Tom ran to the coat closet and found his slicker. "I'm going to help. Keep the girls inside." Of course she would, but Tom had to say it anyway. He glanced down and realized he still had on his good shoes. He needed his boots.

Upstairs he grabbed his oldest pair of high boots and pulled them on. Now properly clad, he raced down the stairs. He waved to his mother in the kitchen. "Be sure to latch this door behind me so the wind doesn't take it."

"Go on. I'll take care of everything here."

He'd no sooner reached the road leading to the creek than the rain began in earnest. Good thing he was so familiar with the creek road or he'd be lost in this blinding downpour.

The wind pushed Tom down the road, and shouts from up ahead let him know he neared the creek. He drew closer to find men in rain slickers piling bags of sand high along the banks. They'd never get a wall built to be high enough and thick enough to stop Stoney Creek if it flooded. Still, they needed to try, and Tom joined the men.

The sand bags, now waterlogged, were too heavy to lift more than one at a time. Two wagonloads remained to be unloaded. Tom climbed up on top to help hand the bags down to waiting hands. When the last bag had been tossed down, Tom bent at the waist, his breath coming in gasps.

Sheriff Bolton hollered for the men to gather round. After he had their attention, more instructions were issued. "I don't think these bags are enough to prevent flooding. The town will be okay since it's on a hill and the houses are built up." He called out to the blacksmith. "How does it look in your area, Burt?"

"We're high enough up. We'll be okay. It's those farmers and the cattle out on the range that worry me." The lightning flashed and thunder rolled through the sky.

"Then take your men and go on back to your homes and make sure your families are secure." The sheriff began dividing people into groups. "Those of you living in the lower areas go back home and evacuate. Bring everything you can as quick as you can and come to the town hall. We'll set it up as a relief center." He scanned the crowd as groups left. "Anyone know who wasn't here that might need help?" Several hands rose in the air. "Then go warn them and get them out if it looks like they might flood."

When the last group left, the sheriff pulled his collar up around his neck. "Okay, the rest of you need to get back to town. Looks like we're in for a long night."

Tom slogged his way home through mud puddles, glad for the old boots covering his feet. The wind wasn't as strong as before, but the rain seemed to be heavier. Now evening darkness would take over that created earlier by the storm and make any work that needed to be done more difficult.

An arm came around his shoulders, and his Pa's umbrella offered welcome relief from the constant rain.

"Well, Son, this is going to be some night. I'm going to the infirmary and make sure I have everything ready in case of any emergencies. Why don't you go to the town hall and see what may be needed there? Maybe your ma and some of the other ladies can help with food."

"All right, but I'm going to change into dry clothes first. I'll get wet again, but at least I'll be dry for a little while."

Twenty minutes later Tom trudged through the pouring rain with his father's umbrella. The weather didn't look like it'd let up anytime soon. At the town hall men and women from the two churches laid out bedding and organized the groups now filling the shelter.

Mrs. Weatherby passed by, and Tom grabbed her arm. "What can I do to help? Do you need food or supplies?"

"Mrs. Delmont and Miss Ruby are preparing sandwiches and coffee to bring over from the bakery. Angela and her mother are helping with the bedding. You can help set up those tables so we'll have a place for the food. We're expecting at least ten to fifteen families from the farmlands to come in for the night." She hurried away to set up more sleeping areas.

If that many farmers brought their families, they could end up with well over fifty people. Faith would be busy helping her mother, so maybe she'd come over with the sandwiches and other food later. Joe waved to him from the corner filled with stacked chairs. Tom waved back and headed in that direction. Even if Faith came later, most likely he'd have no time to speak with her anyway. Right now his task was to help get those tables and chairs set up for the evening meal.

CHAPTER 22

THE RAIN CONTINUED to come down. Although not pounding hard as earlier, it still came steady and heavy. Faith helped her mother pack sandwiches and cookies into boxes to take to the town hall. They'd been told that nearly fifty people were already there, but more were expected as the creek rose past the flood stage. Homes nearest the creek on the outskirts of town were now in danger of flooding.

Aunt Ruby packed the last of the cookies and sealed her box. "This does it for now, but Irene is making more. I'll take these, and you grab the sandwich boxes. We'll have to hurry before we get soaked as well."

Faith untied her apron. The slickers the sheriff had given them would keep them dry enough, but they needed to protect the boxes and their contents. "I'm going to run out to the storage shed and get some of that old canvas out there. We can cut it and use it to cover the boxes."

"Good idea. I'll wait here for you." Aunt Ruby stacked the boxes on the counter.

In a few minutes Faith returned with two pieces of the canvas. She and her aunt wrapped the stacks. "This should keep them dry."

Aunt Ruby nodded and slipped on her slicker. "Let's go."

Rivulets of water flowed down Main Street. Once again Faith gave thanks for the bricks used to pave the streets from the courthouse down through the main part of town. They would have puddles of water, but no mud on the streets. With the protection over the sidewalks, they had only to run across the street here and then the one at the next block before being at the town hall.

Sloshing through the puddles sent water up onto her stockings and soaked the hem of her skirt in the short distances between covered walkways. She couldn't remember a rain as heavy, long, and steady as this had been since the afternoon. Darkness swallowed up everything in sight, and if Faith and her aunt hadn't been so familiar with the streets, they could have been lost because no light came from any of the stores or businesses. Lanterns and lamps at the town hall helped give them a goal to reach.

As they reached the town hall, a bolt of lightning split the sky, lighting up everything around it. Thunder roared less than a second later and shook the boardwalk on which she stood. The thunder hadn't bothered her as much as what the moment of light had revealed. Water covered the ground beyond Main Street and flowed down from the church.

She pushed through the door to the town hall to find frightened children crying and parents glancing about with fear in their eyes. Tom ran over to her.

"Thank goodness you're here with food. I hope more is on the way because more people have come since the mayor sent word to you." He wrapped his arms around her load. "I'll set these over on the table."

Faith followed him. "Mama is baking more cookies, and Aunt Ruby and I will go back and help with the sandwiches." So many more people than she had imagined milled about the room or sat in small groups talking.

Mrs. Whiteman came into the building carrying an armload of blankets. "I brought these extra from the infirmary in case anyone didn't have one, and we have extra sheets and pillows as well."

Tom hurried up to take her load. "Thanks, Ma. I'm sure these will be put to good use. Faith and her aunt brought over the food just now, but they're going back for more."

Angela appeared from behind a screen. "I'll take that bedding and put it out, Mrs. Whiteman."

"Oh, thank you, dear. I'll go with Faith and help with the food."

Faith bit her lip. "I'm worried about the town. The water seems to be rising down at your end, Mrs. Whiteman."

"It is, but the horse and buggy got through. The doctor is back getting the infirmary ready with all the supplies he might need in case of injuries."

"I pray it won't come to that." Faith adjusted her slicker. "I'm ready to go back out. I hope we can still get across the street."

Mrs. Whiteman squeezed Faith's shoulders. "I think we'll be okay if the water doesn't become too swift."

Tom handed his mother an umbrella. "Here, take Papa's umbrella. It'll protect you walking across to the bakery."

"Thank you, Son. Now, ladies, let's go."

She headed toward the door, and Aunt Ruby followed. Faith grasped Tom's hand. "This is the worst rain I've ever seen."

Tom patted her hand. "Me too, but it's going to be okay. Some homes may be flooded, but we'll make it through."

She peered into his eyes searching for any doubts he might have, but all she found was confidence. If he believed that, she could as well. "All right, I'll be back as soon as I can with more food."

On her way out she spotted Joe talking with two of the men who had brought their families in to safety. Somehow that man seemed to be everywhere at once these days. She didn't have time to speculate about him now, but she wanted to talk with Tom about recent events.

The rain still fell, but it had lessened quite a bit. Thunder boomed in the distance, but nothing came as close as the one she'd felt earlier. Maybe this meant the water would recede and not flood the town. Then she realized the storm had come in from the south, probably off the Gulf, and was headed north. That meant waters from the north would flow south and fill the creek even if the rain stopped here. No, Stoney Creek was far from being out of danger. This could turn into a long night with little or no sleep.

She ran through the now larger puddles of water to cross the street and get to the bakery. Mrs. Whiteman would be a blessing for Mama. More hands meant more sandwiches could be made in a shorter amount of time.

⟫⟫⟫⟪⟪⟪

Tom yawned and pulled his watch from his pocket. Well after midnight, and most of the refugees from the storm had settled for the night. The younger single and family men had left to help the sheriff do what they could to protect the lowland properties. He would have gone with them, but the sheriff had asked him to stay and take care of those seeking haven from the storm. A small group of older men sat huddled together discussing the storm. Joe stood on the fringes of the group.

After he'd listened a few minutes, Joe meandered among the beds made on the floor, writing something on a pad. Tom sat still and observed Joe's actions through half-closed eyes. Interesting. What could he be taking notes about? Tom had already written down what he planned to put in his news article, so what could be Joe's interest?

When a hand touched his shoulder, Tom jumped up to find Joe standing beside him.

"Didn't mean to startle you, but I wasn't sure if you were asleep or not."

Tom shook his head to clear it. How had he dosed off like that? "I'm fine. Do you need something?"

"No, I wanted to let you know I'm heading back to the boardinghouse to check on Mrs. Hutchins and the women. I left them there when I heard they needed help here. We won't be able to assess any damage until morning, so we may as well get some sleep."

There he went again, using language no hobo or tramp would speak. "I think I'll stay here. Mrs. Weatherby said she, Ma, and Mrs. Booker planned to be at the diner in the morning. The cook there is putting together a hot meal, and Mrs. Delmont is baking bread to go with it."

"That sounds fine." He settled his hat on his head and headed for the door. "See you tomorrow."

Tom sat with a frown on his face. Somehow he had to figure out who Joe really was and what his purpose could be in Stoney Creek. Somebody somewhere had to know about the man.

Now that his mind had gone into gear, sleep fled. Tom stretched and walked around the room to wake up the rest of his body. He pulled from his pocket the notes he'd taken about the storm and read them by the light of the dim lamps placed about the room. Words and phrases became sentences and the entire article formed in his mind. The end wouldn't come until tomorrow or maybe the next day, but he had the beginnings.

He made note of the sleeping families whose names he knew. Gretchen could use them to write a few human interest stories as well. After everyone in the room had fallen asleep and the lamps has been put out, Tom made his way to the front and peered out the window. The rain had stopped, but the wind still blew in gusts. How much better things would be if they already had electricity and street lamps installed.

With even the saloon shut up and dark, he could barely make out the buildings across the street. Rather than trying to find his way back in the dark to where he'd been earlier, Tom sank to the floor by the doors and rested against the walls.

He bowed his head and prayed for the safety of those in the building and their homes. He prayed for his uncle and the families out on ranches who had to make sure their cattle reached high ground. The quieter it became inside, the louder the sounds outside became. One sound he recognized and feared...flowing water.

He opened the doors and stepped outside to find water flowing in the streets. At this rate it wouldn't take long for the water to rise over the boardwalks and invade the stores. He prayed the water would flow on down south where it would join with the river again and go on to the Gulf. A flood in town before the holidays would not bode well for Stoney Creek businesses.

>>>><<<<

Joe sat by the window in his room and stared out at the darkened streets below. When the rain ceased, he opened his window, and the sound of rippling water replaced that of the rain.

How much water was actually out there? The last time he'd checked the front of the boardinghouse, the water had been a good foot from the top of the porch, but more could have come by now. Mrs. Hutchins and the other boarders had not seemed concerned, so apparently the house had seen floods like this before.

He'd heard stories of tornadoes and how they could rip through a town in a few minutes and create havoc, but this had been no tornado. The only other storm he could imagine was a hurricane. That kind of storm would account for the prolonged winds and rain, but the winds hadn't been strong enough to do much damage that he could see. When a cold breeze blew in, he closed his window.

A growl in his stomach reminded him how long it'd been since he'd last eaten. Maybe there'd be a few leftovers in the kitchen. He lit a candle and placed it in the stand. When he reached the bottom of the stairs, he detected a light in the kitchen.

Mrs. Hutchins sat at the kitchen table with her hands wrapped around a pottery cup. She glanced up when he entered.

"I see you couldn't sleep either. Grab a cup of hot coffee and join me."

While he poured his coffee, she opened the icebox and brought out butter and jam. She placed them on the table. "Some bread and butter will taste good with your coffee."

She reached into the breadbox and brought out a loaf of her bread. After slicing a few pieces, she placed them on a plate. "Maybe this will hold you until breakfast."

Joe buttered a slice of bread and smeared it over with apple butter. "How did you know I wanted something to eat?"

"Oh, when a man comes to the kitchen in the middle of the night, it's usually because his stomach called out to him in hunger." Mrs. Hutchins grinned at him over the rim of her cup.

"I'm grateful you know that." He swallowed a bite and picked up his mug.

Mrs. Hutchins leaned forward on her elbows. "You know, if things get any worse out there with the rising water, people are going to need your help."

He almost choked on the hot liquid. He set it down and coughed. "What...what...do you mean?" His chest tightened, and his hands shook.

"I mean what with your skill at carpentry and building things, people will need your help. I hope you weren't planning to leave anytime soon."

"Um, I'm not sure when that will be." He relaxed in his chair and sipped his coffee again. He set the cup on the table. "If I can be of aid to anyone with rebuilding, I'll be available."

"I figured you would. That rocking chair you made me is the finest I've seen in a long time. You're a fine man, Joe Fitzgerald, and you're very talented. This town is lucky you stopped by for a visit."

Mrs. Hutchins was a good woman, and he did want to stay around to help with any repairs and rebuilding that had to be done. The one thing he couldn't predict was how his health would hold out. If the pain became too unbearable, he'd be on the next train back to home.

CHAPTER 23

TOM JERKED AWAKE. Gray light beamed through the windows, indicating an overcast sky. All about the hall women and children awoke and prepared for the day. Most of the men had not yet returned from their nightlong duties. He stood and stretched to remove the kinks formed in his muscles from a night on the floor.

Sheriff Bolton pushed open the town hall door. He nodded to Tom before addressing the crowded room. "Listen up, folks. The streets in town are near knee-deep with water. All the homes in the lowlands near the creek and not built on a raised foundation have water in them. We were able to lead livestock to higher ground. We don't know when the water will go down or how much rain fell north of us that might impact our area. Until then you'll need to stay here. Your men are taking care of your homes and seeing about the damage. When they can, they'll come in and let you know the conditions at your places."

The women murmured among themselves until one stepped forward, her hands clasped tight against her chest. "Sheriff, what are we supposed to do if we can't go back to our homes?"

The sheriff pushed his hat back from his face and scrubbed his forehead. "I'm not real sure about that, ma'am. The mayor and the preachers are talking and organizing.

We should have information for you soon. Until then stay here where you're safe and dry."

This brought more talk among the women, worried frowns creased many faces, and several sat down with their heads resting on their hands. The children, oblivious to the crisis, laughed and played with each other while a few older girls tried to keep the younger ones in check.

"As soon as we can tell you more, you will hear it." Sheriff Bolton blew out his breath and opened the door. "Tom, I saw Mr. Blake headed to the news office. I think maybe y'all got a little water down there. I got a boat to bring food supplies for the people here. Mr. Delmont will bring the food. I don't want the ladies to risk getting in the boat."

"What about my mother and the ladies from the church?"

"The women have been advised to stay at home or get to a shelter. Two of my deputies have a boat searching for anyone who may be stranded. They'll bring whoever they find back here."

He lowered his voice and leaned toward Tom. "It looks bad. The water's much higher down by the creek and is over three feet deep in many areas. It'll take awhile for things to get cleaned up."

"I understand. I'll go over to the newspaper office and see what help Mr. Blake may need."

"Fine, but be careful and be prepared to wade across in knee-deep water. Some of the businesses did get water. Since the hall is on the higher end of town, everyone should be okay here."

Tom's gaze once again went around the room. "We need to organize some leadership here and set up some routine to keep the people here under control." With over fifty women and children plus those older men who didn't need to be out helping, things would be in chaos unless someone took charge.

He followed Sheriff Bolton out to the boardwalk. Water sloshed over the edge but didn't flood across it.

"You're right about organizing things, Tom. The mayor has called an emergency meeting of the town council to get everyone organized and ready to help. They'll take care of the people at town hall. We really didn't have time to think last night since this all happened so fast. Maybe we'll get it all done today." He waved and waded across to the courthouse and the mayor's office.

Tom looked up the street. The brown water flowing past sent chills up his spine. Nobody should be out in this mess, but just then he spotted the boat with Mr. Delmont and Carl, the diner cook, making its way down from the bakery.

Mr. Delmont waved. "Hey, Tom, we have food here for the refugees. We need help setting it up."

"I'll take care of it." He headed back inside to find two of the women he had met earlier. They were in their sections talking and organizing activities for the children.

"Mrs. Dietrich, Mrs. Calhoun, the food is on its way. If you ladies could help spread it out and get the others in line or something, they'll be served more quickly."

"We know exactly what to do." Mrs. Calhoun looked serious. "How is it out there?"

"We're okay. It's not over the walks."

"My John is out there, and he hasn't been back to tell me anything." Mrs. Calhoun peered at him, her eyes filled with concern.

"I don't know any more than what the sheriff told us a few minutes ago. He said he'd let us know more later, so we'll have to go with that. Right now I need you two ladies to help organize the others and get the food ready. See, Mr. Delmont and Carl are coming in the door now."

"Oh, my, of course. Let's go, Hettie." Mrs. Dietrich marched over to the tables and began organizing and delegating nonstop.

With the meal in good hands, Tom once again headed to the newspaper. Wading through the knee-deep water at street crossings slowed him down and reminded him of the seriousness of the situation. He stopped at the door and spotted Mr. Blake already with a mop in hand sopping up water. Tom found close to an inch of water on the office floor.

"How did this get in here? It's not over the walk." Tom splashed over to his desk and stood surveying the mess.

Mr. Blake handed Tom a mop. "Here, you can help. A window busted and let in the rain. I've got it about under control. I don't think there's any major damage, but I won't know until I start the presses."

Tom swished his mop across the floor and directed the water toward the front door and outside. "How deep was it when you came in?"

"Not much more than it is now. Just got started a few minutes before you arrived." Mr. Blake resumed mopping.

They worked for another half hour and removed the water, leaving damp floorboards and chair legs. Mr. Blake approached the printing press to inspect the damage. "Don't see much it could have hurt. Let me get it started."

A few minutes later, the welcome sound of grinding gears filled the room. Mr. Blake waved his hands and shouted, "Hallelujah, praise the Lord, it works."

Tom clapped. This good news meant they could get right to work on the stories and news that had to be written to inform the people. "I'm going out and see what's going on with the mayor and the town council. Sheriff Bolton said the mayor was organizing people to help those who lost their homes or had significant damage to them."

"Good, Tom. You do that, and I'll go investigate where the floodwaters are. In the meantime, things will dry out here."

Tom nodded, grabbed his pad and pencil, and headed out for his story. Now was the time for the town of Stoney Creek to unite in the effort to take care of its own. If he used the past as a guide, everyone would come together in the next few days and do whatever they could to help.

⇒⇒⇒⇐⇐⇐

Joe changed into his work clothes. Herbert Spooner planned to go into town to the bank. Mr. Swenson might need help, although the bank most likely wouldn't open today. Joe wanted to talk more with Mr. Swenson, so he'd asked Herbert to share the boat they'd found in the storage barn behind the boardinghouse.

He joined Herbert downstairs and followed him out to the back. The barn sat on a hill above the waterline, so they lugged the boat to where the water rippled deep enough for the vessel. Herbert held the boat while Joe climbed aboard. Herbert joined him and picked up the oar.

"The water can't be more than about two feet deep, but I don't relish the idea of walking in it." Herbert dipped the oar into the water and steered the boat toward Main Street.

All along the way shop owners swept water off the walks. Most of them had placed sandbags at their doorways to keep water from their stores, so little damage would be seen in town thankfully.

When they reached the bank, Mr. Swenson met them at the door. "Good morning. Glad to see you. The mayor called a meeting of the town council. I'm on my way there now. Got room in that boat for me?"

"Sure do, Mr. Swenson. I'll drop you off and come back to the bank if you want me to."

"That'll be fine, Herbert. My daughter may try to come in later and help. Don't know if we'll have any business, but I'll feel good knowing you're there to take care of things."

He said nothing to Joe until they reached the town square and both climbed out of the boat at the courthouse. Mr. Swenson waited until Herb backed away and rowed back to the bank before speaking to Joe.

"Before I go inside, I want to tell you how much it's going to mean to the town for you to be here for our recovery. Mayor Gladstone has already told me that one of the things on the agenda at this meeting will be setting up a relief fund to help those who need it. With what you've told me, we can open up a line of credit at the bank for those seeking loans for repairs and rebuilding."

"I'm glad my attorney wasted no time getting the trust arranged. Remember, any money paid back goes straight back into the trust, and there's to be no interest charged for the loans."

"I remember, and this is a good thing you're doing, but I do wish you'd let them know it's you."

"That's part of the deal. If they know it's me, they'll be asking a million questions. No, it's better for me to simply disappear when I decide to go back home, and let them benefit from it all." The last thing Joe wanted now was publicity and notoriety. He simply wanted to go home and die in peace knowing that his good fortune could be passed on to others.

Tom waded across the street, waving at them in greeting. "Good morning, gentlemen. Mr. Swenson, I take it you're on your way to the meeting with Mayor Gladstone."

"That I am, and I assume you're going to write a story about what we decide to do. If so, then let's not waste any more time."

Joe bade them good-bye but stayed in place until the two men climbed the steps and entered the courthouse. The sun had begun to peek through the clouds, promising a beautiful day after a night of fear and destruction. Some buildings had suffered damage, some livestock was likely lost, and trees had been downed by the winds, but so far he hadn't heard any reports of lives lost, and that was a blessing. Property could be restored and buildings rebuilt, but a lost life would never return.

Joe grinned and rocked on his feet as he gazed toward heaven. "Well, Lord, looks like You sent me here for this very reason." He chuckled and remembered the story of Esther and how she had been used "for such a time as this" to help save her people. Yes, he was here by God's hand and planning. Now it was time to give back what the good Lord had been so generous in providing to one Joe Fitzgerald Mayfield.

$\mathcal{T}$OM'S PRIDE IN his hometown grew each day as the flood victims and townspeople came together to help each other. Mayor Gladstone's idea of a fund for recovery had met with the town council's approval, and Mr. Swenson at the bank had announced loans without interest for those hardest hit. Every news story Tom wrote told of more generosity and thoughtful, practical care.

Gretchen's human interest stories had also aroused civic pride as more and more families joined together to assist one another. Tom sauntered over to Gretchen's desk. A little over a week had passed since the flood, and now, three days before Thanksgiving, already one home and two barns had been restored.

"Whose story are you writing this week?"

Gretchen stopped typing and looked up at Tom. "This one is about the house rebuilding this past weekend at the Calhoun farm. The Kirks' place will be the next on the list the Saturday after Thanksgiving. I've heard about how small towns always come together in times of crisis, but this is the first time I've witnessed it firsthand."

"I'm proud of our Stoney Creek people. Those families who lost everything are getting back on their feet through the efforts of both churches. The clothing drive at Reverend Booker's church brought in more than I could ever expect. What did they decide to do with what was left over?"

"That's part of another story. They're going to have a place at their church for people who may have tragedy or needs to come and find clothes and food. Mr. Hempstead donated several boxes filled with canned food, and Reverend Weatherby's church will have a food pantry as well. Looks like the flood may have started more than just helping those in the flood."

Gretchen pulled the piece of paper from her typing machine and laid it on her desk. "Now that one is finished, I'm starting on the one about the tree lighting ceremony. Mayor Gladstone said it will go on as scheduled." She laughed and inserted a clean sheet into her machine. "The next time I complain about so many steps up onto the boardwalks, I'll remember how that kept the waters from flooding the shops and businesses during the storm. At first I thought that height off the ground was a little absurd, but now I'm thankful for it."

"The big flood they had back in 1875 really took a toll. The best thing to come out of it was the rebuilding of the town. Not much can be done about those farmlands and ranches closer to the creek unless they build up high, but maybe they'll come up with something next time around."

"I hope so. Now back to work." Gretchen turned her attention to her machine and the notes she had close by.

With his work ready for Wednesday's edition and on Mr. Blake's desk, Tom decided to check in at the bakery. A cup of coffee and a cinnamon roll always satisfied his hunger this time of day.

When he stepped outside, a wind gust swept around the corner of the building. A hint of the winter to come filled the air, and Tom buttoned up his suit coat. Soon he'd need to add another layer. South Central Texas usually stayed warm a little longer than the towns to the north, but the slight chill today indicated those days wouldn't last much longer.

He opened the door to the bakery, and the warmth welcomed him with aromas of the array of rolls, scones, and muffins in the display cases. Mrs. Delmont greeted him.

"Hello, Tom. What can I serve you?"

"Coffee and one of those cinnamon buns, please." He glanced about the room. "Where is Faith? In the back?" Since the flood they had had little time to talk, and he found himself missing her.

"No, she's down at the church helping Angela finalize the plans for the joint Thanksgiving service Wednesday night. They decided to use the town hall since it'll seat more people and it's been cleared out of everyone from the flood."

As much as Tom wanted to see Faith, doubt filled him about seeing her with Angela. He was fairly sure he had no interest in Angela, but still it might be awkward to see the two of them together.

Mrs. Delmont set the roll and a mug of coffee on the counter. He handed her the money. "Thank you." He picked up the food and strolled to a table that overlooked Main Street.

Down the way Hempstead's store had a steady stream of customers. Women came out with baskets loaded with ingredients for their Thanksgiving meals. With Reverend Booker's church taking on the clothing drive, Reverend Weatherby's congregation had charge of the food distribution and planned a meal before the Wednesday evening services for all who didn't have the facilities to provide their own this year.

In fact, most of the stores appeared to be busy this Monday before the holiday. He loved this time of year partly because of all the good food and festivities to enjoy, but mainly because the Christmas season seemed to bring out the good in people, and generosity took over. Then, besides the holidays, there would be Clara and Theodore's wedding as well this year. What a busy, happy time they could look forward to! It would certainly be a nice change from dealing with the cleanup from the storm.

Faith appeared down the way coming in the direction of the bakery. Tom gulped down the last bite of cinnamon bun and the last dregs of coffee. If he hurried, he'd catch her before she got here. He wanted time to talk with her alone.

He met her in the middle of the street. "Hello, Faith. I was just asking your mother about you. She said you were helping with the plans for the services Wednesday."

She peered up at him with raised eyebrows. "I was, and it's going to be a beautiful one, but why were you asking about me?"

Tom swallowed hard. What was wrong with him? This was Faith, his friend. "Um, I hoped we might have a few minutes together before you go back to work."

"All right. Ma doesn't expect me back for another ten minutes or so. Where do you want to go?"

Tom gulped and scanned the area around them. "Let's go down the block to the hotel. We can sit in the lobby out of the chilly air." He waved in that direction and grasped her elbow.

When they reached the hotel, they entered the lobby and Tom headed for the corner where two wingback chairs offered some privacy. After Faith was seated, Tom sat down.

Faith said nothing but sat there with an expectant look filling her eyes. Finally words came to Tom. He breathed deeply before blurting out, "Will you go to the church service with me Wednesday night and then to the tree lighting on Thursday?"

"Of course I will. Don't we always do those kinds of things together?" She tilted her head with a puzzled expression written across her features.

Yes, they did, but he wanted it to be official this time rather than simply meeting up somewhere. How could he show her that this time was somehow different? Try as he might, he couldn't think of a way. So he said simply, "Yes, well, then I'll be by your house on Wednesday evening before the service."

"Better make that the church because my parents and I volunteered to help serve the meal there."

Of course they would. He should have thought of that. If his family hadn't planned on being out at the Gordon ranch, his mother would be doing the same thing. "That's fine. I'll be coming from Aunt Hannah's, so I'll come on to the church and meet you there."

Faith stood and pulled her shawl up over her shoulders. "I'll see you then, but now I must get back to the bakery. We have a lot of Thanksgiving orders to fill."

Tom stayed back on the boardwalk until she entered the bakery. That had not gone exactly like he'd planned, but he had until Wednesday night to figure how to let her know he wanted to see her as more than a friend.

>>><<<

That was the strangest meeting she'd ever had with Tom. What had happened to him that he decided to ask her to attend something with him that they usually did together anyway? She bit her lip. He had asked her instead of Angela. Maybe that meant something. Still confused, she shrugged and hurried on into the bakery. They'd be spending time this evening getting orders ready for delivery tomorrow and Wednesday, so she had no time to worry herself with Tom's behavior.

When she entered the bakery, the early afternoon patrons were leaving. The door closed behind the last customer, and Faith turned over the sign to let people know the bakery was closed for serving but open for orders. When she entered the kitchen, Aunt Ruby rolled out pie crusts and Ma stacked the last of the dishes into the sink.

"How did it go with planning the services for Wednesday night?" Ma poured hot water over the dishes.

"Everything is all set. Hannah Gordon will play the piano, and Mrs. Grubbs the pump organ. Reverend Weatherby and Reverend Booker will both speak. Angela will sing a solo, and the choirs from both churches will combine to sing one hymn of thanks. Reverend Booker says the response to the service has been very good."

Aunt Ruby slipped a round piece of dough into a pie plate. "I would think so after all we've been through this past week. People of Stoney Creek are coming together like family. It's good to see, and it bodes well for the Christmas Eve service as well."

Faith had always seen Stoney Creek as a family town anyway, so she had expected them to come together after the flood, but they had outdone themselves. Joe had been restoring damaged furniture, and from what she'd heard, he had plenty of orders to keep him busy in the workshop

Mrs. Hutchins had set up for him in her storage shed. That man did have a way with a hammer and saw.

The bell over their front door jangled. That meant someone needed baked goods. "I'll get it, Ma."

Joe Fitzgerald greeted her when she came into the bakery. "Miss Delmont, I'd like a dozen of those chocolate cookies your mother makes so well. If you don't have them, I'll take plain sugar cookies."

"I have both." She reached in with a piece of parchment in her hand to select the cookies.

"Then give me a dozen of each. Little ones tend to get hungry for good cookies."

"Little children? Who are the lucky ones?"

"I'm delivering a new table to the Kirk family. The one they had was really rickety and the storm didn't help any. This and the cookies are my gift to them. Mr. Kirk had to cut down some trees, so we used the lumber to build the table."

"How nice for them. I'm sure the table is a beautiful piece of work." Maybe someday she and Tom would have use for a new table in their home. She bit her lip and placed the cookies in a bag. She had to slow down on that dream; he'd only asked to take her to the tree lighting, not to marry him.

She handed the cookies to Joe. "Will you be at the Thanksgiving service and the tree lighting? The electric lights will be a special treat this year."

"Hoping to be there. I've grown very fond of Stoney Creek and the people here. Don't know how much longer I can stay, but I plan to enjoy every minute of it while I'm here."

He headed for the door when Ma ran from the kitchen. "Help! The stove's on fire! Quick, get help!"

Indeed smoke billowed from the kitchen and Aunt Ruby ran out flapping her apron and coughing. "I think it's more smoke than fire in the room. The fire must be in the stove pipe."

Joe ran out to the street and yelled, "Fire! Fire! Fire at the bakery!"

Faith's eyes watered and her throat burned. She grabbed her shawl and followed her mother and aunt out to the street. People had come running from every direction. Tears flowed in rivers down Faith's cheeks. *Dear God, please help us!* What in the world would they do about filling all their Thanksgiving orders? This could ruin Ma and Pa.

≫ CHAPTER 25 ≪

*W*HEN JOE'S CRY for help reached the newspaper office, Tom raced from the building, followed by Gretchen and Mr. Blake. The street filled with those who formed the volunteer fire department, with Mr. Hempstead being the captain of the group. He divided the group in two sections and sent one around to the back of the bakery and one to the front.

Smoke rolled out of the building, but no visible flames could be seen. Mr. Hempstead asked for any able-bodied men to help, so Tom rolled up his sleeves and joined the others in the water brigade. Some flames could now be seen through the window. Even as he passed bucket after bucket along the row, he searched for Faith and her mother.

He finally spied them huddled together with Aunt Ruby near the bank. His heart sank at the sadness in their faces. With all the orders for the holidays the bakery should be booming with business. What would happen to them now?

In less than forty-five minutes the fire was out, but what a mess remained. He dropped his bucket and raced to Faith's side. He wrapped his arms around her shoulders and held her close.

"I'm so sorry about the building, but so thankful you and your family are okay."

Tears dampened his shirt when she buried her face against his chest. "Oh, Tom, what are we going to do? How will we ever get back to cooking?"

He stroked her hair and rested his cheek against the top of her head. "Let's see how much damage there is and what needs to be done. I didn't see a lot of flames, so maybe all isn't lost."

"It was that old stove. Ma said it was going to ruin more than food one day." She sniffed and stepped back from him. After pulling her shawl tighter about her shoulders, she grabbed her mother's hand. "Well, let's go see what's left."

Tom followed them back to the bakery, where Mr. Delmont met them. "It's not all bad, but we won't be able to live or work here for a while. The stove is history, as are the cabinets and equipment in the kitchen. What didn't burn is water soaked and smoke damaged."

Mrs. Delmont stepped around Tom. "I have to see."

Sheriff Bolton tried to stop her from entering the building, but she pushed him aside and went inside. Faith glared at her father and the sheriff as she followed her mother. Her expression dared them to stop her, and neither man even attempted.

A chuckle rose in Tom's throat and then burst into a laugh. He caught it and slapped his hand over his mouth. The situation wasn't funny, but the determination and grit on Faith's face was. He'd never seen her quite that riled up.

A smile winked at the corner of the sheriff's mouth. "I wasn't about to try and stop her. She's a woman on a mission." He waved his hand at the door. "Care to follow them, Gus?"

Mr. Delmont snapped his head in a nod. After he had gone, the sheriff shoved his hat back. "Most of the flames were contained in the stove pipe, but they spread enough to make the ceiling and second floor dangerous. The flames that did escape charred and blistered the walls and cabinets. Hempstead and I checked, and it's nothing but residual smoke now, so the only danger would be in the structure, but from what I can tell, they'll be able to rebuild."

"I'm thankful for that." Tom peered through the door, but saw only waterlogged cases with drowned pastries and cookies. "Looks like they poured water over everything."

"They did, and they kept the fire contained in the kitchen area. Mr. Hempstead had a crew at the back pump hauling water to the kitchen, and the line out here dumped some on the floors and displays to keep them from sparking. It'll take some repairs and time, but he'll open again."

Which was good in the long run, but it didn't answer the question of the here and now and holiday baking orders. He jerked around when a familiar voice called his name. Might have known his mother would be with the first group of ladies coming to offer help. "Hello, Mama. I see you've brought your helpers."

"Oh, Tom, we're all in this together. How much damage was done? What can we do to help?"

"I haven't seen the damage, but the sheriff said it can be repaired and restored."

"But most likely not in time for this week's orders to be filled." She snapped her fingers and conferred with the ladies who had come with her.

Tom shook his head and grinned. His mother would have them organized and working quicker than a cat pouncing on a mouse. Sure enough, she turned back to him with the most satisfied smile. She said nothing, and

Tom itched to know what she had going in that brain of hers. It would be something good for certain.

Mrs. Delmont and Faith exited the bakery. Tears dampened the cheeks of both women. They came to an abrupt halt when they realized the size of the crowd assembled in the street. Ma stepped forward. "Irene, we know this is your busy season, so some of us are offering our kitchens to help you get your orders filled."

Mrs. Delmont's mouth gaped open and her hand flew up to cover it. Faith wrapped her arms around her mother's shoulders. Aunt Ruby lifted the corner of her apron and dabbed at her eyes.

"Sallie, that's the kindest offer I've ever heard. But how will we get all the supplies we need? The flour and sugar are ruined and most of the spices will need replacing."

Mr. Hempstead strode forward. "Mrs. Delmont, you can have anything in the store you need to get your orders filled."

Tom grasped Faith's hand in his and pulled her aside. "See, it's going to be okay."

She shook her head. "I'm not sure. Papa won't take anything on credit, and I don't know how we'll pay for everything we need."

Just then Faith heard her mother gasp and exclaim, "You said what?"

Faith hurried back to her mother. "What's going on?"

Mr. Hempstead grinned. "I said, a new stove for the bakery was ordered a week or so ago and should be here next week. It's a larger, commercial-size one like the one at the hotel."

Mr. Delmont wrapped his arm around his wife's shoulders. "I didn't order any such stove, and we can't pay for something like that with all the repairs that need to be done."

Red flushed Mr. Hempstead's face. "Um...well...you see...um...it's already paid for. Someone"—he held up his hands and shook his head—"and I don't know who, ordered it from a catalog and paid for it. I got notice it was being shipped."

A scowl filled Mr. Delmont's face. "We can't accept such an offering, and we won't buy the supplies until we have the money to pay for them."

Mr. Swenson from the bank and Mayor Gladstone pulled Mr. Hempstead aside and conferred with him in whispers. The man nodded and spoke again to Mr. Delmont. "Mr. Swenson and the mayor said to let you know it's from the Community Service Fund that's been set up to aid those who had damage from the flood and for anyone else who needs repairs or rebuilding after a fire or tornado or other disaster. There's plenty of money there to take care of the bakery until you're back in business and can repay."

Faith peered up at Tom and bit her lip. "I've never heard of such a thing as a Community Service Fund. Where in the world did it come from?"

Tom had his suspicions but had no facts or proofs, simply his journalistic instincts. He scanned the crowd for any sign of Joe, but he was nowhere in sight. One thing for sure, since Joe had arrived, for every bad thing that had happened, far better things came along to take care of them. For some reason God had chosen Stoney Creek for the greatest blessings they'd ever seen.

⟫⟩⟫⟨⟨⟨

Mama clasped her hands to her chest. "Saints preserve us. I can't believe this is happening."

Aunt Ruby fisted her hands on her hips. "With my kitchen and these other ladies' help, we'll do fine."

Faith wrapped her arms around her mother's shoulders. "It's a miracle, Mama. Now we can get every order filled with the help of Mrs. Whiteman and the other women. We can spread out with you, Aunt Ruby, and me in three kitchens, and we can get it all done."

A smile brightened Mama's face. "I'm so thankful for their help, and yes, I do believe we can do it. We can collect the pans and mixing things we need and clean them up to use. Water and smoke wouldn't damage them."

"See, things really do look better." Faith grasped her mother's hand and nodded to Aunt Ruby. "Now, let's go see what we can salvage."

Back in the ruined kitchen Faith rummaged through the drawers and cabinets to find the cake pans, baking sheets, cast iron skillets, and muffin tins all sooty but easily cleaned. She set them on the floor to divide and take with them to the different kitchens.

Mama added the big pottery and metal mixing bowls, and Aunt Ruby salvaged wire whisks, beaters, spoons, ladles, and tin measuring utensils. Soon they had assembled a good start on what they needed. They pulled out waterlogged bags of sugar, flour, and meal to throw away.

"Here, let us handle those for you."

Faith jerked around to find Tom, Pa, and the sheriff in the kitchen. She handed Tom the bag of sugar.

"I'm so glad you're here. After we get rid of all this stuff we can't use, we can use your help carrying these other things to where we'll need them to bake tomorrow to fill our Thanksgiving pie and cake orders."

Mama hugged Papa. "This is a miracle, Gus. Look at the equipment we saved."

"I do see, and I'm very thankful for this. I've been upstairs and it was pretty much filled with smoke, and the floor over the kitchen is damaged enough that it's not safe. The sheriff says it's better if we don't try to stay there tonight. The floor around where the flue came up the back wall of our kitchen and the wall are damaged as well. We will have to go to the hotel for a few nights until we can find other living arrangements."

"You'll do no such thing," Aunt Ruby declared. "You're staying with me. I got that big house with just me, and there's plenty of room for you. Now get what you need and get it on over to my place."

Mama hugged her sister. "Thank you, Ruby. We'd be delighted to stay with you."

"Ma, do you have the recipes for the orders so we can divide them up and start on the orders for Thursday?"

"The ones on paper were ruined, but I have them all in my head, and I can rewrite them for you."

Aunt Ruby laughed. "I think I have most of them in my head too. We've baked so much lately, we have them memorized."

"Well, I guess that means it's my turn to start memorizing." Faith joined in a hug with her mother and aunt.

Pa raised his hand. "This calls for a prayer of thanks to our great God." He bowed his head, and his gentle bass voice lifted in praise. "Our Father God, You've taken what could have been the greatest tragedy for this family and turned it into a project of unselfish love and sharing. We shall be eternally grateful for the generosity of whoever purchased the stove and for this new community fund. We may be down, but we are not out because You have provided out of Your great storehouse of riches in Your Son, Jesus Christ. In Your mighty name we pray. Amen."

A chorus of "amens" rose around them. Tom hugged her close to his side and bent his head to whisper in her ear, "We've just seen God at work." He kissed her forehead. "Now He has work for us to do."

Faith's heart skipped a beat. Maybe he did care about her. She shook her head. No time to think about that now.

Tom picked up another bag to haul out to the back. Mama divided the pans into three piles. When they had finished and were ready to move the piles to the three kitchens, Pa came back and told them three wagons were outside ready to take the equipment and supplies to their destinations.

Mama picked up her shawl. "Then let's get to the store and get what we need, Ruby. Faith, you go with the menfolk and get everything in the right place. Then we can decide who will work where and when."

Mama and Aunt Ruby left to find Mr. Hempstead. Faith picked up an armload of pots and pans to take to the wagons. With wonderful friends and neighbors like those in Stoney Creek, they would recover. All the Thanksgiving orders would be filled. Faith breathed a prayer of thanks and set her load on the bed of the wagon.

⫸ CHAPTER 26 ⫷

OM FOLLOWED HIS nose to the kitchen late Thanksgiving morning. Although dinner would be later in the afternoon, his stomach still reacted to all the delicious aromas from roasting turkey, cornbread, and pecan pie.

Voices from the kitchen reminded him of all that had transpired in the past two days. He pushed open the door from the dining room to find his mother and Mrs. Delmont sipping tea at the table.

"You must be all done with the bakery orders." Tom reached for a mug in the cabinet.

"Yes, we are. Your mother has been such a great help. She knows what it is to cook for a crowd."

"She sure does, but we never have any leftovers for the next day. With my uncles and cousins around, food disappears in a hurry." He pulled out a chair. "Mind if I join you?"

Ma laughed. "Now, I know you well enough to know you're not sitting here to keep two older ladies company. You want a story."

Tom shrugged and picked up his coffee mug. "Well, I am a reporter, so that's what I do." He gulped down a bit then set the mug on the table.

"Were you able to get all the orders filled? How did you divide up the orders? When were they all delivered?"

"Goodness, you don't give a body time to think on one question before you ask another. Let me think on it." Mrs. Delmont sipped tea and furrowed her brow.

"Faith was over with Mrs. Weatherby at her house, and your sister, Mrs. Stone, worked in her kitchen with Mrs. Booker, and you were here with Ma. Didn't that get confusing?"

Mrs. Delmont set her cup on the table and leaned toward Tom. "Your mother and I did the pastries, Ruby took care of the cakes, and Faith baked cookies. Mr. Hempstead sent over his delivery boy to help deliver groceries, and your brother, Daniel, helped him. Once we relegated the recipes, it wasn't difficult to get it all done."

"That sounds very organized."

"It was, and if everyone hadn't worked together, we'd have had one big problem."

"When do you think the bakery will be back in operation?"

"Of that I'm not sure, but Mr. Delmont, Burt, Reverend Booker, and Reverend Weatherby were there yesterday to take out the furniture and belongings from our living quarters. Most of the clothes will have to be cleaned because of the smoke, but our belongings upstairs are in relatively good shape otherwise. The men are organizing a cleaning and repair crew. We may not have a barn, but it'll be like the old barn raisings we had when I was a girl."

"Strange about that stove, isn't it?" Tom studied Mrs. Delmont's facial expression, which could sometimes reveal more than any words.

"Yes, it is. We asked Mr. Hempstead about it again, and he still has no clue who ordered it. If there is an invoice, that may give a clue. Otherwise, we're all in the dark."

Not exactly the answer Tom wanted, but it did confirm his notion that no one else had any idea who the benefactor might be. Joe's name had not come up one time in all the conversations he'd had and heard concerning the mysterious good fortunes falling on people.

"I think I have enough for my story, so I'll leave you two to do whatever it is you need to do to be ready for today." He ambled through the door to the dining room. Behind him Mrs. Delmont said she had to leave to go help her sister with their family dinner.

That reminded him of Faith. He planned to go over to Mrs. Stone's house after dinner at the ranch and escort Faith to the tree lighting ceremony. The evening he'd planned for last night never materialized because Faith and her family were the center of attention, and he never really got a moment alone with her. He'd make sure that didn't happen tonight.

Faith dropped down into a chair in Aunt Ruby's parlor after setting the table for the dinner with her family. Never had she been so tired. The last of the Thanksgiving orders had been delivered yesterday evening before the church services. Then she and her mother had spent the evening helping serve the meal for all those who had lost their homes and belongings in the flood.

A few stayed with families in town, but some had elected to erect tents on their own property and live there until they could rebuild. They had plenty of food thanks to the hotel kitchen, Mr. Hempstead, and Carl from the diner.

Seemed as though she'd been on her feet forever. How had Aunt Ruby and Mama done it all these years? The past days had been a baking nightmare. Right now she didn't care if she never saw an oatmeal or sugar cookie again, or at least not until next week.

As tired as she was, the wonderful aroma of roasting turkey lured her to the kitchen. As she passed the dining table, she again admired Aunt Ruby's good china dishes and crystal, which sparkled in the sunlight shining through the windows.

When she entered the kitchen, she found Aunt Ruby and Mama filling bowls to take to the table. Her mother ladled green beans into a bowl. Looking up, she said, "If the table's all ready, call your father and we'll eat. I think he's in the back parlor reading."

"It's all set, so I'll get him. It smells so good in here, my stomach is growling."

Faith hurried back through the dining room and to the back parlor where Aunt Ruby had one wall of bookshelves filled with books of all kinds. She found her father seated in a dark blue wingback chair by the window holding a book, but his head leaned to one side against a wing, and his glasses had slipped down his nose. Small flames glowed red and orange in the fireplace. She stopped to admire the perfect fall afternoon scene.

She reached over and patted her father's arm. "Papa, dinner's ready. Mama and Aunt Ruby are putting it on the table."

He jerked awake and blinked his eyes. "Oh, Faith, my dear girl, I didn't hear you come in."

Faith grinned and kissed his forehead. "I guess I was too quiet."

He laid his book aside, adjusted his glasses, and stood to follow Faith to the table. After he blessed the food, Mama handed him the carving knife to slice the turkey.

Faith served her plate with turkey, dressing, vegetables, and spiced peaches canned last summer. This was truly a day for giving thanks. Their home and bakery had been damaged, true, but they were together and had food on the table. Everything else was stuff that could be replaced.

After dinner Faith volunteered to wash and dry the dishes. Aunt Ruby argued for a few minutes but finally gave in. She and Mama covered the serving dishes with a cloth then left Faith to her cleaning up.

Alone with her hands in hot, soapy water, she had time to think about Tom and his strange behavior the past weeks. He'd never kissed her before until now. Then he had actually formally asked to escort her to the tree lighting tonight. It had come to the point she didn't really know what to expect from him anymore. She finished the dishwashing and carried the pan to the back door, where she threw out the water over the grass.

Back inside she dried the dishes and placed them back in the cabinet. As she stacked them on the shelf, a smile filled her heart. Perhaps Tom's strange behavior would lead to a closer relationship. She closed her eyes and imagined the two of them in their own home with several children. What a pretty picture they would make.

She closed the cabinet door and leaned her forehead against it. How nice it would have been to have spent time with him last evening as they'd planned. Things had been so hectic at the church supper, and then the attention from the people at the joint church service had given them no time at all alone.

He'd said he'd be in from the Gordon ranch before the ceremony to pick her up. She checked the watch pinned to her shirtwaist. He wouldn't be here for at least several more hours. With the kitchen now clean she wandered out to the back parlor. The house was quiet with the only sound coming from the fire hissing and popping in the grate.

Everyone else would be upstairs taking a nap before this evening's festivities, but sleep didn't appeal to Faith. She gazed out the back windows toward Aunt Ruby's rose garden. Aunt Ruby has been a widow for ten years now, and she had kept her home and garden just as beautiful as ever.

Faith's heart ached for her dear aunt who never had children of her own. She could have become a bitter woman with no husband or children, but she had filled her time helping Ma with the bakery and helping women all over town with their children. Many a Sunday afternoon found Aunt Ruby with a passel of young ones gathered around for storytelling or games. As wonderful as that was for her aunt, Faith prayed her own life would be different. She wanted children of her own, preferably with Tom.

She removed her shoes and settled back in the chair where her father had dozed earlier. Pulling her knees to her chest, she rested her chin on her knees. Perhaps that day wasn't as far off as she thought. Joy filled her heart. Yes, she was definitely going to show one Tom Whiteman how much she cared for him.

⇛⇚

After the hearty meal served by Mrs. Hutchins to her boarders, Joe retired to his room to rest. Today his body had reminded him once again of the urgency of his business here in Stoney Creek. The medication Doc had given him helped relieve the pain, but the times he needed it came closer together.

He lay on his bed and stared at the ceiling then closed his eyes.

Dear Lord, time is getting short, but there is still much to do. You've been good to me all these years, and I'm thankful for the time I've had. Thank You for leading me to Stoney Creek and the people here. Whatever I can do for them is little in comparison to what You've done for me. I sure would like it if You'd let me stay long enough for Clara and Theodore's wedding and the Christmas program. I'll have to leave soon after that to get back home before the new year begins. Thank You in advance for the blessings still ahead. Amen.

The list of things the town still needed ran through his mind. He'd already talked with Mr. Swenson about ordering a fire wagon for Stoney Creek's volunteer fire team. A bucket brigade wasn't of much use in case of a fire much larger than the one in the bakery. Mr. Swenson had promised to speak with Mayor Gladstone about it before tonight so he could announce it at the ceremony.

For the first time the town would have electric lights on the tree, and that was a sight he wanted to behold. He'd seen the faces of children back home when the lights came on, and the wonder and awe in their eyes and smiles warmed his heart every time. It would be no different here in Stoney Creek.

A knock on his door followed by Mrs. Hutchins's voice stirred him from his reverie. "One moment, I'm coming."

He padded to the door in stocking feet and cracked it open. "What is it?"

"Oh, I wanted you to know that the coffee is hot and the pies are warm. So if you want to come down for dessert before we go to town, it's all ready and waiting."

"Thank you, I believe I'll do just that."

If the pecan and pumpkin pies he'd seen on the sideboard earlier tasted as good as they looked, they'd all be in for a great treat. Thinking of those pies reminded him of the Delmont family. If the stove had arrived a week sooner, maybe the fire could have been prevented.

Too late to second guess the timing on the order now. It'd be here in a day or so, and with all the help the town offered, the bakery wouldn't be out of its building for very long.

Downstairs all but Miss Simmons sat around the table. The teacher had taken the train to spend the holiday with her family up near Dallas. Everyone chatted about the services last night and the ceremony to come later.

He had grown to love his fellow lodgers, and he regretted having to leave them, but he wanted to die at home in his own bed with his two close friends from his church at his bedside and his lawyer who knew what to do after Joe left this earth. His business here was finished, and now he could return home and die in peace knowing that the legacy he left behind would be put to good use in the hands of the one he most trusted here in Stoney Creek besides Mr. Swenson. Now he just needed to write a letter to that person to let him know of his plan.

CHAPTER 27

S THE SUN began to set, Tom settled his horse in the stable before starting for Mrs. Stone's house to meet Faith. His hands shook when he removed the bridle and bit from Hero's mouth. "Sorry, boy, but my nerves are getting the best of me tonight."

All through dinner out at the Gordon ranch today he'd thought of tonight and what he might say to Faith. Should he declare his love now or wait? With all that had happened to her family the past week, now may not be the best time, but then would any time be the best?

Daniel had ridden back from the ranch with him, and the usually talkative young man had been silent most of the way home. Tom hung his saddle over the railing and glanced at his brother, who was filling a bag with oats for his horse.

"Daniel, something seems to be troubling you. You didn't say much on the way home. What's on your mind?"

Red flushed his cheeks. "It's nothing really."

"'Nothing really' wouldn't cause that red in your face. So something's going on."

Daniel fed his horse. "I asked Mary Sue Duncan to the tree lighting, and now I wish I hadn't."

A smile rose in Tom. "And why is that?" His little brother was growing up. Now at age fifteen, he stood eye to eye with Tom. About time he took notice of the girls.

"I don't know what to say to her or how I should act or anything like that. I rode home with you to ask your advice, but I didn't know for sure what to ask."

"I see." Tom busied himself a moment with Hero before answering. "Seems to me it's like this. You've known Mary Sue a while, so you know what she likes. Talk about those things and ask her about herself. Girls like to talk about themselves just like we talk about the things we like to do. Think of how you are at school or at church. Be relaxed and be yourself." He reached up and ruffled Daniel's hair. "You're a pretty good guy, and if you don't quit growing, I won't even be able to reach the top of your head."

Daniel laughed and squirmed away from Tom's hand. "I hope I grow to be as tall as Uncle Will in Louisiana."

"Most likely you will. Now, remember what I said about relaxing and being yourself. Mary Sue must like you as well since she said she'd go to the ceremony with you."

"Thanks, Tom. I knew you'd be able to help me." He jammed his cap back on his head and sauntered out of the barn, whistling under his breath.

Tom stood beside Hero's stall a moment longer. His words to Daniel filled his head. That was the exact advice he should be giving himself. He'd always been relaxed and natural around Faith. Why should that change now that he wanted more than simply friendship? He shuddered. Because he might lose that friendship if she didn't return his feelings.

He slapped Hero's rump. "Well, it looks like I need to take my own advice. I can wait to see how things go in the next few weeks. Don't you think I should have some idea of her feelings by Christmas? I do, so that's what I'll aim for."

His own laughter rang out in the stable. "Now I'm talking to horses for advice. You've got it bad, Tom, old man." He turned on his heel and strode from the barn. Just enough time to clean up before heading to Mrs. Stone's.

>>><<<

Faith eyed the skirt and shirtwaist she'd worn the day of the fire and frowned. Not really very festive for the launching of the Christmas season, but almost everything else still reeked of smoke. Maybe Aunt Ruby had something to liven up the drab black and white ensemble.

She knocked on her aunt's door. "Aunt Ruby, it's Faith. May I come in?"

At her aunt's affirmative answer Faith entered. Aunt Ruby sat at her dressing table in a red, white, and green plaid skirt with a red shirtwaist completing it. "Oh my, I love the red and green. Do you have anything that would brighten up this?" She held her skirt out to one side.

Aunt Ruby tilted her head with her fingers perched on her cheek. "I do believe I have just the thing." She opened a drawer and pulled out a length of red ribbon. "This should do for a bit of red around the collar of your top. If you weren't so much smaller than I am, you could wear my green wool skirt."

Then Aunt Ruby sorted through the hangers in her wardrobe. "I thought this was still here. Haven't worn it in ages." She held up a red wool half cape trimmed in black braid. "This will add a bit of festive color, and it'll be warm as well."

"It's beautiful." Faith fit the cape around her shoulders. It fell to hip length and brightened the look of her skirt and top. "With the red bow at my neck and the red cape, I do feel more like Christmas."

"Hmm, and could that young Whiteman boy have anything to do with why you want to look your best?"

Heat flushed Faith's face and neck. "I guess he does. He's been acting real strange lately. In fact, he actually asked to take me to the lighting tonight. Usually we just end up together once we're there."

Aunt Ruby laughed and hugged Faith. "You grab hold of that young man and don't let him go. He's one of the finest in town."

"I think so too, and if I do get hold of him, I won't let go."

Voices from downstairs caused a gasp from Faith. "Oh, my, I think Tom is here and I'm not quite ready." She hugged her aunt again and kissed her cheek. "Thank you for the cape. I'll take good care of it."

She raced back to her room to put the finishing touches on her hair. After pinching her cheeks to add a little color, she grabbed up her skirt and rushed out to meet Tom.

Halfway down the staircase she spotted him talking with her father. She paused a moment to observe him. He stood several inches taller than her father, and Tom's red hair curled about his neck. His broad shoulders filled his coat in a most becoming way. A smile played about her lips. Not only was he one of the finest men in Stoney Creek, he was also the most handsome.

>>><<<

Tom sensed someone behind him and turned to see Faith midway on the stairs. Her smile sent shivers down his spine. Words stuck in his throat as she descended and joined him in the foyer.

"I hope I didn't keep you waiting too long. I was talking with Aunt Ruby and let time get away from me."

He'd have waited all night for her if he had to. His voice reappeared. "I haven't been here but a few minutes and was having conversation with your father." He tucked her hand in his elbow. Inhaling the scent of gardenia, he decided it was his favorite flower.

After saying good-bye to her parents, Tom escorted her down the steps of her aunt's home. He'd always admired the Victorian style with the wraparound front porch, high windows, and intricate trim. It was the kind of house he wanted someday.

"It's nice you have your aunt to turn to in time of need. I remember her husband and the work he did to make Stoney Creek a better place."

"It's funny, he had so many investments, and yet Aunt Ruby chose to work in the bakery because she and Ma loved to cook and wanted to do something special with it."

A chill in the air caused Faith to wrap the cape more tightly around her shoulders and arms. "I've always loved her house, and Andrew and I had some fun times there. I've always been sorry that she never had children for us to play with. It would have been nice to have a larger family, like you do."

"That is too bad. She's so good with the little ones at church."

Idle chatter was not on his agenda, but then he had no words to truly convey what he was thinking at this particular moment. He held her arm and pulled her close as they joined the throngs of people headed for the town square.

A giant tree stood waiting in the dark. The gas streetlights cast a rosy glow about the square and revealed the tinsel decorations hung by Mayor Gladstone's wife and her committee. Cloth-wrapped boxes with decorative ribbons lay in stacks beneath the tree. Tom spotted Gretchen across the way.

"Look, there's Gretchen. She's covering the ceremony tonight for the lead story in Saturday's edition of the paper. Is that Deputy Cooper with her?"

Faith peered in the direction he pointed and giggled. "It sure is. I remember how he vied for her attention her first day in town."

He shrugged. "It's none of my business anyway. Let's see if we can get a little closer to the tree. Looks like Mayor Gladstone is about ready to begin."

Tom led Faith to a spot only a row or so back from the edge of the crowd. Mayor Gladstone held up his hands and asked for quiet. Reverend Weatherby stepped up to the podium and offered a prayer of thanksgiving and blessing for the coming season celebrating the birth of Jesus.

Then the mayor spoke. "Before we light our tree and officially begin the Christmas season here in Stoney Creek, I have some exciting news for our townspeople. I had a letter this week from the power company in Dallas. They are extending the lines between their city and San Antonio, which puts us right on the line. By this time next year we should have our own electric lines and not have to depend on a generator for our tree, street lights, and even our homes."

A roar of approval rose from the crowd with a thunder of applause, whistles, and shouts of joy. Tom grinned down at Faith. "That could make a great difference for your bakery."

Her face shone with delight, and her eyes sparkled. "Oh, my, yes. I'm so glad we know this now so Pa can make sure we can add whatever is needed for an electrical supply."

"Yes, with the new railroad lines and the power plant, Stoney Creek will thrive even more. I can't wait to interview the mayor tomorrow and write this story." He turned his attention back to the mayor, who now stood beside Catherine Hempstead. The mercantile owner's granddaughter had won an essay contest at school that earned her the privilege of pulling the switch to light the tree.

"Before Miss Hempstead here pulls the switch, I have one other bit of news. An anonymous donor has ordered a fire engine for our volunteer fire department. No more bucket brigades!" After the crowd quieted down again, the mayor raised his hand. "Now on the count of three, Catherine, pull the switch. One, two, three."

She pulled it, and the tree lit up in a myriad of bright colors that sparkled like jewels. More whistles and cheers rose from the people gathered, and the children were urged forward, where Mr. Swenson greeted them dressed in the red velvet of Santa Claus.

Faith squeezed Tom's hand. "I can't believe he looks just like the Santa on the cover of that book by Moore, *A Visit from Saint Nicholas*. Mrs. Rivers has a copy at the library."

"Yes, I've seen it." The crowd began to thin out except for the children and their parents. Tom guided Faith away from the square, and they walked back up Main Street.

Faith inhaled deeply and expelled her breath. "A perfect evening to end a wonderful day. We have so much to thank God for today."

Tom had no disagreement with that. The family time at Micah and Hannah's today had been extra special with

Theodore Gladstone joining them. In just a few weeks his little sister Clara would be married and beginning a home of her own. Had he waited too long to take that road for himself? Faith was...well, Faith was Faith, his best friend.

They walked along in silence back to Aunt Ruby's. Words spun around in Tom's head faster than a toy top out of control. Everything he wanted to say to Faith became garbled and nonsensical. She had never affected him this way before, and now it ruined the fun they had always experienced at the tree lighting. Was it ruining their friendship as well?

At the steps up to the porch at her aunt's Tom stopped Faith and peered into her face. "I had some things I wanted to say to you, but for some reason I can't figure out how to say it properly. We've known each other about all our lives, and we have a wonderful friendship that has grown over those years. I don't want to lose that."

The look in her eyes questioned him, but she said nothing. "I guess I'm going about this all wrong. I treasure our relationship as friends, but—"

Her fingers touched his lips. "Don't say another word. I too treasure our friendship, and nothing is ever going to change that. Thank you for a lovely evening. I enjoyed the ceremony and walking with you." She pulled her cape tighter and raced up the steps. At the door she stopped. "We'll always be friends, and whatever you decide to do with your life, I know you will be doing what God wants you to do."

Tom swallowed hard as she closed the door behind her. What had just happened? That hadn't gone the way he'd planned it at all. Maybe it was a good thing he hadn't told her he loved her. She obviously didn't feel more than friendship for him.

His shoulders slumped, and he dug his hands deep into his pockets. His eyes turned heavenward. "Lord, I could sure use a little help down here. I've lost my heart, but I don't think the one I lost it to wants to find it."

He kicked at a stone in his path. Why hadn't he simply kept his mouth shut?

CHAPTER 28

FTER A NIGHT of crying Faith awakened to a pillow still damp with tears. Although sun streamed through her window and promised a beautiful day, no sun lightened her heart. The dark shadows of last night remained to hover with clouds of doubt. Oh, how she had hoped Tom would declare his intentions for a closer relationship between them.

Friendship! Yes, they had a good one, and apparently that's all he wanted, and he didn't want to ruin it. But she could no more turn off her new feelings for Tom than she could turn off the light from the sun, moon, or stars.

She rubbed her lips with the back of her hand. Those kisses he'd given her had meant nothing to him. They were simply a thank-you for whatever she'd uncovered about Joe. Allowing God to be in control of her future with Tom sure didn't feel good right now, but she'd promised to do it, and she would keep silent until His answer came.

Ma called through the door, "Faith, it's time for you to get dressed and get over to Mrs. Weatherby's. Remember we have Clara's party tomorrow to bake for. I'm leaving now for Mrs. Whiteman's house."

Faith scrambled from the bed. "I'm coming, Ma." She'd clean forgotten about Clara's bridal party that the ladies at the church had planned. Best to get her mind off Tom and onto the things that needed to be done.

After finishing her ablutions in record time, Faith rushed downstairs to the kitchen. Aunt Ruby handed her a plate of eggs and bacon.

"There's a biscuit on the stove and coffee. Help yourself, but eat quickly. I have to get started on the cake for tomorrow. Mrs. Weatherby gave specific instructions for the colors and flavor ordered by the Ladies' Guild."

Faith carried her plate to the table and sat down. No coffee for her, but no time for tea either. Mrs. Weatherby would not be able to help much with the baking Faith had to do today. She was even more surprised when the reverend's wife offered her kitchen. Their son, David, had brought home his girl to meet his parents, so Mrs. Weatherby would be busy with entertaining her guest.

Most likely Tom and David would spend a lot of time together as well since the two had been best friends ever since they were little boys. Too bad Kenny Davis couldn't be here as well. Those three boys had been in more scrapes and given Faith and a few other girls more misery than any three boys she'd ever known.

Aunt Ruby assembled the ingredients on the counter for her cake baking. "Did you and Tom have fun at the tree lighting last evening? You were already home when we arrived."

The bit of eggs she'd just eaten became sawdust in her mouth. Faith took a swig of coffee to wash down the bite. "The tree was beautiful, and the children were adorable when they ran up to see Santa."

"Um, yes, they were, but what about you and Tom?"

Why did she have to be so curious this particular morning? "We had fun like we've had all the other times we've been. I love Mr. Swenson as Santa Claus. I don't know where he got the red velvet suit this year, but it sure looked better than last year."

Her appetite now gone, Faith picked up her plate, scraped the remainder of her breakfast into the scrap bucket, and then washed the plate. After drying it, she kissed her aunt on the cheek. "I'm off to do my baking."

Five minutes later she'd walked the distance to the reverend's home. When she reached the steps, Tom and David burst through the door laughing and poking each other.

Putting aside her jumble of feelings, Faith called out playfully, "I declare, you two haven't changed a bit since we were children." David had grown as tall as Tom, and his light brown hair still curled about his neck.

David's deep brown eyes sparked with amusement as he greeted her. "Oh now, Faith, is that any way to greet a longtime friend?"

"I suppose not. I'd hoped we'd see you and Miss Barstow last night, but there was too much of a crowd."

David pulled open the door. "Speaking of whom, you need to meet her." He disappeared inside, and Faith and Tom were left alone. Great. She wasn't sure she was ready to talk to him, friend or not.

Tom stood at the top step with his hands in his pockets. "I suppose you're here to use Mrs. Weatherby's kitchen again today." Why wasn't he looking at her? Had she grown two horns on her head since last night?

"I am, but why aren't you at the newspaper? Isn't there an edition coming out tomorrow?"

He nodded casually, still looking away from her. "Yes, there is, and I've already turned in my stories and am ready to spend the day with David. We're on our way to the livery to get David a horse to ride out to Uncle Micah's."

Before she had time to answer, David reappeared with a very pretty girl holding his hand.

"Faith, I'd like you to meet Katherine Barstow. She's a classmate of mine at the university."

Relieved at the distraction, Faith smiled as they descended the steps toward her. "I'm so glad to meet you. Mrs. Weatherby has talked about you all week. I hope you will enjoy Stoney Creek."

Katherine's smile revealed deep dimples in both cheeks, and her blue eyes sparkled. "I'm happy to meet you as well. David told me so much about you and Tom and your childhood while we traveled from my parents' home."

David nodded at both women. "As much as we hate to leave such lovely company, Tom and I are off to the livery. You two get acquainted, and maybe we can plan something for us all to do later this evening."

Tom smiled, but still his gaze did not quite connect with Faith's. What was wrong with him today? Before Faith could puzzle it out, the men were on their way, and Katherine was waving her up the steps and into the house, chatting all the way.

"David has been so eager to get on a horse and go out to the Gordon ranch. He says one of the first things he'll buy on graduation next spring is a horse. I understand Mr. Gordon and Mr. Elliot have some of the best horse stock in the state."

"Yes, they do, but let's not talk about horses. I'd love to hear more about you and David, that is, if you don't mind being in the kitchen. I have some pastries to make for Clara Whiteman's bridal party tomorrow." Much as she liked Katherine, Faith had work to do today. Maybe talking with her would help pass the time.

Still talking, Katherine led her to the kitchen. "Yes, Mrs. Weatherby told me all about it. It's wonderful how your church family takes care of everyone in the church. I never thought much about the responsibilities of a preacher's wife until I met David and learned he plans to be a preacher."

Faith unfolded the apron she'd been carrying and tied it around her waist. "Oh, are things that serious with you two?"

Katherine held out her left hand. "David spoke with my father before we came here. This is his grandmother's ring, and he gave it to me last night after the tree lighting." A blue sapphire sparkled on her finger.

A stab of envy hit Faith. "Oh, my, that's beautiful. You're so lucky. David is a wonderful man." How many more of their school friends would be married before Faith even had a chance? Without Tom in the picture, she sure didn't have many choices left. Clara and Katherine both had beautiful rings from their intended families. After last night, she'd never have any kind of ring from Tom.

"But what about you and Tom? David seems to think the two of you should be getting married as well."

Heat rushed up Faith's neck and filled her face. Her heart ached with the truth, but she couldn't gloss it over. "It seems that he cares more for another preacher's daughter, Angela Booker."

"Really? I certainly didn't get that impression from David."

Mrs. Weatherby strolled into the kitchen with a broad smile covering her face. "Good morning, Faith. I see you've meet Katherine, and I'm sure she's told you the wonderful news. We'll be having a wedding in our family next summer."

"We were just talking about Faith and Tom. She seems to think he's interested in a girl named Angela Booker."

Faith wanted to sink into the floor. Did her personal business have to be the talk of the entire town?

Mrs. Weatherby poured herself a cup of coffee and sat down at the table beside Katherine. "Angela is a very pretty girl, and her mother and I have become good friends, but I'm surprised Tom is interested in Angela. Her mother told me she plans to go away and be a missionary next year."

Angela a missionary? She'd hinted at it, but when had she decided? Tom's words from last night confused her even more. She pulled out the pottery mixing bowl and prepared her mind for the task ahead.

An awkward silence developed in the room. Mrs. Weatherby finally broke in. "Katherine, if we're going to do that shopping today and have lunch at the hotel, we need to get busy. Mr. Weatherby has a meeting with the town council today, and they always have lunch brought in by Carl from the diner. Can you be ready in fifteen minutes?"

"Yes, I'm sure I can." A chair pushed across the floor.

Katherine placed her hand on Faith's shoulder. "Maybe we can talk more when we're both not so busy."

Faith nodded and cracked an egg on the edge of the mixing bowl. "That would be nice."

The two women left, leaving Faith to her baking. A tear trickled down her cheek. Why did everyone else have to be so happy when her own life was crumbling around her? First the fire, then Tom declaring he wanted to be just friends.

For the first time in her life Faith dreaded the Christmas season ahead.

Tom rode beside David on their trek out to the Gordon ranch. "I'm happy to hear about you and Katherine. She is a very pretty young woman."

"She's just as sweet as she is pretty. I met her in a Bible class at school. I think I was smitten the moment I saw her. Took her a little longer to feel the same about me, but I'm glad she agreed. I think she'll be the perfect preacher's wife."

"I hope so. She'll have to untangle the messes you get into." Tom winked and laughed at the startled look in David's eyes.

"I do believe I've grown up some since those days, but maybe you haven't. If you had, you'd be walking Miss Delmont down the aisle by now."

Heat flooded Tom's face, and David laughed at him. "That's a nice combination there with your face and hair. Can't tell where one begins and the other ends."

The teasing banter took Tom back to those days when their biggest concern had been how to torment the girls at recess. At least he and David had been ready to graduate by the time Molly came along to teach, or there would have been no end to real punishment.

"Seriously, why aren't you and Faith either married or at least engaged?"

"I'm not really sure about the reason for that. Faith and I have been good friends for so long, and I'm afraid to spoil it by seeking a deeper relationship."

"Do you really believe that would spoil your friendship? That's hogwash, and you know it. I heard mention of an Angela Booker. Isn't she the new preacher's daughter? Is there something there you're not telling me about?"

"Yes, she's Reverend Booker's daughter, and no, there's nothing there to tell about." Although Angela was completely out of his plans for the future, others in town must think differently. Perhaps that's why Faith responded the way she had last night.

While he was lost in thought, David said something else.

"What was that you said?"

"I said if Faith is your best friend now, it could only get better with marriage. At least that's what my mother told me when I asked her about Katherine and our future. I believe her. Since we started to view our relationship in a more serious, lasting light, we've become even closer."

Molly had told him the same thing. "I have to confess, I did kiss her quickly one night just as I was leaving because I've really fallen in love with her. Last night when I started to try to explain my feelings, she went off on this thing about being good friends and we'd always be good friends and so on. I got the feeling she doesn't want any more than that. So, if I push too hard for a relationship, she might run away from me completely, and I couldn't bear not having her in my life."

David's eyebrows raised, and he pushed up the brim of his hat. "I think that's about the longest spiel I've ever heard from you, and you know what? It's a bunch of nothing. Katherine has told me more than a time or two that a kiss from me is a kiss no matter if it's on the forehead, cheek, or lips, and it's important to her."

And it had been important to Tom, but Faith didn't act like it had been to her. "How in the world do you know if it means anything to the girl?"

A smirk appeared on David's lips and he shook his head. "If you kiss her like you mean it, and she starts responding, it means something, and you'd better grab hold of that gal and never let her go."

David's words went straight to Tom's heart. If the opportunity ever rose again, he'd do just what David suggested. If Faith didn't respond, then he'd know for sure she didn't love him. He furrowed his brow and bit his lip.

David pulled up on his horse's reins. "What's the matter? I know that look, and something's gone sour."

"I don't know. What if Faith doesn't respond and gets upset because I've pushed her and she doesn't want it? What if I lose her as my friend?"

"Ah, but what if she does respond, and you find the love you want with her? You gotta take a chance, my friend. And I'd say she's worth every bit of the risk."

With that Tom had to agree. Now he had to get up the courage to take that risk.

⋙ CHAPTER 29 ⋘

CROWD GATHERED IN the street in front of the bakery. A huge, red bow decorated the door. Mr. and Mrs. Delmont and Faith stood on the boardwalk and conversed with Mayor Gladstone. Tom glanced at his pocket watch. Only five more minutes and the new bakery with its new stove would be open for business.

He had no opportunity to be alone with Faith the past week. With her time being spent at Mrs. Weatherby's house and his spent covering state and national news, their paths didn't have an opportunity to cross. He had missed stopping in at the bakery for a pastry every morning. With this reopening, maybe their routines would get back to normal.

A builder from Austin had been hired, and his crew had worked hard to repair and rebuild the bakery and tea room to be even better than it had been before. Tom caught sight of Gretchen and waved her over.

"You've had your hands full with all the social events and the real-life dramas playing out in our town. I'm really glad you're here to take care of all those."

"Yes, and it's been fun. The flood stories were the most interesting, and I loved the way the town pulled together to help the flood victims. My last story went in today for tomorrow's edition of the *Herald*. It's hard to believe all the homes have been cleaned up or repaired and all the families moved back in." She jotted a few notes on the pad she always carried with her.

"By the way, I heard from my father, and he may have a lead on the mysterious Joe Fitzgerald. Soon as he knows for sure, he'll send us the information."

Tom's spirits lifted and his pulse quickened. "I hope the lead goes somewhere. I can't wait to know exactly who Joe is and what he's doing in Stoney Creek."

"In the meantime we need to write about the people here who do good deeds all the time. Your mother and the Ladies' Guild are my next story."

Tom grinned. "That will make our family proud."

She tapped a finger to her lips. "Shh, I think they're ready to begin."

Mrs. Delmont stepped to one side with her husband's arm around her. Faith held a giant pair of cardboard scissors in her hand. She reached across and snipped at the ribbon, which fell to the ground. She grinned out toward the crowd. "Delmont Bakery and Tea Room is officially open once again. No tea room today, but the cases are filled with new pastries and cookies. Come and enjoy. Today there are free samples."

A roar filled the afternoon air as people cheered, clapped, and whistled even more than they had at the tree lighting last week.

Gretchen tapped his arm. "I'll catch you back at the office. I have a story to write."

Tom nodded but kept his gaze on Faith. She wore the same red cape she'd worn last week, but this time it was over a plaid skirt in red, green, black, and yellow. She looked so festive and pretty that he wanted to take her away for some time alone, but that was not to be.

A throng of patrons filled the bakery and the board-walk out front. He'd have to wait until later when business slowed down, if it ever did. Faith would be at his house with Clara tonight. She and her attendants were to have the final fittings of their dresses for the wedding. Maybe he could catch her before she left.

With over half a day before that would happen, he returned to newspaper office to work on his stories. Gretchen sat at her desk, her fingers flying over her type-writer keys. Tom sat at his desk and inserted a clean sheet of paper into his machine. May as well get started on his next story. He consulted the notes he'd gathered and began formulating his thoughts.

⇒⟫⟫⫯⟪⟪⇐

Joe turned away from the crowd still filling Main Street for the bakery reopening. His gut hurt, and his pills had nearly run out. The attacks of pain came closer together. He prayed as he walked down for another visit with Doc Whiteman. All he wanted from the Lord was one more week in Stoney Creek so he could see Clara married. After that he'd make plans to return home.

Hannah Gordon welcomed him at the infirmary. She nodded toward the doctor's office. "He's in there going over some patient records. He'll be happy to see you."

"Thank you, Hannah." Joe knocked on the slightly ajar door. When the doctor bade him come in, Joe pushed the door and entered the office.

Doc Whiteman stood and reached out for Joe's hand. "Hello, Joe. I was expecting to see you. Your pills about to run out?"

Joe nodded and shook the doctor's hand. "The pains are more frequent, and they're a little worse each few days."

"I see. That means you'll be leaving us soon."

"Yes, it does. I still have a few things I want to do before leaving, like Clara's wedding, but I do need more medicine." He eased down into the chair across the desk from Doc Whiteman.

The doctor pulled a pad toward him. "I'll write this one for a little stronger dosage this time. Normally I would never suggest anyone using this much, but since your disease is in its final stages, I don't believe there is a problem of becoming dependent on the drug. Shall I turn it in and pick it up for you same as last time?"

"Please, if you don't mind. I know the pharmacist won't say anything about the prescription in my name, but I'd rather not have people see me visiting the apothecary." Only Mrs. Hutchins had noticed his bouts of pain, and astute as she was, she did not press him for details or fuss over him, as if sensing that he wanted to be left to handle it in his own way.

Joe gazed about the doctor's office. What could he possibly do to make things easier for the doctor? "Doc, you look like you're pretty well equipped here. Is there anything you don't have?"

Doc Whiteman leaned back in his chair. "We do have a fairly up-to-date infirmary here, but new tools are being developed all the time. Ever since my time in the Confederate Army, I've been impressed with the absolute need for sterility in things like surgery or treating open wounds. We wash our hands frequently around here."

"I noticed that. I suppose that does keep germs from spreading."

"Yes, and because of the need for sterility I'd like to have one of those new autoclaves that hold surgical equipment and sterilize them after surgeries. The one we have is small, and only the smallest of our scalpels and retractors fit into it."

Joe made a mental note to give that information to Mr. Swenson. He pulled a bill from his pocket and laid it on the doctor's desk. "This is for taking care of me. I haven't had any expenses, so I've been able to save what I've made with my carpentry."

Doc Whiteman opened his mouth as though to protest but shut it and leaned back. "That's more than enough to cover your medicine and your visits with me. However, I know this is your way of saying thank you, so I accept your generosity."

At last he'd met a man who understood how to accept a gift without refusing it first and getting into a discussion about it. He'd make sure now that Mr. Swenson added something extra to the Whiteman account.

"Thank you for your time and the medicine. I'll check in with you tomorrow to pick it up." Once again he shook hands with the doctor.

As he left the building, his heart filled yet again with the love he'd developed for this town nestled in the hill country of Texas. What little he could do for them paled in comparison to the blessing the good Lord had given in bringing these people into Joe's life.

>>>><<<<

Faith perched on Clara's bed with Juliet and Alice on the floor. Mrs. Bennett smoothed the skirt of the ivory satin dress and straightened the train.

"Oh, Clara, it's absolutely beautiful." Faith clasped her hands to her chest. "Those sleeves are perfect." They were an exaggerated form of the popular balloon top with the sleeve fitting tight from just above the elbow to the wrist. Lace appliqués adorned the back of the skirt and train with the same lace in smaller detail trimming the bodice and lower sleeves.

Mrs. Bennett handed a deep gold mound of lace and silk to Faith. "I hope you like yours as well."

"Mine? But we didn't order one for me. I thought I was to wear my green one." She hugged the new dress, her gaze darting between Mrs. Bennett and Mrs. Whiteman.

"This is our gift to you, dear Faith. Your mother was worried that none of your good dresses could be cleaned of the smoke from the fire in time for the wedding. You and Clara are the same size, so I asked Mrs. Bennett to make this one for you."

Tears filled Faith's eyes and spilled down her cheeks. When she had last inspected her green dress, the smell of soot and ashes still lingered. "Oh, Mrs. Whiteman, this is beautiful." She hopped down from the bed, and with Mrs. Bennett and Mrs. Whiteman's help she removed her yellow-sprigged calico to replace it with the gold creation. Mrs. Bennett fastened the buttons down the back.

It fit her perfectly. Faith ran her hands down the smooth front and turned so she could see the skirt pulled up in a very modified bustle effect with a fabric rose at the back waist. Her sleeves were a smaller version of Clara's.

Mrs. Whiteman adjusted the lace at the neck. "I knew this color would be perfect with your dark hair and eyes. You look stunning."

Faith blinked back tears. "How can I ever thank you for such an elegant gift! Does my mother know?"

"Yes, we asked her permission first, and she was reluctant but then agreed. You're like a part of our family, and we wanted to surprise you."

"Well, you did that, all right." If only she were truly a part of the family, she'd be the happiest young woman in the world.

She spent another half hour with Clara and Mrs. Bennett before the seamstress declared she had all she needed and would have the dresses back to them next week. After she redressed, Faith gathered up her belongings to go back home. Home. How nice it would be to sleep in her own bed tonight. As much as she loved Aunt Ruby's house, it wasn't home.

When she and Clara descended the stairs to the foyer, Tom greeted them at the bottom.

"I'm here to take you home. We don't want you walking in the dark alone."

Papa had planned to come pick her up, but this was so much better. "Thank you, I'd like that very much."

He escorted her out to the street where his father's buggy sat hitched and ready to go. "Pa was happy to loan out his buggy this evening." He helped her up onto the seat then went around and climbed aboard. "I even have an extra quilt in case you get cold. Supposed to be another good frost tonight."

A quilt wouldn't be necessary. Just being this close to Tom provided all the warmth she needed. Forget being good friends. She wanted that and so much more.

The horse took off in a lazy trot, clip-clopping along the bricked street leading to the bakery. Tom pulled on the reins to keep the black horse to a slower pace, which suited Faith fine. The longer the ride home, the longer she'd be next to Tom. The moon on the verge of being completely full offered a silvery night light in a cloudless sky that sparkled with a million gems.

"I'm glad you're back in your home. They did a good job of getting it rebuilt before the holidays."

"I'm glad too. The carpenters worked a few extra hours to get us back in by this weekend. Aunt Ruby's house is plenty big enough for all of us, but being back in our own place is so much better." Why were they talking about her aunt and the bakery? Words she'd like to say lodged in her throat and wouldn't budge.

Tom cleared his throat. "Um...I've been meaning to talk to you about what I said after the Christmas tree lighting."

Faith's nerves cringed, and a vise gripped her heart. Suddenly the words poured out of her in a rush. "I understand what you were trying to say. You want us to remain good friends even though you want to be with someone else."

He jerked the reins and halted the buggy. "What? Want someone else? That's not what I meant at all."

Hope fluttered in her chest. "Well, what did you mean?"

"Will you listen and let me finish and not interrupt?" He gripped the reins in one hand and faced her with his other hand on the back of the seat.

"Yes, I will." No matter what he had to say, she'd be polite to the end. After that she couldn't promise anything.

He dropped the reins and took both her hands in his. "You've been one of the best friends a person could ever want in a lifetime, but..." He breathed in deeply.

She closed her eyes, waiting for the "but."

His breath expelled in a swoosh. "I want more than friendship with you. I want to court you properly and call on you at your home."

Faith's eyes flew open, and her head jerked back. "What did you say?"

His hands squeezed hers. "I...I love you, Faith Elaine Delmont."

Love for Tom filled her heart to the point of bursting. "I thought I'd never hear you say that. I love you too, Thomas Dyer Whiteman."

With the moonlight glowing on his face, Tom reached up to cup her cheeks between his hands. He leaned forward, and she did the same to meet him halfway. His lips touched hers, lightly at first, and then his hands moved and his arms went around her in an embrace she'd remember the rest of her life.

As the kiss deepened with great promise, every year of waiting had been worth every moment to bring them to this point.

Tom pulled away. "I have to get you home now, or I can't be responsible for whatever happens." He grabbed up the reins and flipped them to get the buggy moving again.

Faith slipped her arm under his and snuggled against his shoulder. A smile tickled her lips. As much as she enjoyed his kisses, he did need to get her home before her heart simply burst with joy. Aunt Ruby, Mama, and Katherine had all been right. Now this Christmas would be her happiest ever.

᚛᚛᚛᚛᚛

At the top of the stairs leading to the Delmont home, Tom kissed Faith one more time before she closed the door behind her. Tom wanted to shout, run, laugh, and kick up his heels. He loped down the stairs and back to the buggy.

David had been right. Her response had been more than he ever dreamed. The moon couldn't shine any brighter than his future did. Maybe it had taken longer to get up the nerve to express his feelings, but the result exceeded anything he could ever have imagined or dreamed.

⋙ CHAPTER 30 ⋘

AITH SIPPED PUNCH and gazed about the room. This had been the most beautiful wedding she'd ever attended. Ma and Aunt Ruby had outdone themselves. The cake and other delectable sweets filled the table and beckoned people to come and enjoy. Because she was a part of Clara's wedding party, Faith had been given the night free of any duties at the reception.

The ballroom at the hotel glowed from the gaslight chandeliers. Greenery and candles decorated tables set around for guests to enjoy the refreshments. A string quartet provided music for both listening and dancing. As far as Faith could tell, over half of Stoney Creek attended the wedding of the doctor's daughter and the mayor's son.

The ceremony had been so romantic. Theodore and Clara exchanged their vows in the glow of candles with the light of love shining bright in their faces.

A hand tapped her shoulder. "Your eyes have stars in them, my friend."

Clara's words sent heat rising up Faith's neck to her cheeks. "Only because your wedding was the prettiest I've seen. You look even more beautiful in your dress today."

Clara leaned close. "And maybe you will wear it someday in the near future."

Faith's eyes opened wide, and her mouth fell open. Clara giggled. "I've seen the looks between you and my brother. You're as much in love as Teddy and I are. A wedding isn't too far off in the future for you."

Warmth wrapped around her heart and filled it with love for Tom. He had declared his love, but no proposal had come with it. "He hasn't even asked me to marry him."

"Oh, but he will; you wait and see." She grinned and grabbed Faith's hand. "Now, come on and let's find those men of ours."

Faith set her punch cup on the tray for used ones and allowed Clara to pull her across the room where Tom and Theodore conversed with Reverend Weatherby. A smile lit up Tom's face when she reached his side, and Theodore pulled Clara closer to him.

Reverend Weatherby chuckled. "Looks like you young men have much better company now, so I think I'll find Mrs. Weatherby and enjoy some of that cake."

Theodore kissed Clara's forehead. He winked at Tom and said, "Hope you don't mind if I steal my bride away for this dance."

The nearness of Tom after all that had happened last weekend turned her insides upside down. This was the first time they'd had a chance to be alone together this week. Once again Tom had been out of town covering state news and had only arrived back in town yesterday. She would have joined him at the ranch with his family last night if she hadn't stayed in town to help Ma and Aunt Ruby with the last-minute preparations for today.

"I missed you last night." Tom's breath stirred the curls above her ears.

"I missed you as well." She leaned closer to him.

He wrapped his arm around her waist and took her hand in his free one. "Shall we join Theodore and Clara?"

Before she could answer, he'd swung her onto the dance floor.

The heat of his hand at her waist sent tremors of delight up and down her spine and into her heart. Her grandest dreams had begun to unfold in even more wonderful ways than her dreams ever portrayed. They had danced at many a town social, but this time his love for her spread through her with a rhythm that didn't come from the music.

The quartet ended the set, and couples moved off the floor. Faith couldn't be sure if the heat surrounding her came from the nearness of Tom or the liveliness of the dance. Whichever it was, she needed a cool breath of air.

As if reading her mind, Tom led her to the lobby of the hotel and the sofa there. "It's cooler out here, don't you think?"

"Yes, it is." How she wished for the fan that lay with her other belongings back in the ballroom.

Tom held her hands in his. "I've missed you this week, not just last night. It's been the longest week of my life."

"I know. If we hadn't been so busy at the bakery, I'd have died from loneliness. How did the trip go?"

"Fine. The government has shut down now for the holidays, but they had a few bills to get passed before the recess. What about your week?"

"It was so much better with that new stove. Ma and Aunt Ruby outdid themselves with the baking, and the tearoom stayed so busy I hardly had time to sit down." Why were they talking about the bakery and the government?

Tom must have thought the same for he leaned close. "If this were not such a public place, I'd kiss you right here and now."

"And I'd let you." She lifted her chin, but someone called their names.

"Here you are. I've been looking for you two." Gretchen hurried toward them waving a piece of paper in her hand.

She stopped to catch her breath and handed the paper to Tom. "This came in the mail today from my father. It's from a friend of his in Chicago."

Faith leaned over to see the picture Tom now held. An elderly man with a beard stared at them from a news photo. The caption said that Joseph Mayfield, a prominent businessman from northern Illinois, had been missing for several months.

Tom turned the picture over. "This is dated from last summer. Could this possibly have any connection to our Joe?"

Gretchen sat down in the chair next to them. "It doesn't really look like him, but it's the closest thing we've had to a lead."

Faith tried to imagine the man in the picture without the beard. Something was familiar. The eyes. That was it. "Look closely at this man. Those are Joe's eyes."

Tom peered at the photo then handed it to Gretchen. "I think she may be right."

Gretchen stared a moment before nodding. "I agree, but how can we get him to admit it? We can't just go up to him and say we know who he is. What I want to know is why he's keeping his identity a secret."

"I do too, but let's go slowly with this. I've got an idea." He leaned forward. "But we need to keep this among ourselves. Don't show anyone else that picture. Not even Mr. Blake."

※»—««

Joe slumped against the wall next to the doorway to the lobby. They'd found him. He had to leave before they started nosing around too much. Tom had lowered his voice, but Joe had heard enough to know they'd learn his secret if he stayed in town. Tom and Gretchen were both too good at their professions to leave this alone.

He made a mental checklist. The sets for the Christmas play were built and ready for painting. The letters for Tom and the town were safe in the hands of Mr. Swenson. The sterilizer for Doc Whiteman had been ordered. He'd picked up his last prescription from the doctor. All the funds he'd requested had been transferred to the Stoney Creek Bank. Mr. Hightower had drawn up the legal documents, and Joe had signed them.

Joe straightened his shoulders and stood tall. His work was done. He could leave with assurance that Stoney Creek would be in good hands. He made his way to the kitchen, hoping to slip out unnoticed from the back door.

Mayor Gladstone caught Joe's arm at the kitchen entrance. "I've been looking for you. Mrs. Gladstone wants to add some cabinets in our kitchen. You did such fine work for Mrs. Hutchins that we thought maybe you'd do the same for us."

"I'm not sure, Mayor. I haven't felt well these past few weeks, so I can't make any promises. I will think on it and let you know."

"Oh, I'm sorry you've been ill. No one has said anything." He patted Joe's shoulder. "I sure hope you feel better soon, and I'll be waiting to hear from you about those cabinets."

After the mayor walked away, Joe glanced around to make sure no one else noticed him before he slipped through the deserted kitchen for the back door.

Once outside he headed for the depot to check the train schedule. A lone gas lamp illuminated the chart hanging by the ticket window. Just as he'd thought. No trains on Sunday. The first one headed north wouldn't be through here until late Monday morning. Where would he stay, and what would he do until he could slip out, get his ticket, and be on his way home?

He trudged back to the boardinghouse with these questions crowding his mind. Slowly a plan formulated.

Light shone from the windows of the boardinghouse. Mrs. Hutchins must be back from the wedding party already. When he stepped into the entryway, she greeted him.

"I see you're home from the party early too."

"Yes, I'm not feeling well at all. I'm going up to my room. If I'm not down for breakfast, don't worry about me. I most likely won't make it to church either."

She laid down her sewing and looked up. "I'm sorry to hear that. What is it? Your stomach? Your throat?"

"It's nothing, Mrs. Hutchins. I got chilled yesterday, so I may be coming down with a cold. Nothing for you to fret about."

"If you say so, but you let me know if you need anything. I can call Doc Whiteman for you, and he'll come check on you."

"No need for that. I'll be fine. Think I need some rest, that's all."

"Well, you have been working mighty hard on those sets for the Christmas program. I say it's time for you to quit working so much and get your rest."

"Thank you. Now if you'll excuse me, I'm going upstairs."

Once in the privacy of his room Joe found his old knap-sack and set it out to fill in the morning while everyone was at church. He sat on the edge of the bed and slipped off his shoes. The pillow behind him looked very inviting. After pulling back the quilt, he slipped between the covers, fully clothed. Remembering he had on the suit Zachariah had made, Joe rose from the bed and undressed. This was the suit he planned to be buried in, and from the way the past two days had been, that day would come sooner rather than later.

After taking Faith home and sharing a good-night kiss, Tom drove the buggy past the boardinghouse on his way home.

He pulled up on the reins and stopped in front of the house. He stared up at the window in Joe's room. "Who are you really, Joe Fitzgerald? Are you behind all the good things that have happened in Stoney Creek? I think you are, but how can I prove it?"

Tom sat in the quiet of the night and contemplated the old man who had become a good friend to the town. All the contradictions he, Faith, and Gretchen had noticed now made sense. Joseph Mayfield was a wealthy man and, according to the news article, very active in many chari-table activities. He'd been married but lost his wife and only daughter. Everything said about Mayfield matched what they had seen in Joe except the money. If either Gretchen or Tom approached Joe and began asking too many questions, they'd most likely cause him to leave town. The plan he'd devised tonight with Gretchen and Faith wasn't the best, but it was all they had for now.

His plan called for them to treat Joe the same as always, but whenever any of them were with him or talked to him, the conversations would include comments about things that had been done for the town like the stove for the bakery, the town emergency fund, and the extra money in the Kirk family's bank account. Then they would watch for Joe's reaction to the comments.

Gretchen had a great sense of people's ideas and feelings from observing them in various situations, and Tom's friendship with Joe would help as well. Faith didn't have the expertise, but she did have an uncanny ability to get people to open up to her. He counted on that for her time with Joe.

His mind drifted away from Joe and onto Faith. Contentment and happiness flowed together to fill his heart with love as he snapped the reins and headed home. Why had he waited so long to tell her he loved her? Thinking it would spoil their friendship had been as dumb as David Weatherby had made it sound. That didn't matter now. He'd told her, and she loved him back. He hadn't asked her to marry him yet, but he wanted the perfect moment, and that would be Christmas Eve, the most magical night of the year.

⋙ CHAPTER 31 ⋘

OE'S PLAN HAD worked perfectly. He'd left the house early on Monday before breakfast and hastened to the depot, where he'd purchased a ticket to Dallas, planning to stop there and buy another ticket to Chicago. He'd then returned to the boardinghouse in time for breakfast. No one had seen him leave and return, so no one questioned him.

While others spoke of their plans for the day, Joe had sat quietly eating his breakfast. Mrs. Hutchins had inquired about his health, and Herb Spooner had inquired as to Joe's plans for the day. He'd been evasive but had given the impression he'd be about town like he had been most days.

He'd paid one last visit to Mr. Swenson at the bank to make sure everything was in place to carry out the plans they'd made together. Once assured that all was in order, Joe had gone to the depot, where he stashed his knapsack and hid out until the train arrived.

Now he stared out the window at the countryside as the train pushed on. He wouldn't need the ragged clothes he'd worn into town, so those had been left behind for Mrs. Hutchins to dispose of later. Now he was clean-shaven and wearing a pair of trousers, shirt, and jacket Doctor and Mrs. Whiteman had provided for him.

On this return trip people no longer avoided him. What a difference a comb, razor, and clean clothes could make in a person's attitude toward another. No matter what happened back in Stoney Creek today after they discovered his absence, he believed he'd left everything in good hands, and all of his hopes for the town would come to fruition.

Joe sighed and leaned back against the seat. Just a few more days and he'd be home, and then not long after that he'd be home with his Lord and Savior, safe and secure for all of eternity.

⋙⋘

"What? He can't be gone! He was at the wedding on Saturday night." Tom's stomach plunged to his toes. Joe had to still be here.

Mrs. Hutchins shook her head. "I tell you, Tom, he's gone. He left after breakfast saying he'd be in town for a while. I went up to this room to change the linens on the bed and all his things are gone. He left his grungy old clothes in a pile on the floor, but everything else is gone."

Tom had planned to have lunch with Joe, but now that appeared unlikely. Mrs. Hutchins nudged him out of the way to place a large soup tureen on the table. He'd best get out of her way or he'd have hungry boarders out for his head.

Coming into the room, Herb Spooner overheard their conversation. "Hi, Tom. Looking for Joe? I believe he left town this morning. He came into the bank and talked with Mr. Swenson awhile. I spotted him heading over to the depot after he left the bank."

"Thanks, Herb. I'll check with the ticket counter at the depot. Sure is strange his leaving like that."

The bank teller swayed back and forth on the balls of his feet. "Yes, I had really come to like him. He made frequent trips to see Mr. Swenson a number of times in the past few weeks. I think it's strange too that he'd leave town without telling anyone."

"I think I'll mosey on down to the depot now. Maybe I can find out the direction he was heading." He left Herb Spooner in the room scratching his head.

At the depot he questioned the ticket man. "Yeah, he came in early this morning and bought a ticket to Dallas. Didn't say why or nothing, just that it was time for him to leave. Sure do wish he'd stayed around awhile longer."

Tom thanked him and headed back to the newspaper office. He wished Joe had stayed around too. He had a lot of unanswered questions left dangling like the worm on the end of a fishing pole. Now he'd never pull in a catch.

He passed by the bakery and yearned to stop in to see Faith. Much as he'd like to do just that and spend a little time with her, he had work to do. The article he'd written after his last trip was ready for Mr. Blake's approval. He wanted to go over it one more time. Maybe he should write an article about the mysterious stranger and his sudden disappearance.

Gretchen was typing away when he entered the office. He hung up his coat and hooked his hat over it. As he passed her on the way to his desk, Gretchen whirled around in her chair. "Is it true Joe's gone?"

"Yes. I checked at the depot, and he left on the train to Dallas this morning. I suppose he's on his way back home. I sure would have liked to talk with him some more. He wasn't at church yesterday, but Mrs. Hutchins said he wasn't feeling well. I'm thinking that was a ruse to keep from seeing me."

Gretchen crossed her arms. "I suppose we shouldn't be surprised. He did say he'd have to leave before long."

"Yes, but I expected he'd at least wait until after the Christmas Eve program. After all, he did do most of the sets for the play." Tom rubbed his hands together and sat down at his desk. This was one mystery he couldn't let go. They had to find out who Joe was and why he had left without telling anyone.

His mind remained as blank as the sheet of paper in his typing machine. "Gretchen, where's that picture and story your father sent you?"

"Right here." She reached into her desk drawer and pulled out the news article. "I read the story again, and some things fit, but others don't." She handed the piece to Tom.

"Would you wire your father and ask him to contact Joe's hometown paper and then to let us know when Joe has returned?"

"I'll send the wire. Anything else I should say?"

"I can't think of anything, but if you do, go ahead and add it. I'm going to the boardinghouse and talk with Mrs. Hutchins. I'm also going to stop at the bakery and talk with Faith."

Gretchen left, and Mr. Blake strolled to Tom's desk. "I overheard what you were saying about Joe. Anything you need me to do? This has become a very interesting story."

Tom thought a moment then snapped his fingers. "How about interviewing some of the people in town for whom he made and repaired stuff. Find out what they might know about him. You never know what little fact he might have let slip out while working on a project."

Mr. Blake grabbed up his hat and coat. "That's a good idea. I'm as anxious as you two are to find out who our Joe really is."

When Tom arrived at the boardinghouse, Mrs. Hutchins invited him to sit and have sugar cookies and tea. Once she served him, she sat down across from him and tilted her head.

"And to what do I owe the pleasure of this return visit? Might it have anything to do with our Joe Fitzgerald?"

Tom picked up a cookie. "Yes, ma'am, it does. What can you tell me about him?"

Mrs. Hutchins shook her head and laughed. "That's a good question. I don't know any more about him than what he's told everyone else in town who asked. He never shared about himself, but he was always asking about others."

"What do you mean by that?" He bit into the cookie and savored it as it all but melted on his tongue.

"I mean he asked about the library and how our town got the books for it. He asked about different families and what kind of things would make Stoney Creek a better place to live."

The library received a new shipment of books, and several families had sure been helped from out of nowhere. The puzzle pieces were there; Tom just had to put them together for the complete picture.

Mrs. Hutchins leaned toward Tom. "I know reporters want news and ask a lot of questions, but this is one time you might want to leave things be."

"What's that supposed to mean?"

"If Joe wanted us to know more about him, he would have told us. It's none of our business about his background. Sheriff Bolton already assured me Joe wasn't a wanted man or a criminal."

Tom opened his mouth to comment, but she held her hand palm forward toward him. "Just wait; I always check out my boarders with the sheriff, and that's not being nosy. I'm being cautious. Anyway, I don't think you should be in such a big hurry to find out who he was. He's gone, so it can't make any difference. I say write a story about a man we all liked, how much he will be missed, and what he did for folks with his carpentry."

What she said had merit, but Tom's curiosity wouldn't let the truth be covered up and tucked away. "Thank you, Mrs. Hutchins. I'll think about your advice, but if we find out anything worth knowing, we have to report on it."

"I understand, son, but a man's privacy is very important, and if he didn't want us to know more about him, then we should not pursue it."

Her words gave Tom a lot to think about. He strolled down toward the bakery. Maybe Faith had some ideas or thoughts about Joe. Anticipation at seeing Faith put spring into his step, and he all but sprinted to the bakery.

⋙⋘

Faith placed the lid back on the cake server and at the ring of the bell over the door glanced up. Her heart skipped a beat then sped up its pace as Tom approached her. A smile tickled her lips. "Good morning."

"Good morning, yourself. Are you busy? Can we talk a minute?"

She nodded as her gaze landed on his lips. Those kisses had been better than she had ever dreamed, and one would be nice about now. Faith shook herself and raised her eyes to his. "Yes, we have a lull. We can sit over there."

Tom followed her to the corner where she had pointed, and they sat down across from each other.

"Look, you know Joe's gone. He left on the train this morning."

"Yes, almost everyone who's come in has had something to say about him. They all seemed to really like him after they got to know him. I'm sad to see him go too. There was something special about him that I can't quite describe. He listened to what I had to say and had wise words to give me." She turned her gaze out the window to the streets half expecting to see Joe meandering his way to the bakery.

"Gretchen is following up on the news article her dad sent. If Joe's return is reported in his local paper, we can pretty well conclude that Joe Fitzgerald and Joseph Mayfield are one and the same person."

"So what if he is? Maybe he simply wanted to take a vacation without being recognized or hounded for interviews." Knowing Tom like she did, he was not going to simply drop his investigation because Joe was gone.

"I don't know, but my journalistic instincts tell me different. What about all those mysterious things happening in town, especially after the flood and your fire?"

Faith bit her lip. "Those were mysterious, but what if Joe did do those things? What can you do about it now? He's gone, so you can't find out why or even if he really was behind it all."

Whether their benefactor had been Joe or some other unknown person didn't really matter. Stoney Creek had been blessed, and as far as she was concerned, God had made provision where the need was greatest.

"Tom, I think you need to leave this one alone." She reached across for his hands. "We don't have a right to pry into a man's private life, no matter how curious we are. We do know that his wife and daughter are both dead and he's alone, so maybe the trip was his way of handling grief."

"Mrs. Hutchins said essentially the same thing. Maybe there's wisdom in that. I'll think about it. If it's better not to write the story after I get a few more facts, then I will leave it alone."

If they weren't in a public place, she'd kiss him right now. Her heart swelled with love and pride. "That's why I love you, Tom Whiteman. You will always do what is best for a person or in a situation. Whatever we find out about him, we'll keep it to ourselves. Right?"

"Right, but if Mr. Blake senses we're holding back on a story, he'll be angry and might print it anyway."

"I don't think so. Mr. Blake is a good newsman, but he has a heart too. He'll do the right thing as well."

"Since we don't know for sure where Joe's going, all we can do is speculate." He pushed back his chair and stood. "I have to get back to the office for now, but I'll be by later this evening."

At the door he brushed his lips across her cheek in a quick kiss before bounding down the steps to the street. Faith leaned against a post and followed his figure until he disappeared into the newspaper office. She loved that man with all her heart and soul, and if there was one person to find out the truth, it would be Tom. She could only pray he'd keep his word and not write a story exposing the truth about Joe.

Even though she believed God had sent Joe, she didn't want to advertise his good deeds. What Joe had done in private, God would honor in heaven because that's the way God worked.

⫸ CHAPTER 32 ⫷

OM SAT AT his desk in his room and stared at the notes in front of him. These scribbled words had the makings of a great story, especially at Christmas time. It had been hard to put the notes aside, but after Mrs. Hutchins and Faith had voiced the same concerns, he'd prayed and God had given him the same answer.

Gretchen had been reluctant to kill the story as well, but she understood that they should honor Joe's privacy. And after she and Tom talked with Mr. Blake, even he agreed with them.

A knock on the door was followed by his father's voice. "Son, may I come in?"

"Sure, Pa. Come on." Tom straightened the papers in his hand and stacked them on the corner of his desk.

"I have something I want to tell you about Joe." His father sat in a chair next to the desk.

"It's okay, Pa. We're not going to run the story about him."

"I know, and I admire you for that, but this is something Joe said I could tell you on Christmas Eve."

"All right, I'm listening."

"For one thing Joe came to me not long after he arrived to get a prescription filled. You see, Joe was dying of cancer. It was eating away at his insides, and there wasn't much we could do except help ease the pain. He wasn't sure how much longer he had to live, but he wanted to go home where he could die with friends from his church and be buried next to his wife and daughter."

Tom blinked back tears. Joe hadn't been in Stoney Creek very long, but it was long enough for Tom to respect and admire him. "I'm so sorry to hear that. I cared a lot about that old man."

"I know you did, or you wouldn't have brought him to us. He's a fine Christian who is ready to meet the good Lord. Not sure why he wanted me to wait until today to tell you, but you know I couldn't have told you at all without his permission."

His father's integrity both as a man and doctor were two of the traits Tom most admired. "Of course, and I'm glad you told me now. I'm sad to know he's dying but happy to know he didn't just up and leave us because he didn't want to stay any longer."

Faith would be devastated by this news. She had come to like Joe more than anyone else he knew in town except maybe for Mrs. Hutchins, whose tears as she asked Tom not to pry into Joe's history said it all.

"We'll be leaving soon for the service. The buggy will be hitched and ready for you to go pick up Faith. Again, thank you for not prying into Joe's background. He wanted it this way." He gripped Tom's shoulder. "I'm proud of you."

After he left, Tom stored the papers in his desk drawer and prepared for his evening with Faith. Clara and Tom had returned from their wedding trip, and Clara would be singing at tonight's service as would Angela, with Aunt Hannah at the piano.

Forty-five minutes later he and Faith arrived at the church. At almost eleven at night, the sky was cloudy but clear enough in spots for the half-moon to light the deep blue background. The air held the chill of frost, but as Faith snuggled next to him, it was perfect for Christmas Eve.

Tom decided to wait until after the services to tell Faith about Joe. That was the time he'd also chosen to ask her to be his wife. He could think of no better Christmas gift than for her to say yes. The thought brought a smile to his face as he helped her down from the buggy.

As they headed toward the church, Mr. Swenson hailed Tom, waving what appeared to be letters. "May I have minute of your time, Tom? I have two letters here from Joe. One he wants you to read to the people at church at the end of the service. The second letter is addressed to you and Faith for you to read together after the services."

Tom frowned and took the envelopes. Would they hold the answers he had sought? "Thank you, Mr. Swenson. Does Reverend Weatherby know I'm to read this at the end?"

"Yes, and you'll read it before the final prayer. Now I must get inside to sit with my daughter and Alex."

Tom slipped the letters into the inside pocket of his coat. He grasped Faith's arm. "Well, maybe these will give us the answers we want." He led her inside and down to the Whiteman family pew. They each picked up a candle at the entrance.

Candles glowed all around the church and at the end of each pew. The light gave a beautiful aura to the holly and ivy and cedar adorning the railings and windows. A manger scene held center focus on the stage area.

His aunt Hannah played the carols they all loved, and the congregation sang out with joy in their voices. When Clara's clear soprano voice filled the church with "Oh,

Holy Night," Tom's heart swelled with pride for his sister. He clutched Faith's hand and squeezed it. She squeezed back and smiled up at him. His heart might burst with love for the girl beside him.

After the play presented by the children, Tom held her hand all through the Christmas message as Reverend Weatherby challenged them to begin the year 1893 with the Lord as their shepherd and Savior.

At the end, before the final carol and prayer, Reverend Weatherby beckoned to Tom. "Tom Whiteman has a letter to read from Joe Fitzgerald. He may have been with us only a short time, but he touched many lives, and we were all sad to see him go." He pointed to Tom. "The podium is yours."

Tom slid the letter from the envelope. He hadn't read it and prayed his voice would hold out until he read it through. He cleared his throat and began.

> *Dear people of Stoney Creek,*
>
> *As Tom reads this letter to you, I am back at home in Rockford, Illinois. I'm sorry I had to leave without saying good-bye to all of you because you made the last few months of this old man's life the best he's had in a long while. You took me in despite the way I looked and smelled that first day. You allowed me to come into your lives and become a part of your community. You gave me odd jobs to do and gifts I never expected. I left, not because I didn't care about you, but because I wanted to go home and be with my church family there.*
>
> *You see, I'm dying, and I wanted to be in my hometown where I could be buried next to my wife and our daughter. I don't know how many days or*

weeks I may have left, but from the bottom of my heart I say thank you. May God bless your town and all its people.

Yours truly,
Joe

Tom blinked his eyes and glanced up to see handkerchiefs and fingers swiping at tearstained cheeks across the congregation. He made his way back to his seat as Reverend Weatherby lit the first candle in the congregation. Aunt Hannah's fingers played across the keyboard, and the strains of "Silent Night" filled the air. One candle after another was lit, and they filled the room with the light of love and hope.

⇶⇷

Faith held Tom's arm and choked back tears as the final words of the song hung over them. She'd never forget this night and the letter from a man who still remained a mystery. Now they'd never know who he really was and why he had come to Stoney Creek to begin with.

After everyone extinguished their candles, voices hummed and buzzed about Joe and his illness. Tom and his father tried to answer their questions, but they had no new information to give.

Angela made her way to Tom and Faith. "I've been looking for the two of you." She hugged Faith and whispered in her ear. "I see the love Tom has for you in his eyes. You two were made for each other." Then she stepped back. "I have something to tell you both."

Angela's statement about Tom wiped away the last strands of guilt still in the deep recesses of Faith's heart.

The sparkle in her friend's eyes spoke of something good for her as well.

"I spoke with my parents last evening, and I'm going away to attend seminary and become a missionary. I'm hoping to be able to go to China where Miss Lottie Moon is serving and help her."

Faith gasped and reached for Angela to wrap her in a hug. "Oh, Angela, you'll be a wonderful missionary."

"Yes, you will. With your love of people, you'll win over the hearts of those in China or wherever you happen to go." Tom grabbed Angela's hand and shook it.

Angela wiped a tear from her eye. "I'm so happy to finally have made the decision, and I know you'll both be praying for me. Thank you so much for your support." With that she spun around and hurried away.

Faith shook her head and grabbed Tom's arm. "That wasn't a complete surprise, but it did come sooner than I expected."

"Yes, and she will be great servant for the Lord." He placed his hand over hers. "Come, it's time to go."

Outside, the sky had completely clouded over and the air was even colder than before. He lifted her up to the buggy seat. "This night isn't over yet. I have another letter Joe addressed to us. I think I want to read it here at the church, but we'll wait until everyone has left."

After lighting the lanterns on either side of the buggy, he climbed up beside her. The last of the worshippers piled into their various vehicles and made their way home. The bells on both churches rang out to announce Christmas morning had arrived.

Tom grinned and opened the second envelope. "This is perfect. I think Joe would be pleased." He smoothed out the page and began to read.

> *Dear Tom and Faith,*
>
> *If you're reading this, then it's either late Christmas Eve or early Christmas morning. I have come to love and admire the two of you as I would a son and daughter of my own. I know you both have been curious about me from the beginning, and I'm sorry I had to keep the truth from you, but it would have spoiled the surprise and the joy I had in doing what I did.*
>
> *My name is Joseph Fitzgerald Mayfield...*

"I knew it! Gretchen and I were right about that picture and article."

Faith squeezed his arm. "Read the rest."

> *...and I'm the founder of one of the largest furniture manufacturing companies in Illinois. I recently sold the company, and with investments made over the years, I've accumulated quite a bit of wealth. I have no family as my wife and I were only children and our only child died young. When I learned I was dying of an incurable illness, I set out to find someone worthy to be my heir. Thus the disguise. If people accepted me as a homeless, dirty vagrant and welcomed me into their homes and lives, I had found the place. Stoney Creek did just that.*
>
> *Tom, I transferred all of my wealth to the bank in Stoney Creek. I have named you as trustee of that account, which is to be used for things like the flood, the library, needy families, the new stove for*

the Delmonts, and for anything else the town needs.
This does not mean you are to freely give money
away to solve all problems, but use it as a means
to help people get back on their feet and start over.
Mr. Swenson has all the details and will answer all
the questions I know you must have as you read this.
My only request is that you reveal none of this to the
people of Stoney Creek.

"That's going to be hard, and he's right about questions.
I have a million of them. I'll have to see Mr. Swenson the
first thing Tuesday morning." He lowered the letter. "Isn't
it just like God to send us this on Christmas Sunday?
What better time to reveal the miracle of love through one
of God's children."

He grinned and continued reading.

Now, you should be reading this with Faith, and
if you haven't declared your love for her and asked
her to marry you, I ask, what is taking you so long?
My love and blessings to you both.
Joe

Heat filled Faith's face at those last words. Tom had
declared his love, but the proposal hadn't followed.
What now?

Tom laughed, laid down the letter, and reached into
his pocket. "Well, Joe sorta spoiled my surprise, but…"
He opened his hand to reveal an opal ring. "This was my
Grandmother Dyer's ring, and I want you to have it. Will
you honor me by consenting to spend the rest of your life
as my wife?"

Love soared through every last fiber of her being. "Of course I will marry you."

He slid the ring onto her finger and embraced her, his heart pounding next to hers. When his lips met hers, she leaned into him and returned it with love flooding her soul with joy. The dream she'd had for so many years had ended in the reality of Tom's love, and a new dream began.

Flakes began falling about them, and Faith squealed. "Tom, it's snowing! This is perfect. I don't ever remember having a white Christmas."

Tom stuck his hand out into the falling flakes. "It's almost as if God is sending us an extra miracle with Joe's revelation. Wait till the children see this tomorrow."

Faith shivered in delight at the snow now falling heavier. A perfect ending to a most unusual day. She snuggled closer to Tom and gazed at her new ring. Now her finger wore a family heirloom, and in the near future she'd be his wife.

Flakes swirled about and settled on the trees and bushes, and love filled her heart to overflowing. Somewhere Joe celebrated Christmas, maybe in heaven, but the miracle of love and generosity he'd left behind in Stoney Creek would live forever in the hearts and souls of the ones whose lives he'd touched.

"Merry Christmas, Joe, wherever you are."

❧ Author's Note ❧

HIS ENTIRE HOMEWARD Journey series has been loosely based on my great-grandparents' love story and their family. My great-grandfather came to Texas in 1880 to begin his medical practice in Victoria, Texas. My grandfather, Thomas Dyer Whiteman, was born in Victoria to Manfred and Sallie, somewhat earlier than in the story.

My grandfather is the hero of *Christmas at Stoney Creek*. He worked for a newspaper in Victoria as a boy and then moved away to try his hand at various other jobs, but he came back to the newspaper as an adult and worked for one until he finally retired when he was in his seventies. The wedding ring my grandfather Tom gave his bride, Lella, is still in the family, as is Sallie's. I told the story of her ring in *Love Stays True*.

My grandmother's gold wedding band was given to me as her oldest granddaughter with the instructions that I was to give it to my oldest granddaughter. I gave the ring to Erin Elizabeth on her sixteenth birthday. She is now thirty-one years of age and the mother of three children and will someday pass it on to her granddaughter. So the legacy begun by Tom and Lella carries on today.

CONNECT WITH US!

**CHARISMA
HOUSE**

(Spiritual Growth)

SILOAM

(Health)

REALMS
(Fiction)